One of the deputie[...] [obscured by barcode sticker]
gigantic black bag[...]
when I realized it was a [...] [...]ed to
us. "Evening, detective. Is this the [...] [...]s with
the victim?"

"Yes, Sam. She's agreed to identify the body. Ms. McKay,
are you sure you're ready?" Detective Hunter's palm
rested on my back as he gazed sympathetically at me.

"As ready as I'll ever be." I swallowed and braced myself
for the unveiling.

Sam unzipped the bag, then looked at me for
confirmation.

His eyes were closed, but the pale face and damp curly
silver hair were undeniably recognizable.

Omigod. I gasped and frantically looked around as the
butterflies in my stomach morphed into an assault team
of flying pterodactyls. Hunter took one look at my face
and led me over to some shrubbery alongside the patio.
A hundred dollar's worth of champagne was eliminated
within seconds.

"Yes." I pressed my hands against my heaving stomach. "I
don't know how you detectives get used to seeing dead
bodies."

"Your first is never easy."

"Well, I'm not planning on making a practice of it."

"Glad to hear it. I'm not sure our sheriff's department is
large enough to handle your social life."

DYING FOR A DATE

CINDY SAMPLE

W☉RLDWIDE®

TORONTO • NEW YORK • LONDON
AMSTERDAM • PARIS • SYDNEY • HAMBURG
STOCKHOLM • ATHENS • TOKYO • MILAN
MADRID • WARSAW • BUDAPEST • AUCKLAND

If you purchased this book without a cover you should be aware that this book is stolen property. It was reported as "unsold and destroyed" to the publisher, and neither the author nor the publisher has received any payment for this "stripped book."

Recycling programs
for this product may
not exist in your area.

DYING FOR A DATE

A Worldwide Mystery/August 2012

First published by L & L Dreamspell

ISBN-13: 978-0-373-26812-2

Copyright © 2010 by Cindy Sample

All rights reserved. No part of this book may be reproduced or transmitted in any form or by any means, electronic or mechanical, including photocopying, recording or by any information storage and retrieval system, without permission in writing from the publisher. For information, contact: L & L Dreamspell, 376 West Quarry Road, London, Texas 76854 U.S.A.

This is a work of fiction. Names, characters, places and incidents are either the product of the author's imagination or are used fictitiously, and any resemblance to actual persons, living or dead, business establishments, events or locales is entirely coincidental.

® and TM are trademarks of Harlequin Enterprises Limited. Trademarks indicated with ® are registered in the United States Patent and Trademark Office, the Canadian Trade Marks Office and in other countries.

Printed in U.S.A.

This book is dedicated to my mother, Harriet Bergstrand, the most supportive mother in the world, and my wonderful children, Dawn and Jeff, who have made me a better person and who bear absolutely no resemblance to any characters in the book.

A special dedication in memory of my friend, Jerry Roberts, who departed her family and friends far too soon.

Acknowledgments

There are so many readers to thank, friends who loved the book, even in its early stages. Thanks to Barb, Cathy, CJ, Diana, Judy, Karen, Lois, Lynne, Madelyn, Marci, Matt, Maxx, Michelle, Nancy, Nora, Penny, Robin, Sandi, Sunny, Sharon B, Sharon W, Tracy, Val, and Vicki. Your positive remarks kept me going. I can't thank my critique group enough for their unwavering support and excellent suggestions (Kathy, Norma, Pat, Rae.) Special thanks to the Cindy Sample fan club (Jaci, Jana, Liz, Nina, and Terri). They read and critiqued, and reread some more. I'd like to give a shout-out to Capitol Crimes, the Sacramento chapter of Sisters in Crime, for their support. My editor, Cindy Davis was a delight to work with as is the rest of the "Dream" team. A big hug for my son, Jeff, who built my fabulous website, and last but not least, thanks to my ex-husband, Ron, for providing me with so much material.

ONE

IF I'D KNOWN MY CLOTHES WOULD be covered in blood by the end of the evening, I probably wouldn't have agonized over my wardrobe selection. But as I prepared for my first date since my divorce, my fashion choice seemed of monumental importance.

Sweaters, slacks and skirts were strewn across my bedroom but I still couldn't decide what to wear. After negotiating my curves into a pair of overpriced tummy control panty hose, I gazed in dismay at the mess on my barely visible bed.

Too short. Too long. Too boring. Too sleazy.

The bright red numbers on my digital clock glared at me. Less than five minutes to get my butt out of the bedroom and into my car. I zipped up a midcalf black skirt, buttoned a long-sleeved white blouse and tucked it into the waistband. The mirror above the dresser reflected its disapproval of my selections.

"Nothing looks right." I sighed. "I either look like Betsy Banker or Bimbo Barbie."

"Are you sure you want to go through with this?" Jenna, my sixteen-year-old daughter, slouched against the door. "You're kind of old to start dating again."

Old? Since when was thirty-nine considered over the hill? According to *Cosmo,* thirty-nine was the new twenty-nine.

My teenage critic flopped on top of my bed, turning the mountain of castoffs into a wrinkled puddle. I didn't need Dr. Phil to realize some passive-aggressive stuff was going on.

I put my hands on my hips and scowled at her. "Look what you did to my clothes."

Jenna slid off the bed with a martyred sigh and disappeared through the doorway. Seconds later a powder-blue cashmere sweater sailed across the room and smacked the back of my head.

The loan of the sweater must be Jenna's way of apologizing. Unfortunately it was a gift from her father. No time to ponder the psychological ramifications of wearing an item purchased by my ex-husband for my first date in seventeen years. I slipped the sweater, designed for a smaller frame than mine, over my head and stared at my reflection. Between the tight sweater glued to my chest and the long black skirt on my chunky five-foot-four frame, I'd invented an entirely new look—Bimbo Banker.

I stepped into my new black heels. At least my shoes looked hot. The only reason I was in the middle of a clothing meltdown was that Liz, my best friend, had talked me into joining a dating service called the Love Club—the safe alternative to online dating. As far as I was concerned there was only one safe alternative.

Not dating.

I flew down the stairs then paused to peek in the family room. Red and gold strobes of light swirled over Jenna's auburn curls. Tucked into a chair, iPod earbuds in place, my daughter attempted to concentrate on her book, *The Joy of Calculus,* while her seven-year-old brother, Ben, and his best friend battled it out with their Jedi knight laser swords.

A grapefruit-size lump lodged in my throat as I gazed at my children, reevaluating my decision to start dating. Was I looking for a partner or a male role model for my son? If

I met someone would it harm the close relationship I had with my daughter? Did I really want to find Mr. Right?

Or just Mr. Every Other Saturday Night? Meaningful questions which I needed to ponder when I had more than thirty seconds to spare.

Fifteen minutes later I walked into Leonardo's, a Tuscan-themed restaurant in El Dorado Hills, an expensive residential enclave located thirty miles east of Sacramento. I had lost the battle with a stubborn gas nozzle and reeked of gasoline.

I darted into the ladies' room to wash the pungent smell from my hands. After tracing lipstick over full non-collagen-enhanced lips, I peered in the mirror. Another one of those mysterious silver strands had appeared in my copper-streaked bob. I yanked out the wiry culprit, took a deep breath and threw open the door.

The smell of garlic mixed with flowery perfumes greeted me as I click-clacked across the terra-cotta tiles to the reception desk. The women milling around the lobby were all taller, slimmer and better dressed than me. Any minute now the El Dorado Hills fashion police would hand out a fashion citation.

"My name is Laurel McKay," I said to the size-zero hostess who was barely larger than the menu she held. "Do you know if Garrett Lindstrom has arrived?"

An arm snaked around my waist. "Laurel, sorry I'm late."

I squirmed away to get a better look at my date. This guy chose me? Garrett was even better looking in person than on his DVD. Over six feet tall, with dark brown hair and designer wire rims—a Clark Kent look-alike clad in a black shirt and slacks.

The hostess led us past a three-piece jazz combo to an intimate corner table. My heart pounded in rhythm with the bass player as I folded the white linen napkin on my lap. Garrett bore an amazing resemblance to the intrepid journalist/superhero. Thoughts of the two of us soaring over city skyscrapers flitted through my brain.

"Do you like to fly?" I asked, still hung up on the Clark Kent likeness.

Garrett looked surprised. "Uh, yeah, I enjoy flying. But my accounting practice keeps me busy, so I haven't traveled that much. How about you? Taken any exotic vacations recently?"

It took me all of three seconds to contemplate the exotic trips I'd taken in my lifetime. "The kids and I went to Disneyland two years ago."

Garrett gave me a blank look and I mentally slapped myself. Nothing like mentioning Mickey Mouse on a first date to bring the conversation to a crashing halt.

Our waiter appeared before I could embarrass myself further by elaborating on the joys of riding in oversize teacups. He leaned over and lit the small candle on our table. "My name is Aaron. Can I tell you about tonight's specials?"

Garrett winked at me. "I think my date is pretty special but let's hear about yours."

My cheeks flushed tomato soup–red. It had been years since anyone paid me a compliment. My self-esteem, which had been nonexistent since my ex-husband moved out, jumped up a notch.

Once we placed our orders the silence engulfed us. Silence is not golden in my world. I rushed to fill the gap with anything I could remember from my Accounting 101 class. "Garrett, I'd love to learn about depreciation."

I really needed to get a *Dating for Dummies Guide*.

Ten minutes later when our entrees arrived, he was still discussing depreciation methods. The glow of meeting my superhero dissipated, as Garrett morphed into an IBA—Incredibly Boring Accountant. When he lined up his dining utensils to display the merits of straight-line depreciation, I could see the writing on the spreadsheet. There would not be a second date.

I peeked at my watch. If we skipped dessert I could make it home in time to watch *CSI.* It crossed my mind that I might not be ready for dating if the thought of viewing dead bodies on television was preferable to being out with a live male.

I tuned back in to hear Garrett say, "If you structure it right, it's like getting free money."

Free money? My ears perked up at his statement but my eyes were diverted by the mocha-and-cream confection placed between us. I could always make time for tiramisu.

Once the server cleared our plates and brought the bill, I was ready for the evening to end. Garrett insisted on pulling my chair back for me as I rose from the table. What nice manners…hold on, did his hand graze my right breast?

Nah. Wishful thinking. It had been years since anyone grazed on any part of my anatomy.

The brisk night air felt refreshing after the garlic and basil scents of the restaurant. As we walked through the parking lot, I pawed through my purse. Lipstick, pepper spray, melted gummy bears. No keys and no phone. We approached my car and I peered in the window. The keys dangled from the ignition, right next to the cell phone hanging from the charger.

Some mother I was. Dating was already proving to be too much of a distraction.

"Garrett, my keys are locked inside the car and my phone is in there, too. Can I use your cell to call AAA?" I shivered as the cool night air penetrated my lightweight sweater.

He pointed to a large sedan a few spaces away. "It's getting cold. Why don't you make the call from my car?"

Good idea. I slid into the soft tan leather bench seat of his roomy beige Lincoln Town Car. My date had excellent taste in vehicles. Garrett slipped into the driver's seat and handed me a slim metal phone. I dialed AAA and gave the dispatcher our location. I hung up, turned and…

Thunk.

My head hit the passenger side door as Garrett thrust himself on top of me. His cell fell out of my hand and my purse flew over the headrest and into the backseat, removing the pepper spray out of reach. My right elbow smashed into the windshield as I struggled to push him off. He grabbed both wrists, holding them with a viselike grip, and covered my face with wet, sloppy kisses. The door handle pressed into my back as my superhero was transformed into Dr. Evil.

Garrett finally relaxed his hold on my arms and shifted his attention downstream.

Adrenaline surged though my body as anger replaced fear. I grabbed the first thing I could find then raised my right arm.

Crack!

TWO

BLOOD SPURTED AS THE PHONE connected with Garrett's nose. The back of his head bounced off the driver side window as he roared out a string of obscenities. Although with his mashed nose it sounded more like "Puck" and "Pitch" than the usual expletives.

I yanked my purse from the backseat, jumped out of the car and slammed the door. As I raced back to the restaurant, I silently thanked Nokia for designing such an effective weapon.

The hostess looked startled as I rushed past her into the ladies' room. I dampened a paper towel but it was useless on the bloody splotches splattered all over the sweater. I dropped the towel in the garbage can and leaned against the sink, my hands trembling.

Why had the boring accountant changed into a sex-crazed maniac? Maybe I shouldn't have ordered the tiramisu. Did ordering dessert signify I was willing to be dessert? His behavior didn't seem normal but I was clueless when it came to dating. I'd married my high school sweetheart and Garrett was only the second man I'd gone out with in my thirty-nine years.

By the time I returned to the reception area, Garrett's car was gone and the bright yellow AAA truck was idling in the parking lot. In less than five minutes the door was unlocked and I was on my way home.

I stopped for a red light and then the storm broke. Tears rained down my face and my sweater, enhancing the paisley bloodstains. Between my blurred vision and my heaving chest, I was in no shape to drive. I made a U-turn at the next light and pulled into McDonald's. Waiting in line behind eight cars for a shot of caffeine gave me time to pull myself together. The mascara running down my tear-streaked cheeks had transformed me into Goth Mom but at this time of night, the crew had probably seen it all.

The kids were asleep when I arrived home so I didn't have to explain why mottled red splotches adorned my borrowed sweater. I tossed, turned then tossed again all night, finally falling asleep before dawn. The sun blasted me awake around eight. I tied my fluffy pink chenille robe around my waist and padded down the stairs in my matching pink bunny slippers.

"Morning, boys," I mumbled to Ben and Jimmy, sitting cross-legged on the carpet, playing a Nintendo game, "Pillage and Burn." I could tell them a thing or two about pillaging.

My slippers crunched through a trail of Cheerios leading from the family room into our sunny yellow kitchen. My rooster-covered wallpaper usually cheered me up, but this morning I wasn't in the mood to watch roosters strutting. It might be time to redecorate.

After grinding a few extra tablespoons of fresh roasted beans, I hit the brew button on the coffeemaker then grabbed the Sunday paper. The aroma of Kona coffee wafted through the kitchen as I checked out the advice columnists. Apparently no other single woman clobbered her date last night so I wasn't going to receive any professional advice on my encounter.

The shrill ring of the phone interrupted my reverie. I checked caller ID. Liz.

"What took you so long?" I rested the receiver against

my ear as I poured the first drops of steaming coffee into my mug.

"Thought you might want to sleep in." Her British accent was in full throttle as she deepened her voice. "In case you boinked your date."

"How did you find out I bonked him?"

"You had sex with Garrett!" Liz shrieked.

Sex? Oh, yeah. I forgot that the British definition of *boink* was far different from *bonk,* and did not mean smacking your date with a cell phone.

Liz clucked sympathetically as I recounted each agonizing detail of my encounter. "Well, luv, maybe you were too darn irresistible and he couldn't control himself. Did you wear that luscious lipstick I gave you last week?" Liz owns a full-service spa and she is dedicated to preserving her youth and mine with all-natural products.

"You mean Hottest Hottie Red? Nope, I went with Plain Old Pink."

"Wise move. Otherwise he might have attacked you in the restaurant. I'm sure the next guy you go out with will be a big improvement," she commiserated.

"Nah. I'm done. That was my first and last date. I'm perfectly content to spend the rest of my life alone with my crosswords." And a pound or two of chocolate to get me through those killer puzzles in the Sunday *New York Times.*

"Laurel, you have to get back on that horse."

"Horse?" The closest I'd been to a horse recently was the horse's ass that attacked me last night.

"You know what I mean. You can't quit after one bad date. Don't forget I went out with more than fifty fellas before I met my sweetie. Your wise friend is ordering you to go back to the Love Club. Don't let one rotten apple spoil the apple pie."

My natural inclination was to bury my head in the sand,

or better yet, in a book, but Liz did have a point. The agency needed to hear about Garrett's behavior. Not to mention that my bank account had suffered a serious withdrawal when I signed up for the six-month membership. It wouldn't kill me to go out with one more guy.

After agreeing to visit the agency after Ben's soccer game today, I hung up the phone. My daughter slid into the spindle-back chair across from me, her oversize gray sweats covering up a slender and athletic five-foot-eight frame. Most sixteen-year-old girls spend their days at the mall exhibiting an excess of tanned flesh and drooling over gawky, pimply boys. Not Jenna. My math whiz daughter calculates statistics problems as a hobby. When she grows up she wants to be an astronaut. Or a professional poker player.

"So…how was your date?" Her blue eyes looked anxious as she wound her auburn ponytail around her index finger. Was this the time to have that mother/daughter chat about the perfidy of men? Should I share any details about my oversexed dinner companion?

Someday. But not right now.

"He's not my type," I muttered as I stood up and washed my mug in the sink. Too bad I couldn't scrub away the memory of the previous evening.

"Maybe you should wait a few more years to date." She refused to meet my gaze as she stared at her gnawed nail stubs. "You know…like after Ben and I are out of the house."

"How about if I hold off until I'm ready for assisted living? Then when I meet some hottie in a wheelchair, we can roll off into the sunset together."

Jenna chuckled. "Good one, Mom."

I kissed the top of her head and walked into the family room. It was time to get the boys ready for their first soccer game of the season. I detached the duo from their Nintendo controls, ruffling Ben's hair and adding several more cowlicks to his shaggy chestnut mop. As they raced each other upstairs I noticed the crest on Ben's royal-blue-and-red pajamas. Superman jammies. Was this a reminder I should stick to pint-size supermen and forget about finding a grown-up version?

While I dressed, I reminisced about my high school days. Every Friday night, I sat in the bleachers supporting my boyfriend, Hank, the star quarterback. Back then cheerleaders in short pleated skirts constantly chased after him.

When we married right after college it never occurred to me that adult women in short skirts would continue to chase after my husband decades later. But that was past history. Hank had moved on to greener pastures and so would I. Today my concentration would be focused on my son and the grassy green soccer field.

I threw on a turquoise sleeveless shirt, khaki shorts, and a pair of matching turquoise straw mules I'd found at the mall, fifty percent off. The weather was expected to be in the mid-eighties, sunny with patchy clouds, so I could multitask and work on my tan while I watched the game.

The second grade teams play in a park located four miles from our house. With the influx of so many new residents in the area, the league was forced to hold games on Sundays as well as Saturdays, until a new field could be constructed. Thirty minutes later, I stood on the sidelines of an emerald-green rectangle, cheering along with the other parents.

My son had inherited my athletic genes, or lack thereof, which was a huge disappointment to his jockstrap father. Ben had spent the summer practicing his soccer skills by dribbling his soccer ball back and forth across the front lawn. All I could do was cross my fingers and hope for his success.

A whisper of a cloud temporarily blocked the sun as the ref blew his whistle for the second half kickoff. One of the forwards on Ben's team kicked the ball backward and it smacked into my son's foot. He stood in place, stunned, probably from the shock of having possession of the ball.

Ever the supportive Mom, I screamed, "Go Ben."

Whether it was my yelling or the pack of soccer players bearing down on him, Ben finally began to dribble the ball down the field, a sea of blue and gold hot on his rubber-spiked heels. One of the other team's players, a gold number two emblazoned on his royal-blue shirt, towered over my son.

All of a sudden number two's foot shot out and kicked Ben above his shin guard. My baby flew over the white-and-black patchwork ball. When he landed, his body was as still as...

My heart.

THREE

I SPRINTED ACROSS THE FIELD AS fast as a woman wearing turquoise mules can run. Never having experienced an injury to my child in a soccer game, I assumed it was natural for his mother to run to her baby's rescue. The tiny kitten heel of my left shoe became mired in one of the muddy ruts so I left it behind in my frantic attempt to get to Ben.

By the time I reached my son, his teammates were gathered around his recumbent figure. Ben's coach ambled over and a big guy from the opposite side of the field joined us.

"Honey, are you okay? What hurts?" I clutched his tiny hand as I knelt down beside him. Tears shimmered in Ben's eyes but he didn't cry. I looked up at the craggy-faced coach. "Dan, that little boy intentionally kicked Ben."

The coach ignored me. "Ben, can you stand up?"

"I think I can," Ben whimpered, "but can you make my mom go away?"

I stood up and stomped my remaining sandal, which sank into the soft grass. "That monster should be disqualified from playing soccer forever. I'd like to have a talk with his parents."

A hand tapped my shoulder. I looked up, way up, into a pair of hot fudge sundae–brown eyes, fringed with outrageous black eyelashes. Only a man would be blessed with natural eyelashes like that.

He scowled at me. "I'm Kristy's father. You want to talk with me?"

"Kristy? Your son is named Kristy?"

The bear of a man folded muscular arms over a faded brown T-shirt that matched his faded brown ball cap. The brown eyes that glared at me weren't faded at all. "Kristy is my daughter. I can assure you, ma'am," he said with a pronounced emphasis on the last word, "she would never deliberately kick your son. She's been taught to play soccer fair and square."

He drew his daughter close and she leaned against him. Now that Papa Bear was protecting her, little Goldilocks had resumed her aggressive stance, shooting me a defiant look. Hard to believe the super-size girl was Ben's age. She was almost my size.

"Mrs. McKay, can we get on with the game?" Coach Dan asked, his lined face looking weary. "Ben can rest a few minutes and come back in when he's ready."

Ben struggled to his feet. "I'm fine, Mom. Go back to the sidelines and stay there."

I brushed off the dirt that had caked on my knees.

"Yeah, 'Mom.'" A deep baritone parroted my son. "Go to the sidelines where you belong."

The middle finger of my right hand itched to respond but I restrained myself. Kristy's father turned and I watched as his long legs loped to the opposite side of the field.

"Men," I muttered, frustrated with the bunch of them. Small and tall.

With a valiant attempt to look dignified, I limped across the field and retrieved my ruined sandal. As I approached the sidelines, my eyes made contact with a familiar pair of green eyes. Swamp-green eyes, as our daughter affectionately described them.

"When did you get here?" I asked.

"I arrived just in time to see your performance." My ex

tipped the visor of his black Giants baseball cap to me and snickered. "Nice job embarrassing our son."

I glared at him. "At least he has one parent who cares." Despite the fact he lived only thirty miles away in Sacramento and was a self-employed contractor, Hank's attendance record at Ben's games was far from perfect.

I turned away and tried to concentrate on the game. Ben appeared to be fine. He could have limped a little and made me feel less like an overprotective hysterical mom.

Hank cleared his throat. "I heard you had a date last night."

"Yup." I didn't see any reason to elaborate. One of the kids must have told him I had a date. I'd better institute a "need to know" policy concerning their father. Basically he didn't need to know about my social life.

"Do you think you'll go out with him again?"

Not in a million years, but Hank didn't need to know that. "I don't think that's any of your business."

His face flushed and he shot me an angry look. "Of course it's my business. What kind of mother are you? Your job is to focus on our children, not your love life."

My mouth opened so wide in protest I almost swallowed a wasp that had been circling around in search of sustenance. What kind of mother was I? What kind of father was he, leaving his family and moving in with the woman who had hired him to replace some tiles on her roof? It had taken Nadine Wells less than a week to woo him down from her roof and into her bed.

He didn't just replace her tiles. He'd replaced me.

Cheers from the parents who were not engaged in close verbal contact with their ex-husbands erupted. The game was over and we'd won. I was furious with my ex so I stood off to the side while he and Ben talked. Hank promised Ben he would attend the game the following week. I'd believe it when I saw it. His erratic appearance in our children's lives was one of the reasons I had started the search for a replacement.

The boys clambered into the back of my periwinkle Prius, a tight fit for the seven-year-olds, but my car made me feel like I was contributing to making the world greener, one gallon of gas at a time.

I took the boys out for lunch then dropped them off at Jimmy's house. My next stop was the Love Club, which was located in Placerville, one of the more infamous gold-country towns whose beautiful Victorian houses were portrayed by Thomas Kinkade in his early paintings.

Driving down Main Street, I automatically looked up at the mustached man in frontier clothing hanging from the pole above Hangman's Tree Tavern. The man is a dummy but it's still kind of cool. During the gold rush, the locals used two enormous oak trees downtown to eliminate a couple of troublemakers. After the hanging of "Bloody Dick" it was called Hangtown for a brief period. I thought about my encounter with bloody Garrett and decided those pioneer women would have been proud of me.

The Love Club is housed in the refurbished brick Cary House, best known as the hotel that provided beds for Mark Twain, Buffalo Bill and Ulysses S. Grant. Too bad Buffalo Bill wasn't around last night. I wouldn't have minded if a few shots of lead had pelted Garrett's posterior.

The Club's young receptionist greeted me as I pushed open the heavy oak door. With her perky nose, violet-blue eyes and blond-streaked mane of hair you could tell she wasn't a member.

I grabbed a few books from the shelves and settled into a chestnut-colored leather club chair. The agency wasn't large but it claimed to be the most successful matchmaking service in Northern California. Hard to argue with a seventy-five percent success rate.

Member profiles are separated by gender and divided alphabetically by first name into individual volumes. Garrett had been the one to select me, so I decided this time, I would do the choosing. I skimmed through the *H, I* and *J* books. If I found a profile I liked, I could watch their DVD. Unlike the online dating sites, the agency required that photos and videos be updated annually. No false advertising at the Love Club.

The Harrys, Henrys and Hermans were all too old. On the plus side, they were probably too feeble to attack me. The *I* prospects looked like baby-faced boys, too young for me. I wasn't ready to be a cougar. I moved on to the *J* book.

The Love Club required that all clientele go through a credit check and complete a comprehensive psychological profile, supposedly to weed out any weirdos. Evidently they needed a little help with their system. But like Liz said, Garrett was probably an aberration.

New members filled out a six-page questionnaire, which included vital statistics like age, religion and education, hobbies, pet peeves, ideas for a romantic evening. A more practical approach would be to ask if the men left the toilet seat up, dropped their clothes all over the floor and were attached at the wrist to the TV remote.

There were enough potential suitors in the *J* book to keep me occupied for my entire enrollment. I entered one of the screening rooms, sat down and scrutinized the videos of four men. One of the reasons I had agreed to go out with Garrett was that not only was he attractive, his video had portrayed him as a man of integrity.

Did his attack mean that when it came to judging men,

I was clueless? Maybe I couldn't tell the good guys from the bad ones. Or was I such a hot babe Garrett couldn't help himself?

In my dreams.

After reviewing their bios once more, I finally ended up choosing a doctor named Jeremy and an engineer named Jack. Neither of them made my heart hum, but they both appeared stable, if a little dull. After last night's excitement, dull sounded kind of appealing.

Once I turned in my choices, the club would notify the member by both email and voicemail that someone had selected them. If Jack or Jeremy was interested in me, they would be given my email address and phone number. A simple concept, but it worked. I scribbled my selections on the blank member request form then walked up to the glossy cherrywood reception counter.

"Hi, Laurel," said the gorgeous blonde, batting her two inch eyelash extensions at me. "Did you choose anyone today?"

"Hi, Sunny. I thought these two men looked interesting. And safe. You wouldn't believe what happened last night when I went out with this guy named Garrett Lindstrom."

Her face grew paler than the white forms I held in my hand. "You were with Garrett last night?" she squealed.

"Uh, yes. Why? Did he tell you what I did to him?" I was surprised Garrett would have divulged what happened.

"You mean, you're admitting it?" Her voice rose to a crescendo, her eyelashes flickering so fast they were creating a draft.

"Of course. I'd do it again if the same thing happened on my next date."

Sunny looked at me like I was crazy. I was beginning to think she was missing a few screws herself.

I leaned forward, resting my elbows on the counter. "So what exactly did Garrett say?"

Sunny pointed her crimson-tipped index finger at me. "Garrett didn't say anything. He's dead. You killed him."

FOUR

"You killed him. You killed him." Sunny was now backed against the paneled wall, right and left forefingers crossed in front of her, as if she was trying to ward off a vampire. Or prevent the homicidal woman standing in the reception area from attacking her.

"What are you talking about—Garrett's dead?" The room started to tilt so I dropped into one of the overstuffed chairs, bent over and breathed deeply. I lifted my head and stared at the receptionist. "Are you sure we're talking about the same person? Garrett Lindstrom?"

Sunny picked up a black cordless phone, staring at me with anxious eyes. Was she going to call the police? Or use it as a weapon against the supposed murderer in the lobby?

"A sheriff's deputy stopped by a few minutes ago. A neighbor found Garrett this morning. Sitting in his car. In his driveway." Her arms performed mini calisthenics as she expostulated. "His head was bashed in."

I shuddered and slumped back against the chair. This couldn't be happening. All I did was hit Garrett on the nose with his phone. You can't kill anyone that way. Although his head did hit the window and there was blood everywhere, but I thought that was normal with any head injury.

"You really didn't know he was dead?" Sunny was clutching the phone like she'd been given an extra lifeline, but at least she hadn't dialed the police. Yet.

"No," I whimpered.

She hesitated then set the phone down, inching closer to the reception counter. "You don't look like a killer."

I chose to take her comment as a compliment. "Um, thanks," I said with a halfhearted smile.

Sunny must have decided my nonthreatening visage meant it was okay to confide in me. "The deputy said they found one of our invoices on Garrett's desk and guessed he was a member. They want me to find the women who chose him, and who he picked in the last few months. I found twenty so far, but I didn't come across your name yet."

Twenty women? Who did this guy think he was—Don Juan Lindstrom? Well, with his amorous assault-style maneuvers, it was unlikely he ever went on a second date with anyone.

My head buzzed with unanswered questions, but a line of single females had formed, waving their selection forms at Sunny. I stared at the women waiting in line. Had any of these women been on a date with Garrett? Perhaps they, too, fought off an attack by him.

Or…killed him.

The line of restless women distracted Sunny as she immersed herself in paperwork. I slipped out the door and walked through the parking lot, mulling over this startling development. Sunny wasn't the brightest bulb in the chandelier. She could have mixed Garrett up with someone else.

During our dinner, Garrett mentioned he lived in Villa Dolce, one of the gated subdivisions that comprise the massive Serrano housing development in El Dorado Hills. It couldn't hurt to do a brief drive-by, and it might make me feel better.

Fifteen minutes later I was driving up Serrano Parkway. Villa Dolce was located near the top of the parkway on the south side of the street. By riding the bumper of a black SUV, I was able to sneak through the gated stone entry. After aimlessly driving up one street and down another, all lined with earth-colored stucco McMansions that blended into the earth-colored hills, the futility of my mission sank in.

Hoping to find an escape out of the maize maze, I turned right then slammed on my brakes. It would be impossible to miss the spacious one-story house with the beige Lincoln Town Car in the driveway. The two sheriff's cars parked in front of the house. And the yellow tape stretched...everywhere.

Sunny was right.

My first thought was that Garrett must have been one heck of a CPA in order to afford a house this expensive. Or maybe he was involved in something shady. One of his clients might have disagreed with his method of depreciation and accelerated Garrett's death.

As my car crawled down the street in the direction of the house, two of the county deputies, clad in pressed khaki shirts and forest-green pants, glanced up. The dark-haired officer with the miniature Hitler mustache frowned at me. Time to move on. My pastel vehicle wasn't designed for undercover detecting.

As I drove to Jimmy's house to collect my son, I pondered my predicament. Should I contact the police and tell them what happened on our date? I didn't think the *Dating for Dummies Guide* had any advice on what to do when your date is found dead less than twenty-four hours after you hit him with a cell phone.

The car rolled to a stop in Jimmy's driveway. Before I could open my door, Ben ran out of the house and slid into the backseat. His navy backpack, which reeked of antique bananas, was unzipped as usual, and its messy contents scattered everywhere. "Mom, I'm so hungry I could eat a tyrannosaurus rex." He rubbed his stomach for emphasis.

"Sorry, Ben, no T-Rex burgers tonight. Maybe tomorrow."

"For real, Mom?" he squealed in delight.

Since I had to dash Ben's hopes for a prehistoric burger I promised to whip up his favorite fudge for dessert. If he cleaned up the gummy bears, banana peels and G.I. Joes strewn across the back of the car.

The message light was blinking on our phone when I got home. "This is your mother, Barbara Bingham. Call me."

Did she think her only daughter forgot her name? Mom would have to wait until I called my best friend. The last thing I needed was maternal advice from the woman who could do no wrong. At least in her own mind.

I didn't want the kids to overhear my conversation so I went upstairs, plopped on my bed and speed-dialed Liz. "It's me. He's dead," I sputtered into the mouthpiece.

"Laurel? What are you talking about? Who's dead?"

"Garrett. My date. I went to the Love Club this afternoon to complain about him and they told me he was found in his car. Dead."

"Oh, my. That's a bit of a downer."

Talk about British understatement.

"You don't think there's any way I could have—" I gulped "—killed him?"

"Don't be silly. With a cell?" She paused as if she were contemplating the odds of a mobile phone killing. "There must be a reasonable explanation for his death."

"I hope you're right. What should I do?"

"Let me see if Brian has heard anything. I'll call you back."

Brian, her fiancé, was not only an assistant District Attorney for El Dorado County but he was a terrific guy. I blew out the breath I'd been holding. "Thanks. I appreciate it."

"Don't worry. Everything will be fine. Trust your auntie Liz."

Humph. If Auntie Liz hadn't talked me into joining the Love Club I wouldn't be in this situation. I tried to calm myself by cooking dinner, an old family recipe called Pasta à la Ragu. I washed the dishes, made a batch of my special gold nugget fudge, then a batch of brownies. I figured it was better to work off my angst chewing on chocolate than chewing off my nails.

The doorbell rang while I was upstairs in the bathroom. I heard voices then the sound of Jenna's size tens pounding up the stairs. "There are two men from the sheriff's department downstairs. What's going on?" she whispered. "You're not dating both of them, are you?"

The anxiety in her cornflower-blue eyes mirrored mine. I hadn't expected an official visit this soon. I pulled her close and attempted a reassuring smile. "No, I think they're investigating an accident. Nothing to fret over." There was no point in worrying my daughter about my situation.

"Oh, okay." She smiled suddenly. "Too bad. One of them is a real hunk."

Hunk? Despite her scholarly pursuits, Jenna wasn't totally oblivious to the opposite sex. It was probably one of the baby-faced deputies I'd noticed in front of Garrett's house today. I told her to tell the men I'd be down in a couple of minutes.

I changed from my sweats to a denim skirt and white blouse. I swiped gloss over my gnawed lower lip and slapped on extra blush. Murder suspects probably look pale and wan. Hopefully my rosy cheeks would proclaim my innocence.

My mind and heart raced as I trod down the stairs. Was it normal for the sheriff's department to appear on your doorstep without any warning? Did they consider me a suspect or was this a routine questioning? And despite the fact I heard the phrase repeatedly on TV, what the heck was a routine questioning?

Lost in thought, I tripped down the two stairs leading into our sunken living room, landing with my legs spread out in a position I hadn't been in since my divorce. The muscular arm that lifted me up made me feel as light as a marshmallow. A familiar pair of Godiva-brown eyes gazed back into mine.

"You?" It was the annoying guy from the soccer match today; the dad with the super-size daughter.

His eyes registered recognition and he responded with a tight-lipped smile. "Oh, yeah. The shoeless soccer mom. Small world, isn't it?" He held out his right hand. "Detective Hunter."

"Hello, Detective Hunk, I mean Detective Hunter." I floundered as his large, capable hand engulfed my much smaller one.

His face remained expressionless so he must have missed my faux pas. Evidently my daughter did not. Muffled laughter emanated from the stairs, followed by a growl originating from one of the mauve velour wing chairs in the corner of the living room. I turned and caught a fleeting glimpse of Jenna's shoes disappearing up the steps. I glanced at the wing chair. Who or what was growling?

The creature in the corner unfurled his gangly legs and introduced himself as Detective Bradford. Tall and bald, with a bulbous nose and bags under his eyes the size of dinner plates. The steel-gray eyes that gazed at me were as sharp as my steak knives.

"Please sit down, Ms. McKay," he said in a gravelly voice, as he lowered his oversize frame back into the chair. I tried not to wince as it creaked in response.

I walked over to my outdated blue flowered sofa and

perched on one corner. Detective Hunter looked at the remaining delicate wing chair and wisely decided to join me on the more comfortable couch. He settled into the cushions, uncapped a pen and pulled a small navy notepad from his sport coat pocket. "We have some questions about a friend of yours."

"Of course, oh, before we start, would you like some coffee, brownies, fudge?"

"Not now, perhaps later," Hunter said.

As I settled against the sofa cushions, my skirt slid up my thighs. Hunter's gaze briefly drifted to my bare legs then quickly returned to his notes.

"We understand you dined with Garrett Lindstrom yesterday evening. Evidently you and he are members of a matchmaking agency called the, uh, Love Club." A smile briefly flickered across his normally impassive face but he quickly stifled it behind his hand.

I glared at the younger detective. "Garrett was my first encounter with someone from the Love Club. Our date didn't go that well."

"Would you care to elaborate?" Hunter sat poised with his notebook and pen, probably waiting for some sizzling comments.

I could talk all night about that evening, but that wasn't the point. Wasn't he going to inform me Garrett was murdered? Was Sunny not supposed to tell me? Was he trying to trip me up with trick questions?

"Are you are aware Lindstrom was found dead in his car Sunday morning?" he asked.

"Yes, I am." I slumped against the cushions. "One of the Love Club staff told me when I stopped in today. You don't think I had anything to do with it, do you?"

"That's why we're here asking questions. How about you tell us more about your not-so-great date."

I proceeded to give the detectives all of the gory details. When I mentioned I Nokia-ed Garrett's nose, Detective Bradford grunted, his only input into the conversation so far.

"That was the extent of our time together. His car was gone when I returned to the parking lot and met the AAA driver. I was back home before ten. Garrett couldn't have died from me hitting him with the cell, could he?"

"We haven't seen the full autopsy report yet, but I can tell you the examiner discovered a significant contusion on the back of his head as well as a broken nose. Do you remember anything else about your, um...altercation?" Hunter asked.

All I remembered was rolling around the front seat of Garrett's car while I tried to extract myself from his unwanted embraces. My fingerprints must be plastered all over the seat and the windshield.

A strange expression flitted across Hunter's face. I could feel the heat rising up my face then working its way down to another zone.

"How did you find out about our date?"

"His laptop. He used Outlook to manage his appointments. The time and the name of the restaurant. And the initials—LM. It might have taken us a while to figure out whom he met with but we received a call from one of the Love Club employees a few hours ago. She confirmed you went out with him last night."

Gee thanks, Sunny.

"Did Lindstrom mention anything during dinner that could help our investigation?"

I tried to recall if Garrett had said anything revealing during his monologue on depreciation. All I could remember was blah, blah, blah.

"How about anything suspicious inside Leonardo's?"

Detective Hunter asked. "Or maybe later when you walked through the parking lot?"

I crinkled my nose at him, puzzled. "Suspicious, like what?"

"Someone observing you while you were eating. Following you outside." He shot a questioning look at me. "You do realize you could have been attacked, as well."

My stomach did a backflip cartwheel combination. It never once crossed my mind that I could also have been in danger. "What time was Garrett killed?"

"The medical examiner said it was sometime between ten and midnight."

I didn't like the sound of this at all.

"Can you account for your whereabouts after leaving the restaurant, Ms. McKay?" boomed Tall and Bald.

I jumped. "Whereabouts? Like where I was, uh…about?"

Hunter snorted but maintained his deadpan expression. "Yes. Did you stop anywhere on your way home? Can your children confirm what time you arrived?"

"They were in bed by the time I got here. After I drove out of the parking lot I went through the McDonald's drive-through and bought a coffee because I felt kind of shook up. I don't know if anyone would remember me."

They exchanged glances, which must have been some type of secret signal because Detective Hunter stood up, slipping the tiny notepad into his pocket. Detective Bradford unfurled himself from my chair, lumbering out the door without a goodbye.

The younger detective followed, pausing to shake my hand.

"Thank you, Ms. McKay. Perhaps the next time we see each other it will be under more pleasant circumstances— like another soccer game."

I wouldn't describe meeting over Ben's prostrate body as pleasant, but it was preferable to being involved in a murder.

"Please call if you have any more questions. I'm anxious for you to solve this crime. And I promise not to injure any more dates."

I thought my comment might get a laugh out of the detective, but his expression remained blank. This guy had absolutely no sense of humor.

I leaned against the door. "Goodbye, Detective Hunter."

He paused on the sidewalk and looked back over his shoulder, a slight smile briefly flitting across his face. His response filled the chilly night air.

"Don't you mean Detective Hunk?"

FIVE

THE THUMP OF THE HEAVY OAK door slamming shut couldn't mask the thuds of two children pounding down the stairs. Ben landed first, Jenna close on his heels.

"What happened? Why were those detectives here?"

I curled an arm around each child's waist. It was time for full disclosure.

"Okay, kids. My dinner date Saturday night turned into a disaster. I locked my keys and my cell in the Prius and my date offered to let me sit in his car and use his phone to call AAA. He got a little too friendly, so I hit him in the nose with his cell phone. It turns out someone murdered him in his car later that night and the police wanted some details from me."

Ben bounced up and down. "Murder. Sweet."

"Mother, that is so gross," Jenna said. "How could you do this to me? What if my friends hear about it?"

"Hey, Mom, can I tell Jimmy?"

"No. Let's forget about this incident. I had nothing to do with the murder and we don't need to share this information with any of our friends. Now go upstairs and get ready for bed."

The best advice I could give myself was to forget about Garrett. If he could attack me on a first date, imagine what other nasty things he was involved in. He probably had a drug habit and his supplier did him in. That theory worked for me.

My thoughts turned to Detective Hunter's parting remark but the shrill sound of the phone interrupted my reverie. I peeked at the caller ID. Mother.

"Laurel, dear, how was your weekend?" I visualized my mother, from the top of her frosted blond flawlessly cut hair to her frosted pink pedicured toenails.

"Hectic." Talk about the understatement of the year.

"Honey, you have no idea how hectic life can be unless you're in the real-estate business. It's nonstop 24/7. I sold two of my listings this weekend but of course they were priced realistically. Something the other agents need to learn in this kind of market."

I sighed with relief. I would receive a short lecture on the foibles of the real-estate industry from the thirty-five-year veteran on the other end of the line and hopefully escape any maternal nagging.

She paused for a second. Uh-oh.

"Laurel, I heard the strangest rumor tonight. Since the rumor included *your* name and the term *corpse* I thought there might be something you wanted to share with me."

Not really, but in a small town like ours who knew what kind of stories would be flying around. I gave her a brief update on the demise of my date. She was quiet for a few seconds before she let me have it. "I told you signing up for that Love Club would be a huge mistake. It's undoubtedly full of psychopaths and con men."

My mother. The optimist.

"Mother, I keep telling you the agency is designed for professionals. It's too difficult for single working people to meet each other, especially here in the foothills. You wouldn't believe the horror stories my friends have shared about online dating." I grabbed one of the glossy agency brochures and read the verbiage out loud. "'The Love Club is a highly intellectual process for discovering your future mate.'"

"Humph. Well, I wish you would forget about that stupid club. I don't think it's safe. You know, there's a new agent in my office you should meet. Peter is about your age, single and highly successful. He recently transferred from the Folsom office. Wouldn't you rather go out with someone I can vouch for?"

Would I rather go out with someone my mother worked with every day? No, not really. We wrangled over the merits of the dating agency for a few more minutes. I finally told her it was late and time to say good-night to the kids. I hung up the phone and trudged up the stairs to Ben's room. At his age he didn't need me to tuck him in bed, but it's part of our nightly regimen and something we both look forward to each evening.

I crossed the threshold into Ben's unique fantasy world. Posters of a prehistoric triceratops and a brontosaurus hung between glossy prints of Chewbacca and Batman. He was already in bed, his blue-and-gray lightsaber resting on top of his Spider-Man bedspread.

"Honey, you know you're not supposed to sleep with your toys." I held out my hand for the plastic sword.

"No. Mom. I need it." He grabbed the saber and hid it under his Batman sheets.

"Now, Ben…"

He sat upright against crumpled pillows. "I need it… to protect you. What if the murderer comes here?" A tear rolled down his cheek and he quickly swiped at it. "I'm the man of the house now."

Tiny droplets welled up in my eyes. What kind of mother was I, subjecting my impressionable young son to murder? When you're raising children, it sometimes feels like you make one bad decision after another. I sure didn't remember Dr. Spock covering a situation like this one.

I climbed in the twin bed and wrapped my arms around

my son. I held him close as I explained it was a coincidence that I had gone on a date with Garrett and he died the same evening. The murder had nothing to do with me. And absolutely nothing to do with the kids. The detectives were merely hoping I would have some information to share.

Ben seemed satisfied with my explanation. We nestled together, his shaggy brown mane that was so overdue for a haircut tickling my chin. I made sure Ben was sound asleep before I slipped out from under the covers. He could sleep with his sword tonight. Not a battle worth fighting right now.

As I closed his bedroom door I once again pondered my decision to start dating. Maybe my daughter was right and I should hold off until both kids were out of the house. Of course that meant by the time I started the search for eligible men I would also be eligible for early-bird dinners.

Considering what happened the previous night that would be just fine with me.

SIX

THE NEXT DAY WAS MONDAY, THE start of a fresh new week. Unfortunately it looked like everyone had woken up on the wrong side of their respective beds.

"Mom, there's no bread for my sandwich," Ben whined. He waved the empty plastic bag in front of my face. My son was not a morning person, another gene we shared.

Drat. "You can have cheese and crackers. Won't that be a treat?"

He crossed his arms and frowned. "Jimmy's mother would never run out of bread."

Okay, so I wasn't the West Coast's answer to Martha Stewart. "I'll bet Jimmy's mom would never let him have four cookies for lunch." The bribe produced a beaming smile. Sometimes working moms have to compromise to save their sanity.

Jenna had misplaced her homework, which she finally located under the kitchen phone, so we left five minutes late. The kids jumped into the car and I zoomed down our street. I turned right on Wagon Wheel Lane and glimpsed the canary-yellow bus pulling away.

That bus driver and I had a love-hate relationship. I was positive she waited at the bus stop until she saw my car fly around the corner. Then she shifted gears and hauled you-know-what, forcing me to follow her to the next stop.

I stomped on the gas pedal with a vengeance, and all four cylinders responded with a resounding "ping" as we caught up to my nemesis. Ben's pals waved at us from the back window of the bus. At the next stop Ben flew out of the car and jumped on board. One kid down. One to go.

My daughter refused to ride in a school bus filled with freshmen and sophomores so our next stop was the high school.

"I'm probably the only kid in the junior class who doesn't have her own car," Jenna complained as I pulled up to the loading and unloading area in front of the high school.

"Great. That means there are three hundred sixty-one kids who can give you a ride." I chuckled, silently patting myself on the back.

"Very funny." She grabbed her forest-green backpack and slogged up the sidewalk toward the ponderosa pined campus. I watched as two of her friends joined her. Within seconds they were giggling, heads close together.

I would have loved to provide my daughter with her own transportation. Jenna was a straight A student, and other than her penchant for playing Texas Hold 'Em, a good kid. But a car, even a junker, was not in our budget. I made a left turn out of the school parking lot and headed to the office. My job might not be a cash cow but it was the only cash coming in right now.

My employer is Hangtown Bank, established one hundred fifty years ago and located only a few doors down from the infamous hanging tree in Placerville. Before Ben was born, I was employed as a manager for one of the bank's local branches. Someone had to bring home the bacon and eggs since my ex kept getting involved in one idiotic get-rich scheme after another.

When the last feathered mammal was sold from his ostrich-farming venture, Hank decided to go into construction. The real-estate boom combined with a surprising knack for building spec homes provided us with sufficient income so I could quit work and stay home for a couple of years. After Hank and I split up over his extracurricular female activity, the only available position at the bank was mortgage loan underwriter.

I pushed open the glass double doors and smiled at Vivian Vaughn, the bank's receptionist, who also specialized in nosiness. The seven-foot carved wooden bear that the president of the bank had purchased to enhance the lobby decor greeted me with a snarl. I snarled back a good morning, walked past the old-fashioned oak teller stations to the area reserved for the mortgage staff. I had barely stuffed my purse away when my cubicle neighbor popped her head over the five-foot wall of gray tweed that divided us.

"How was your date?" Mary Lou, a five-ten Barbie doll look-alike who maximized her assets and minimized nothing, had discovered online dating to be an underwhelming experience. My coworker had gone on twenty-five "meet and greets," as she referred to her first-time meetings with online matches. The men she met through a website called Supermatch.com were either forty pounds heavier, three inches shorter or far balder than their online photos. She swore some of them posted their high school yearbook pictures.

Vivian had joined a different online site, which proved to be even worse. Three of the four men she met over the internet turned out to be married. We had warned her about those profiles that said "ask me for my photograph." We dubbed her dating site Mismatch.com.

Rosa Martinez, an unmarried processor, and Stan Winters, my underwriting assistant, joined us. "I want to know everything," Rosa said, her dark eyes hopeful that one of us would find success with the match game. Rosa had signed up for a third online site that analyzed your personality profile then provided matches with potential partners. Members weren't allowed to make selections themselves. So far the fifty-year-old processor had been rejected by thirty-nine of their forty suggested matches. The reason being "other." At five foot one Rosa didn't know if she was too short, too chunky or too old. She only knew she couldn't take much more online rejection.

I didn't want everyone to freak out so I withheld a few facts, such as the fact that my date was now deceased. Mary Lou spit out her coffee when I admitted I'd discovered a new use for a cell phone.

"Hey, Laurel, I wouldn't mind taking your rejects," snickered Stan. "As long as they're not battered and bruised." Gay men have their own unique brand of humor.

"Ahem." Our boss stood in the doorway, glaring at the assemblage. Within seconds, my coworkers vanished to their respective cubicles. I wondered if he noticed that none of his direct reports had been doing anything remotely related to work in the past ten minutes.

Earl Fisher leaned forward, his double cheeseburger stuffed stomach resting on my desk. "How was your weekend?"

My weekend basically sucked. I didn't think it was any of his business although I couldn't afford to annoy the head of the mortgage division. "Why?"

"Just making conversation. Always interested in the welfare of my staff." He winked and drifted down to Mary Lou's desk.

I grabbed a loan file and soon became absorbed reading the borrowers' letter of explanation for multiple credit card delinquencies. They claimed their mail carrier had deliberately not delivered their credit card statements because their basset hound had bitten the carrier's ankle. They scored a nine for originality. Zero for integrity.

Reject.

I grabbed another file but my mind drifted to the events of the past weekend. It was hard concentrating on loans when there was a high probability I could be involved in a murder investigation. I finally confided in Stan and Mary Lou.

"Your date was killed? As in dead?" The furrow in Mary Lou's brow deepened. "And I thought my date was a disaster. Does this mean you're a suspect?"

"I don't think so," I said.

"Are you kidding? Of course you're a suspect. You need to hire an attorney," advised Stan, our resident crime show aficionado. "Otherwise they'll try to trap you into saying something you'll regret."

"But I don't know anything. How can they trap me?"

Stan rolled his eyes and graced me with a pitying look. "Trust me. If the detectives think you're the killer, they sure aren't going to waste time looking for anyone else. The next thing you know you'll be wearing matching metal bracelets."

"And an orange jumpsuit," Mary Lou chimed in.

As far as I was concerned, the words *orange* and *jumpsuit* should never be combined, particularly in a sentence referring to me.

It was only Monday but already I could tell it was going to be a long week.

SEVEN

WHETHER THE DETECTIVES WERE busy hunting bad guys or not, there were no further calls or visits from the sheriff's department in the next couple of days. Wednesday evening I received a call from Jeremy Slater, the physician I selected during my last trip to the Love Club. I had totally forgotten about the two agency choices I'd made the previous weekend. Right before Sunny shared the news about Garrett.

The last thing I felt like doing was go on another date, but after conversing for over an hour, I decided Jeremy might be a pleasant diversion. We exchanged the usual information hapless singles share, number of kids—zero for him, number of divorces—another zero for him, where we worked, what we liked to do, etc. Jeremy suggested we meet for lunch on Friday. A lunch date seemed safe. I shouldn't have to worry about any front seat acrobatics during daylight hours.

Friday morning turned into another wardrobe time waster. I couldn't decide what to wear to the office that would be suitable for lunch with Jeremy. I didn't want to reprise my Bimbo Banker look, so I finally selected a tailored white blouse, my good black suit and black heels.

Fridays are always dress-down days at the bank, so my appearance in a suit created a buzz. Stan was the first to investigate. He plopped his slight frame in my gray tweed visitor chair, pushed his wire-rimmed glasses up his pointed nose and whistled.

"My, my, all dressed up, aren't we?" His deep basso

voice was at odds with his slight physique. "Do we have an outing planned for today? Any more love bugs circling?"

"Stan, some days you are a royal pain in the patootie."

My smart-ass responses needed a little work.

"Sweetie, you're looking good. And you know we all want you to meet the man of your dreams. I'm sure the other Love Club members won't be like that first jerk."

"Thanks. I hope you meet the man of your dreams, too." Stan had recently broken up with his partner of ten years. It wasn't that easy meeting gay men in the foothills, but Stan grew up here and he preferred living in a small town to the big-city social scene.

Since Jeremy's medical practice closed at noon on Fridays we had agreed to meet at a restaurant in downtown Placerville. I entered the Main Street Bistro a socially correct five minutes late. Jeremy was easily recognizable from his video. An inch or two over six feet, with a full head of curly gray hair, a big Roman nose and a disarming smile. Not even remotely drop-dead gorgeous, which was fine with me. I didn't need any more drop-dead dates in my life.

"Laurel, it's a pleasure to meet you." He proffered his hand from a safe distance of at least two feet away. We were shown directly to a green marble-topped table overlooking a tiny fern garden. The soothing sound of a waterfall helped diffuse the noise of the other diners.

Jeremy quickly peeked at the glossy menu then laid it on the table. I checked out their salad selections, pleased with the variety.

"What are you going to order?" I asked.

"Oh, I'm kind of a boring diner. I usually order turkey on whole wheat, with a small salad on the side. Fiber, fiber, fiber, I always say."

Yeah. I always say that, too. In between devouring candy

bars. His fiber mantra seemed a little weird but doctors need to be serious about nutrition.

"Have you tried any of the new diets, like South Beach or the Zone?" he asked.

That was an awfully personal question. Was Jeremy intimating I needed to lose weight? "I did try the South Beach Diet last spring," I said with a wry smile. "It lasted for all of six hours. I'm afraid the only diet that works for me is the 'See no chocolate, eat no chocolate' diet."

He chuckled. "You're not alone on that one. It's certainly not unusual for women to crave sweets. Of course, the more refined carbohydrates you eat, the more you'll want. But you can overcome those cravings if you change your lifestyle." He gazed at me with intensity. "Soon you'll discover you desire something else."

Oh, dear. Not another man with an overactive libido. First there was Lindstrom the Lech. Was I now dining with Slater the Sex Fiend?

Fortunately our waitress arrived to take our orders. A turkey sandwich for Jeremy and a healthy Cobb salad for me—with plenty of fiber, just like the doctor ordered. I wasn't going to worry about the other fattening ingredients. I reached for a piece of garlic bread and Jeremy grabbed my hand.

"Laurel, that's exactly what I'm talking about. If you avoid bad carbohydrates, eventually you won't crave them anymore. You'll crave the healthy foods your body needs."

"Oh…right." I pulled my hand from his and shook my head at my unsavory thoughts. He was concerned about my health. That was sweet. Nevertheless, I kept my hands under the table until our food arrived.

We continued to talk throughout lunch. Technically Jeremy talked and I listened, which gave me the opportunity to demolish my Cobb salad—fiber, fat and all. Other than his fetish for fiber, Jeremy was personable and the time flew by. He barely touched his turkey on whole wheat, probably the reason he was so slim. I wasn't sure what to do when the bill arrived. Did the man pay on the first date? Was lunch considered a date? Somebody needed to write a rule book on this subject.

Our middle-aged waitress must have had her own set of rules because she plopped the bill next to Jeremy's plate. She smiled at me as she cleared the table. Jeremy picked up the bill and reached for his wallet.

"Can I split that with you?" I asked.

"Thanks for the offer, but it's my treat. I do have a question for you, though."

Uh-oh. I hoped he didn't want my daily carbohydrate count.

"I'm in the middle of applying for a loan and I've experienced some problems so I'd love to pick your brain about the mortgage application process. Not to mention I enjoyed your company at lunch. Would you like to go to dinner next Saturday? I haven't been to the River Inn for a while and they have an excellent and healthy menu."

Decisions, decisions. I fiddled with the cloth napkin as I tried to decide whether to accept his invitation. Jeremy seemed nice, although a trifle obsessed about nutrition. One of the articles I'd read in a women's magazine said you should go on a minimum of six dates with someone before you decide they aren't right for you. I couldn't imagine six dates with someone I wasn't interested in, but one dinner with a financially secure doctor wouldn't be such a hardship. He could assault me with loan questions as long as he didn't attack me in his car.

Or deprive me of dessert. "Sure. Saturday will be fine."

"Great. I'll make a reservation. Shall I pick you up at your house?"

Darn, more trick questions. I gnawed at my lower lip, debating whether to let him come to my house. What the heck? He was a doctor. I could always check out his references before he showed up at my front door.

Jeremy escorted me to my car and we shook hands good-bye. We decided to confirm the details of our next date the following week. I returned to the office and decided that a sunny Friday afternoon in mid-October was not conducive to reviewing loans. Usually I'm very conscientious about my loan files. It didn't take more than a few loans going into foreclosure to put a small lender out of business.

Even big banks weren't immune to a foreclosure crisis. One CEO of a failed mega bank bragged about how they funded the most loans in the country. What is it with men? Why do they always think bigger is better?

The phone rang and I grabbed it. "Hi, luv, can you lunch tomorrow? Brian and I were going wine tasting but he has to work instead," Liz said.

Lunching with Liz sounded great. Although wine tasting sounded even better. I pictured a romantic outing at one of the local El Dorado wineries, red checked tablecloth covering a lakeside picnic table. My date stroking my hand, his brown eyes gazing soulfully at me...

"Laurel, are you still there?"

I cleared my head. "Sorry, I was daydreaming. Where do you want to meet—the usual?"

"Sure, there's no place better than Sweetie Pie's as far as I'm concerned."

We settled on one o'clock to meet. Now all I had to do was find a babysitter for Ben. Jenna had made plans to go to the mall with a friend who had just received her driver's license. I still couldn't decide what was worse: letting Jenna ride with a friend, letting her drive my car or chauffeuring her back and forth.

Young mothers with toddlers think their lives are stressful, but nothing can prepare a parent for the daily fear they experience the minute that laminated driver's license is in the possession of their offspring.

I hated to ask Jenna to cancel her plans so I called several of Ben's friends Saturday morning. No one was home, which left me with only one possible babysitter. Mother. She was at the real-estate office—her normal home on the weekends. Heaven forbid she lose out on a potential walk-in customer looking for a real-estate bargain.

In my best suck-up-to-Mom voice, I said, "Hello, Mother. Do you have any showings this afternoon?"

"No, dear. Only paperwork to catch up on. What do you want?"

That's my Mom. She doesn't waste a second.

"Liz and I want to get together for lunch today. Jenna is going to the mall with Katie so she can't watch Ben. Would you be able to babysit him for a few hours? I promise we won't be too long."

Her sigh resonated over the line. My mother loves her grandchildren, but she prefers that familial visits be booked weeks in advance. "Well, there is a potential listing I want to preview in your area. I'll pick him up at your house then take him to McDonald's and get him one of those happy plastic meals."

McDonald's might not be pleased with her description of their kids' meal but Ben would be thrilled to add a new toy to his collection of colorful plastic items that were never played with again.

I donned a sleeveless white top and my denim skirt and was pleasantly surprised to see the waistband was loose on me. Was the stress of dating burning off calories? Or was it the stress of knowing there was a murderer out there?

Jenna agreed to stay with Ben until her grandmother

arrived. I slid into my car, shoved in a Shania Twain CD, and popped open the sunroof. My hair flew in all four directions as Shania belted out "Man! I Feel Like a Woman!" I relaxed for the first time all week as my car zipped past red barns on decades-old farms and newer stucco ranches on five-acre parcels. Horses cantered alongside the road as I careened down the twisty ten-minute drive into Placerville.

The sidewalks in front of the brick and pastel clapboard buildings lining Main Street were clogged with tourists, most likely on their way to Apple Hill, home to more than forty apple and pumpkin farms, as well as wineries famed for their medal-winning Syrahs and Zinfandels.

I finally squeezed my car into a parking space between two massive SUVs. Clusters of hungry people mingled on the sidewalk outside the mauve Victorian house built in 1865 that housed Sweetie Pie's Restaurant. I politely pushed and shoved my way inside, hoping Liz was already seated.

Like a moth to a flame, the cinnamon-scented air drew me to a glass bakery case piled high with their world famous cinnamon rolls drenched in a gooey caramel glaze. My stomach gurgled in response to the mouthwatering display.

I needed to find my friend before I succumbed to eating a two-thousand-calorie cinnamon appetizer. I waved at the owner, who was scurrying around the high-ceilinged room with its flower-sprigged wallpaper, attending to her customers. I walked into the sunny back room and found Liz seated at a corner table, her hazel eyes glued to the menu, gold corkscrew curls askew.

Liz and I became acquainted our sophomore year of college. She had just arrived from Kent, England, as a participant in an exchange program with the University of California at Davis. We met at a fraternity party during which both of our dates decided to drink themselves into stupidity. After hiking the three miles back to campus, we formed a friendship that has lasted twenty years. She's the yin to my yang; or maybe I'm the Abbott to her Costello. Either way, despite our differences, she is my best friend.

While I married immediately after college, embarked on a sensible banking career and bore two children, Liz traveled to exotic locales, seduced by the glamour of foreign countries. Not to mention foreign men of all shapes, sizes and nationalities. After acquiring health and beauty tips from spas all over the world she eventually returned to El Dorado County and opened a state-of-the-art luxury salon in El Dorado Hills. Once her Golden Hills Spa became a success, she moved on to the next goal on her "to do" list. Getting a man. Enter the Love Club and Brian.

I slid into the chair across from my pal, losing one of my red slides in the process.

"Are you ready to order?" Her bracelet-laden wrists jangled as Liz waved her arms wildly at one of the servers.

"Well, hi to you, too." My buddy is always hungry and subsequently always dieting.

"Sorry, luv. I arrived early and I'm starving."

"Give me a second. I think I'll try something on the healthy side for a change." I scrutinized the menu as I tried to wiggle my shoe back on my foot.

"I'll have the fettuccine Alfredo," Liz told our server, snapping her menu shut.

I stared at her. Didn't she have a wedding coming up?

"So I'll spend an extra hour on the StairMaster." Her dimples appeared as she grinned at me. "Their fettuccine is worth it."

I ordered a chicken Caesar salad, dressing on the side. The waitress promised to bring our iced teas right away.

"Do you have any more dates on your calendar? I was afraid you'd give up after what happened with that Garrett guy." She patted my hand, her heavy gold bracelets clanking against the varnished wood table.

"You know if I hadn't already selected a couple of guys from the Love Club before I found out about Garrett, I probably would have dropped out. But I had lunch with a doctor yesterday and we're going out again next week."

"Ah. A doctor. Now we're talking." She lifted her left eyebrow and leered. Liz needed to stop watching soaps. That one eyebrow lift was almost professional.

I shrugged. "I didn't hear any bells ringing, but he was very pleasant."

"Well, don't expect to hear bells right away." She shook her charm bracelet, and it tinkled in response. "It takes time, persistence and patience to find the right guy. Dating isn't a game—it's a full-time occupation. Remember how many losers I went out with?"

How could I forget? Before she met her fiancé, Liz had dated and dumped so many men that I'd lost count. She'd demonstrated classic signs of becoming a serial dumper when Brian popped into her life.

Strangely enough I could have sworn I heard a faint tinkling when Detective Hunter said goodbye the other night. Must have been the brass wind chimes on my porch.

"So tell me what happened with the detectives. Anyone I might know?"

"Some old grump named Bradford and a big burly guy called Hunter."

"Oh…I've heard about that Detective Hunter," Liz said, her eyes dancing. "The dispatcher at the sheriff's department said as far as eye candy goes, he's a Godiva God."

A vision of the detective's chocolate-brown eyes popped through my head.

"I heard he has a cute bum. What did you think?" She winked at me as she reached for a roll.

"I didn't notice."

Liz opened her mouth, aghast at this lack of anatomical perception on my part. Fortunately the server arrived with our entrees and I escaped a lecture. I smiled as she inhaled the creamy fettuccine. "That fettuccine looks and sounds fabulous. Can you find a way to enjoy your pasta and talk about the murder at the same time?"

Patience hadn't made it on my list of virtues.

"Honey, you need to slow down," she admonished me. "Enjoy lunch with your best friend. Remember, *carpe diem*—seize the day."

Carpe diem? I was more worried about *corpus delicti*.

I speared an oversize piece of romaine lettuce. "C'mon. Brian must have shared something about the Lindstrom case. They don't really think I'm a suspect, do they?"

Liz put her fork down and dug through the emerald-green Marc Jacobs tote that perfectly matched her silk blouse. I tried not to slobber on the buttery leather as I admired the craftsmanship. The only chance I had of owning a designer purse was to get lucky at a garage sale.

"I was afraid I would forget what he told me so I took some notes." Liz rummaged through the capacious bag and finally yanked out a sheet of lined pink paper. She grabbed her fork and somehow managed to eat her pasta with her right hand while reading from the page in her left.

"Let's see. The sheriff's department doesn't have any suspects other than you." She raised her perfectly arched eyebrows at me. "Rumor has it there were fingerprints in some unusual places."

My fork dropped out of my hand, clanging against the delicate china plate. I shuddered, remembering Garrett's attack and our front seat gymnastics.

"The coroner said the victim was hit with some kind of blunt object. Brian implied that Garrett's head smacking the window probably wouldn't have created that type of in-jury." She peered at me over her plate of pasta. "You didn't whack him with anything other than his cell, did you?"

"Of course not. What do you think I am?"

She pursed her lips. "Correct me if I'm wrong, but you did hit Hank in the forehead with that dinner plate. The night he announced he was leaving you for Nadine."

I gulped. Oh, yeah. That night.

"That was an accident. It was supposed to fly over his head like a Frisbee. It's not like I wanted to break a hundred-dollar piece of china over his lamebrained head."

She nodded in sympathy. "Men may come and men may go, but Royal Doulton lasts forever."

We finished our lunches, paid our bill and cruised down Main Street. Placerville is an antique road show mecca for buyers who have the energy, time and knowledge to wade through piles of crap.

I mean old stuff.

We stopped in Placerville Hardware, the oldest oper-ating hardware store west of the Mississippi. The scuffed wooden floors creaked as we squeezed our way down the narrow aisles. The bulging floor-to-ceiling shelves looked like they were a sneeze away from toppling over. A few gold pans were stuck next to some shovels so I decided to buy one for Ben. One of these days we'd make it over to Coloma, site of Sutter's mill where the first nugget of gold was discovered.

Liz purchased a bone china teapot in a cream-and-violet pansy pattern in one of the antique stores. As the cashier wrapped the teapot in bubble wrap, Liz turned to me. "He's single, you know." I must have looked confused because she punched me in the forearm. "Detective Hunter. The Godiva God. He's a widower."

"Oh, what a shame," I responded, remembering the detective's protective stance at the soccer game. Poor Kristy. Having lost my father at a young age I could empathize with his motherless daughter.

"Well, keep that in mind, in case your date with the doctor doesn't work out."

I rolled my eyes. "Liz, what are the odds that a widowed detective who's investigating a crazy soccer mom for murder would want to go out with said soccer mom suspect?"

She grabbed the paper bag that held her teapot and smiled. "Good point. Have fun with the doctor."

After supplying me with enough seaweed and cucumber moisturizer samples to keep my face glowing for the next year, we parted. I sped down the hill toward the Centurion Cameron Park office as fast as my little hybrid could move without drawing the attention of the CHP. I couldn't decide which was worse, getting a ticket, being a suspect in a murder case or arriving late and risking the wrath of my mother.

I pulled into the parking lot, jumped out of the car, flung open one of the Centurion Realty glass double doors and found myself chest to stomach with a tall blond-haired guy in a dark suit. He dropped a few manila folders, scattering them across the slate-tiled lobby.

"Oh, let me help you." I bent over to pick up the files.

"No. That's okay. I'll get them." He knelt down and quickly scooped them up.

"I'm so sorry. I'm in a hurry to pick up my son. My mother is Barbara Bingham and she's been watching Ben all afternoon and I'm late as usual," I rambled on.

A broad smile creased his face and a lock of hair fell over his forehead as he nodded sympathetically. "Ah, the formidable Barbara Bingham. I can understand why you wouldn't want to be late." He held out his right hand. "I'm Peter Tyler."

"Laurel McKay," I said, automatically shaking his hand. His handshake was firm, but not crushing.

"It's nice to meet you. I'm new in this office but Barbara has mentioned your name several times."

How embarrassing. I tried to imagine what she could have told him. The chatter of voices and footsteps interrupted us.

"Hi, Mom. Grandmother bought me a happy meal and it came with a Spider-Man. Isn't that cool?" Ben thrust the tiny blue-and-red plastic figure in my face. I admired the miniature toy and thought how uncomplicated life is at seven years old. Maybe if I stuck to small plastic figures my life would be simpler, too.

"Peter, you've met my daughter?" My mother looked only slightly frazzled from the three hours spent with her hyperactive grandson.

"Yes, we've introduced ourselves. She is every bit as delightful as you said."

Delightful? It was far more likely she would refer to me as difficult.

Since I didn't have time for her to admonish me on my tardiness I grabbed Ben's hand and turned to Peter. "It was nice meeting you."

"My pleasure," he said, opening the door for us.

"Mother, thanks for taking care of Ben." She frowned at our hasty departure. I anticipated a lengthy lecture in my future.

By the time Ben and I arrived home, Jenna was already there, having survived the ride to and from the mall. She assured me that everything she'd bought had been reduced by at least eighty percent and showed me the marked down price tags to prove it.

The three of us spent the evening nestled under an afghan on the sofa, munching on a bowl of buttered popcorn and watching a classic Julia Roberts film, *Runaway Bride*. The movie was fascinating because it depicted the way Julia's character redefined her personality every time a new man entered into her life. If the right man came along, would I turn into a totally different person?

I thought about the men who had recently appeared in my life.

The doctor. The real-estate agent. The detective. My ex.

The dead guy.

The metamorphosis was beginning. Whether I liked it or not.

EIGHT

AN ARTIC FROST ICING MY CHEEKS woke me early the next morning. The temperature had dropped more than thirty degrees. With the heat turned off, it was only fifty-five degrees in the house. Dark gray clouds glared balefully at me. I glared back.

After a long dry summer, most Californians welcome the first rain of the season. But rain and soccer are not a great combination from a mother's perspective. The kids revel in it since it gives them an excuse to slip and slide in the mud without getting into trouble. The lucky moms stand on the sidelines getting drenched then we get to launder the muddy clothes afterward.

The game was as awful as I anticipated. Blue and gold merged with muck brown as arms and legs tangled on the sloppy field. If Liz were here she'd say it was peeing rain. I peered through the showers pouring off the rim of my turquoise umbrella, trying to determine which muddy player was my son.

I was so engrossed in the action on the field that I didn't notice the man standing next to me. It wasn't until his size twelve Nike bumped against the toe of my running shoe that I looked up and saw Detective Hunter gazing down, his oversize black umbrella almost a foot above mine.

"You take soccer quite seriously, Ms. McKay. I've been standing here for over five minutes and you haven't blinked once."

Blink? How could I blink? The rain had welded my

waterproof mascara to my eyelids. I opened my mouth to respond when I heard a roar from the parents. I glanced at the field just in time to see my son kick a ball right through the legs of the other team's goalie, a perfect shot.

"That a boy, Ben." I jumped up and raised my fist triumphantly in the air, totally forgetting the man standing next to me.

"That was a well-placed kick, Ms. McKay. Your son is a smart player. He must take after his mother."

My eyes narrowed as I looked up at him. Are detectives allowed to give compliments to murder suspects? "I'll take credit for Ben's intellect, but I'm afraid the only time I received an A in P.E. was in square dancing. I was the do-si-do diva."

"I have no doubt you're quite a hit on the dance floor." He smoothly segued into another question. "So do you have any more Love Club dates on the horizon?"

Odd. Was the detective investigating me or flirting with me?

I shrugged my shoulders nonchalantly. "Well, you know the life of a single woman, one pressing social engagement after another."

His eyes twinkled and a brief smile hovered over his lips. Didn't he believe me?

"For your information, I have a date next weekend with someone else from the Love Club. A doctor." I enunciated the word *doctor*. Who was he to smirk at my social calendar? "We're having dinner at the River Inn."

"Good to know. I might have dinner over there myself." The look he shot at me penetrated through my windbreaker. "Just to make sure nothing happens. To your date."

He checked the gold watch on his left wrist. "I need to get over to Kristy's game. She'll be wondering what's keeping me. My daughter thinks she's going to kick up a storm, so to speak. Congratulations again on your son's goal."

With that remark, he strode down the sidelines toward one of the other playing fields. Remembering Kristy's tenacity in her last game, she undoubtedly would be kicking major butt, so to speak.

I gazed down the field and contemplated her father's broad shoulders and fine posterior as he walked away. Liz would be so proud of me.

But what did his parting comment mean? Did he think Dr. Slater could be at risk going out with me? Was that a warning? As I watched his burly form disappear down the side of the field, I felt the nudge of an umbrella. Swamp eyes.

"How's the game going?" Hank asked, wisps of dark blond hair escaping from beneath his ball cap and brushing the collar of his beige windbreaker. For a second, it looked as if he was going to kiss me, but I checked his advance with my own umbrella.

"Ben made a goal."

"He did? You're kidding?"

I drilled him with a look. How about supporting your son instead of knocking him? Ben would never be the athlete his father was. Thank goodness. The last thing the world needed was another high school quarterback who couldn't stop reliving his victories from two decades ago.

A few seconds passed before Hank broke the silence. "Do you have any more dates coming up?"

I lifted my head from under the umbrella, a major strategic error that resulted in a deluge of rain down my face and chest. Fortunately, I didn't need to make a good impression on Hank. This man had seen me at my worst, during my twenty-plus hour labors with each child.

"Why?"

"I'm worried about you, honey. What if something happens when you're out with one of these bozos? Are you checking these guys out? Googling them. I don't want anyone to hurt you. You need to think about our kids." The gaze he fixed on me surprised me with its intensity. "And us."

Wow. Hank was displaying more passion this afternoon than in our twenty years together. What brought this on? Maybe he finally realized what he'd given up when he broke up our marriage and our family. The impact his leaving had on his young children, not to mention his wife. I was about to question Hank further when I noticed our son slipping and sliding toward us with the apparent intent of giving me a hug.

"Did you see my goal, Mom? Wasn't it awesome?" His grin reached literally from one side of his mud speckled face to the other. Then he noticed his other water-soaked parent.

"Dad. You made it. Did you see my goal?" he squealed.

"I'm real proud of you, big guy. You're a chip off the old block."

I snorted. Chip off the old blockhead was more like it. Hank performed some kind of complicated male bonding fist thing with Ben then attempted another kiss on my cheek. I outmaneuvered him but he grabbed my hand and held it tight.

"Be careful, Laurel. Don't take any chances." He hugged Ben then walked away, leaving me in an unusual state. Stunned silence.

The rest of Sunday passed uneventfully. Ben called all of his buddies to swap stories about their soccer games and make sure they heard about his goal, as well. I did four loads of laundry and pondered my future.

My eagerness for my pending dinner with the health-conscious Jeremy Slater had waned. Since the kids would be with their dad the following weekend maybe I should use Liz's shotgun approach to getting a guy. My friend used to schedule four to five dates a week. But then Liz's goal was to find a husband and the father of her future children before her estrogen clock stopped ticking.

My goal was…what exactly was my goal? Did I want a friend, an escort, a lover or a husband? Was my decision to join the Love Club just a response to my loneliness and the desire for intimacy with someone? Or was I trying to replicate the happy home Hank and I had for most of our marriage? Was I truly ready to spend the rest of my life with that special someone, the man who would keep not only my feet warm but also my heart?

Very heavy thoughts, which should be contemplated when I wasn't so tired. After soccer and a full day of laundry all I really wanted was to hit my four hundred thread count sheets. The phone rang as I brushed and flossed. One of the kids picked it up and a few minutes later Jenna called out, "Hey, Mom, Grandmother Bingham for you."

My mother refused to go by Grandma or Granny.

"Hello, Mother, how are you?" I grabbed the phone and plunked into my overstuffed blue-and-green-plaid wing chair.

"You never told me what happened with that murder investigation. Your name popped up on my 'to do' list."

I could visualize it now. Number twenty on her list— check on status of daughter to determine if necessary to raise bail on Monday. "No need for the bail bondsman yet," I said.

"Good." A few seconds elapsed. I think she really did check me off her list.

"I wondered if you would accompany me to a dinner they're having next Saturday at the country club to honor the top producers in our company. Remember we went together last year."

How could I forget? My mother, the queen of Centurion Realty, had been in her element. I felt like her ugly duckling daughter. She forgot to tell me it was a formal affair so I wore one of my old suits. Thank goodness I didn't have to face that well-coiffed group again.

"Sorry. I have a date Saturday night. Dinner at the River Inn."

"Oh, no, not another of those Love Club people," she groaned. "I thought you were finished with that foolishness."

"I've only been on one date. Just because it ended disastrously doesn't mean I shouldn't try again. His name is Doctor Jeremy Slater."

A doctor. A successful professional as a potential son-in-law.

"Why would a physician resort to joining a club like that? Certainly he can find dates without assistance."

I sighed. There was no pleasing my mother.

"What are you going to wear? The River Inn is quite elegant. I think men are supposed to wear coats and ties," she said.

Coats and ties. That was pretty unusual for a California restaurant. Now I'd have to find time to buy a new dress. Too bad my mother and I weren't built the same. How my five-foot-seven, slender mother produced a short, curvy daughter was beyond me. Guess I had my dearly departed fireplug of a father to blame. I would love to go shopping in her walk-in closet, which was almost the size of my bedroom. Plus all of her designer suits and dresses were organized by color. Talk about anal with a capital *A*.

"I haven't decided what I'm wearing. I'll fill you in at church next weekend."

"I'm sure Pastor Martin will be delighted to see you again."

Did I detect a hint of sarcasm? I opened my mouth to

respond that we'd only missed two services this month but she cut me off. "Try not to ruin your next date."

That was a low blow, but the dial tone came on before I could respond with a pithy reply. I hung up the phone, set my alarm clock and crawled into bed.

The clatter of squirrels rearranging the steel tiles on my roof woke me early the next morning. I love living in the country, but I wished some of my furry neighbors would find a hobby that wasn't so noisy or so expensive to repair. Even so, the joy of living in the foothills is worth it. Starry, smog-free skies, snowcapped mountain vistas, herds of deer grazing peacefully on my front lawn, eating all the petunias in my window boxes.

Okay, it's not pastoral perfection all the time. But I'm only ten minutes from the office. If I lived in Sacramento, a forty-mile commute on clogged highways, I'd have to get up an hour earlier. Or get rid of my children.

Monday morning I arrived early at the bank. I exchanged growls with the wooden bear and with Vivian, who seemed even more surly than usual. After storing my purse, I sauntered down to the break room. The coffee looked and smelled like scorched caffeine, but at least it was caffeine. Mary Lou entertained several of our coworkers with her description of her date the previous Saturday night. I leaned against the counter and nodded sympathetically when she confided that he was a lousy kisser.

At least he was alive and kissing.

I grabbed my mug, scurried past the rows of gray cubicles that lined our office and reached my own minuscule six-by-six cube. The pile of loan applications formed a barricade around my desk. The bank was definitely benefiting from the closing of some of our competitors.

I grabbed the first file and flipped through the pages. The borrower, a hairstylist, claimed to make one hundred thousand a year. Maybe in Beverly Hills, but no way in El Dorado Hills.

Reject.

Considering the crazy loan products that some of our competitors had been offering, the borrower's next stop could be the mortgage company down the street. I was glad I worked for a conservative bank. No mumbo jumbo mortgage products here.

I was grateful that my employer stayed true to its mission statement—making sensible loans to qualified borrowers. Fully documented mortgages. Some of our competitors used to originate NINJA loans. That stood for no income, no job, and no assets. Nothing about the borrower had to be verified. Sometimes it's hard to fathom the cupidity, not to mention the stupidity of mankind.

"Hey, gorgeous." I recognized Stan's deep baritone and looked up.

He might be gay but Stan had one of the sultriest voices of the male persuasion. "What's up? Do anything exciting this weekend?"

Stan draped himself over the tweed chair. His pressed lilac shirt and matching satin tie were perfectly coordinated as usual. "The highlight of my weekend was helping my sister pick out a dress to wear to a wedding if that gives you any idea of my hot social life."

"Hey, I need a new dress. Can you think of someplace suitable for me—as well as my budget?" I added, knowing that with Stan's excellent and expensive taste, further clarification was necessary.

Stan stroked his chin, gray eyes thoughtful behind his wire-rimmed glasses. Not that he had much of a chin to stroke. "Honestly, I think we visited every boutique in Sacramento. Jeannie is such a perfectionist it took *forever* to find something, and she never lets a price tag stand in her way."

"Great." I rubbed my hands together in anticipation of a shopping expedition. "Do you have any evenings free this week?"

"Between my baseball league, knitting class and the church choir, I think I can squeeze you in." We settled on Thursday since most of the stores would be open late.

Wednesday evening I called Coach Dan and he agreed to bring Ben home from practice on Thursday. I could ramp up my Visa to my heart's content and my bank card's limits.

Stan and I left the office together promptly at five. He offered to drive us in his new Beemer. I wasn't about to refuse the offer and entertained myself on the drive to the city by trying out all of the twelve different seating combinations.

"This is such a terrific car. Do you think I'll ever own one like it?"

"If you don't mind being indentured to a finance company for the rest of your life, you too could own a BMW. Just think, if we find the right dress tonight you may end up marrying the doctor. Doesn't the Hippocratic oath state they have to drive a BMW or a Mercedes?"

I chuckled, but his comment made me pause. Could our shopping excursion eventually result in marriage to the respectable Dr. Slater? And was marriage my ultimate goal? The sensible thing would have been to spend the next three hours evaluating what I wanted in a man. Instead, we spent the evening trying to decide what I wanted in a dress.

Stan suggested we start at the Pavilions. Since the Plaza is more than forty miles from my house, I hadn't shopped there in years. As we strolled up the brick-lined sidewalks I ogled the mannequins in the window of one of the stores.

A soft black chiffon number caught my attention. It looked like it would be perfect for my less than perfect figure.

A rhapsody of tinkling bells greeted us as we entered the store. A willowy saleswoman impeccably dressed in a sage-green silk suit, her left hand enhanced with a diamond the size of a snow globe, greeted us. "Hello. Can I help you find anything in particular?"

"How much is that black dress in the window, the floaty one?" I asked.

"The, uh, floaty one? I believe it's either twenty-two ninety-five or twenty-three ninety-five. What size are you?" Her aquamarine eyes sized me up, down and sideways.

"I'm a ten or twelve. I can't believe that dress is less than twenty-five dollars. This is better than Ross."

The saleswoman and Stan gawked at me and managed to synchronize the rolling of their eyes. She turned the price tag over and read out loud, enunciating every patronizing syllable. "This Roberto Cavalli is twenty-three hundred ninety-five dollars. Let me see if I have your size available." She stared down her perfectly shaped nose at me. "If you still wish to try it on."

My cheeks blushed hot pink. What was Stan thinking bringing me here? I was on a Payless budget, not a Prada budget.

"Of course I want to try it on. I'm sure it will be the perfect dress for me," I muttered.

The minute she walked into the back room to look for my size, I grabbed the sleeve of Stan's retro bowling shirt and dragged him over to the front door. "Are you nuts? I can't afford that dress. Twenty-four hundred dollars is the equivalent of three months of house payments. Or eight hundred mochas."

"You said you needed the perfect dress," he said with a sheepish look. "Sorry. Sometimes my champagne taste collides with my common sense. But who knows, it may be exquisite on you." Luckily the exquisitely overpriced dress was unavailable in my size. We browsed through several other stores but couldn't find anything in my price range that made either of us rave.

"Don't get discouraged," Stan said as I slumped in the leather seat of the Beemer. "We still have lots of boutiques to check out in midtown and East Sac."

We found a parking space on H Street in front of a store called Serendipity. Twinkling white miniature lights lent a festive look to the fall fashions in their window. Stuffed pumpkins strewn throughout the display reminded me it was less than a week to Halloween. Ben and I hadn't even discussed his costume yet. This mother had her priorities all screwed up.

"I'm getting some good vibes here." Stan's head swiveled as his eyes scanned the racks of clothes. "You take the racks on the left and I'll head over to the ones on the right."

I had forgotten how tiring shopping could be since I rarely indulged in what used to be my favorite predivorce hobby. I was ready to call it a night when Stan cried out, "Hoochy Mama."

Hoochy Mama?

Hoochy Mama was a sapphire-blue dress with sheer sleeves, ending in beaded cuffs at the wrist. The Empire-style dress with its low rounded neckline would flatter my curves. I snagged the dress from Stan's clutches, walked into the dressing room and closed the louvered door. I held my breath when the zipper came to an abrupt halt, but a little jiggle and it made it to the top. I slipped on my heels and peeked in the mirror.

A young saleswoman tapped on the door. "We have a three-way mirror out front. I'm sure your boyfriend wants to see how you look."

I snickered as I opened the door. "Stan's not my boy-friend. He's just the best personal shopper a girl could have. We'll let him make the final decision."

I model-walked through the store, ending my perfor-mance in front of Stan's chair. The look on his face was pure delight. "Babe. You've been hiding yourself under those Betsy Banker clothes. You look good enough to make a gay man go straight."

"Okaay…I'll take that as a compliment. Guess I'm buy-ing the dress."

I changed back into my slacks and sweater, hung the dress back on its hanger, and walked back into the store straight into—her. Nadine Wells. The golden goddess who for some strange reason clung to the arm of—another man? Not my ex?

"Um, Nadine, um…hello." I turned to Stan. My expres-sion must have screamed help. My buddy jumped in to rescue me.

"Hello. I'm Stan. Laurel and I were just leaving. In fact, we were just getting into my new Beemer, the silver six-sixty parked over there…"

I recovered in time to save Stan from receiving the "gay dork" award of the week. "Where's Hank?"

Nadine tittered as she tottered on four-inch gold stilet-tos. Every time I encountered the woman I expected her to topple over, her super-size man-made breasts at odds with her size double-zero body. At least I had a decent-size frame to haul my excess soft tissue around.

"Honey, I kicked him out a few weeks ago. This is Dr. Hugo Black. Plastic surgeon extraordinaire, aren't you, sweetie?" Her breasts tilted up in homage to the man who must have been responsible for their design and construc-tion.

A plastic surgeon far surpassed Hank financially. Hank

could barely keep up with my child support payments since the bottom fell out of the construction industry. Had Nadine grown tired of supporting him?

The plastic couple sauntered to the back of the store as I paid for my dress. Stan and I were both quiet as we drove up Highway 50 toward Placerville. Nadine's revelation had stunned me. Were Hank's recent overtures due to a realization that our children had suffered when he'd moved out of the house? Or were there financial considerations involved?

Stan dropped me off at the bank parking lot. I thanked him for his help, climbed in my car and headed home to a house ablaze with lights. I couldn't wait for the day when my kids received their very first utility bill.

I parked in the garage and removed my dress from the backseat. Despite the high wattage emanating from every room, neither of the children was downstairs. I walked into the kitchen, the dress in its navy plastic Serendipity bag draped over my arm.

A note lay on the table. Jenna had scrawled the words a mother never wants to read.

NINE

I READ THE NOTE A SECOND TIME. DON'T FORGET—SNACK FOR SCHOOL.

The two most dreaded words in a mother's vocabulary. Snack Mom.

Ben's teacher had decided that every Friday one student should bring a treat for the entire class. It would give the kids something to look forward to at the end of the week. An excellent concept assuming the mother of the designated student remembered her snack-mom detail.

I'd totally spaced out and forgotten it was Ben's week. A quick check on the kids then I'd head out to the supermarket. I climbed the stairs and entered Ben's room. He was sound asleep with a contented smile on his face. Probably dreaming of a soccer goal. I tucked his covers in then crossed the hall to Jenna's room. I knocked on her door and she gave me permission to enter.

She glanced at my garment bag. "Did you find what you were looking for?"

"Uh-huh. I bought this amazing dress. I was going to try it on for you but then I saw Ben's note. I have to drive to the store and buy a snack for his class."

"Nah, you're good. We made brownies and they're stacked in the Tupperware carrier. I wrote the note so he wouldn't forget to take them in the morning. We figured you had enough on your mind and could use a little help. We didn't want you to screw up this date, too."

In my opinion, I *wasn't* the one who screwed up my last

date, but I was thrilled by Jenna's helpful attitude. I plunked down on her apricot embroidered bedspread. "Guess who I ran into tonight?"

She gave me the look that only a sixteen-year-old daughter can give. Okay, maybe she is too old for guessing games. "Nadine. According to her, she and your dad split up."

Jenna's eyes lit up and her smile was the widest I'd seen since our divorce. "Now you and Dad can get together again." She catapulted from her chair and twirled around the room. Her mattress whooshed as she landed in a happy sprawl on the bed.

My heart plummeted. Why hadn't I realized what her reaction would be? With Nadine out of the picture, Jenna assumed Hank and I would reconcile. My garment bag dropped to the floor as I embraced my daughter. She might be four inches taller, but I was still her mother.

"Honey, your dad and I aren't getting back together. It just means he's no longer living with Nadine." I frowned when I realized her father had neglected to inform me he was residing elsewhere. "Did you know he had moved?"

She gave me a sheepish look reminiscent of the man in question. "He told me he and Nadine were having problems so he moved in with his friend Bill. I thought…I thought maybe we could all be a family again…" Her voice trailed off as she slumped against me.

All the anger I felt when Hank left two years ago erupted in full force. How dare he let Jenna get her hopes up for a reconciliation? It was a good thing he wasn't standing in front of me because I definitely had murder on my mind.

I kissed the top of her tangled auburn hair. "We'll discuss it tomorrow." The shopping expedition had worn me out and I didn't have the emotional stamina to think about my ex-husband's deceit right now. It could wait until the next day.

Unfortunately, Hank didn't give me the opportunity. He

left a voicemail Friday morning informing me he would pick up the kids from school. I would have to wait until he brought them home on Sunday before I could berate him. Although our divorce decree granted joint custody, it ended up more like an eighty/twenty split. I hoped their lack of quality time with their father wouldn't make them any more dysfunctional than most children. Considering the amount of time they spent with me, that was probably a given.

Despite Jeremy's courteous demeanor during our previous meeting, I was somewhat apprehensive about having him come to our house. Not to mention he probably wasn't used to tripping over the G.I. Joes and Matchbox cars that normally decorated our family room.

After a restless night, I woke up early, determined my house would be so clean I could invite the first lady to dinner. I swept, vacuumed, scrubbed and polished. Once the house was immaculate it was my turn to be scrubbed and polished. I skipped lunch and by six o'clock, I was ready. Thanks to Liz, my face was aglow with sunny sheen foundation, an organic product that guaranteed I'd look ten years younger. Too bad it couldn't guarantee I'd look ten pounds lighter.

With extra time on my hands, I paced through the house. I was half looking forward to the date and half dreading it. My pacing eventually brought me into the kitchen. A little wine wouldn't hurt and it might relax me. I uncorked a bottle of chardonnay just as the doorbell rang. I took a sip of liquid fortification about the size of a Big Gulp, set the glass on the counter and walked to the front door to greet my suitor.

Jeremy stepped into the entry, tall and slim in a gray suit, blue shirt and darker blue tie. He smiled as his eyes appraised me. "Laurel, you look terrific. Are you ready to go?"

"Yes. I didn't know what time the reservations were. Would you like some wine before we leave? There's a bottle of chardonnay open."

"Sure. Sounds good." He followed me into the kitchen and perched on one of the oak bar stools.

I poured a glass for Jeremy and topped off my own. Our glasses clinked as he toasted, "To a beautiful woman and a beautiful evening."

Aww. What a lovely sentiment. Both his words and the wine made me feel all warm and toasty inside. Jeremy was definitely a step, or an entire staircase up from my last date. I beamed at him. He smiled back then took a sip of wine and grimaced. Evidently the doctor wasn't a connoisseur of the McKay house brand, the infamous Two Buck Chuck. He set the glass on the counter then swiveled around, surveying my kitschy yellow kitchen.

"Nice house. Very cozy."

"Thanks. My ex built it. Lots of flaws just like him."

Jeremy looked taken aback. Complaining about your ex is a no-no on your first date. Love Club rules.

"I guess all men are flawed to some extent. No matter how hard we try, perfection eludes us." He shrugged. "Are you ready to go?"

Strange remark. Jeremy looked troubled but since he didn't elaborate, I didn't push. Maybe once we reached the restaurant he'd feel comfortable confiding in me. I eyed my glass of wine. I hated to waste good chardonnay. I also hated to waste cheap chardonnay. I took one quick sip then put the glass down by the sink.

I locked my front door and we walked out to Jeremy's navy Mercedes. He politely helped me in without making any anatomical detours. I settled into the passenger seat, admiring the gleaming burled walnut paneling and array of controls on the dashboard. "Nice car."

"Your cars are the clothing you drive in." He shot me a sideways glance. If that were true, I was currently riding in a tux. But what did my pastel hybrid say about me?

It was a short drive to the restaurant. Jeremy handed the keys to the valet and we strolled down the slate pathway to the entrance of the River Inn. Between the vaulted ceilings, pine-paneled walls and enormous green plants interspersed throughout the restaurant, it was like entering a primeval forest. The hostess greeted us warmly and we followed her to a romantic corner booth overlooking the American River.

Jeremy immediately started perusing the wine list while I admired the tumultuous river crashing over the rocks below the restaurant. When the waiter appeared, my date lifted his gray curls from the menu. "We'll have a bottle of the 1976 Dom Perignon."

The waiter looked impressed, nodding his head in approval. "Excellent choice, sir. I'll be back shortly."

I was also impressed and displayed my approval by emitting a tiny burp. Uh-oh. Maybe I shouldn't have drunk that chardonnay on an empty stomach. Our waiter arrived with a silver ice bucket, two crystal flutes and the two-hundred-dollar bottle of champagne. A muffled pop and—voila, I was holding a fifty-dollar glass of booze.

The busboy delivered a basket loaded with some garlicky smelling focaccia bread. Jeremy was still engrossed in reviewing the wine list so I withdrew two pieces and slathered on some butter. The doctor was either trying to make a major impression on me or he was a wine connoisseur bar none. I sipped the champagne and munched on the excellent refined carbs while gazing at the churning river below.

My date finally looked up from the two-inch-thick gold embossed wine list. "Laurel, do you have any preferences for reds?"

My only preference was that the wine didn't taste like

grape juice. How could I convince him I was a connoisseur, as well? "I prefer red wines from the Napa Valley." That should narrow it down to a couple hundred choices.

I sipped the champagne while Jeremy examined the list. He smiled, finally selecting a 2006 Heitz Cabernet Sauvignon. Undoubtedly a better choice than the $1.99 bottle I served earlier. The waiter stood, pen in hand, primed for our orders.

I held the menu at arm's length then brought it closer, but it was still out of focus. Why was it that the fancier the restaurant, the smaller the font size. When in doubt, stick with the age-old standards. "I'll have the Caesar salad to start and the prime rib, petite cut."

Jeremy was ready with his order. "Spinach salad with nonfat Italian dressing on the side, and the sautéed sea bass, no sauce." He handed his menu to the waiter.

"You have such control over your diet," I said in admiration.

"Everything in moderation." He traced his index finger around the rim of his crystal champagne flute. "It's an easy motto to follow. But there are those who just can't help their addictive personalities."

I looked down at the crumbs littering my bread plate. Time to turn the conversation in a different direction before another lecture on my diet was forthcoming. "What do you like to do for fun?"

His smile lit up his face and his shoulders relaxed for the first time this evening. "I enjoy going up to Lake Tahoe. I can never get enough of its incredible beauty. Last summer I hiked most of the Tahoe Rim Trail. In fact, I'm thinking of buying a vacation home on the south shore."

My mother would so love to get her hands on Jeremy. A doctor and a multiple homeowner.

"Your practice must be doing well."

His pensive look returned as he drank his champagne. "It is. I've been very fortunate. But something odd came up when I made the offer on the property. Laurel, since you're in the mortgage business, I thought you could explain how..."

A buzzing noise suddenly erupted. I jumped and banged the crystal flute into the table, champagne droplets landing on the beads of my new dress. Jeremy grabbed his pager from his belt and silenced it.

"I didn't realize you were on call tonight." I bent and dabbed the spots with the black linen napkin. Smart restaurant. No white lint speckling our dark clothing. Too bad they couldn't guarantee my dress remain in a spill-free zone.

Jeremy seemed perplexed as he stared at the number on his pager. "It's not an emergency, but I need to make a call. I'll go outside so I don't disturb anyone. Enjoy the champagne. I'll be back shortly."

Being the obliging person that I am, I sipped the bubbly that hadn't landed on my dress. I didn't normally drink champagne but this Dom stuff tasted pretty good. I wondered if Jeremy treated all of his dates to such fine wine and cuisine. It wouldn't be too difficult to become accustomed to such first-class treatment.

My eyes glanced wistfully at the empty breadbasket as I poured more champagne into my flute. The servers must have been waiting until Jeremy returned before they brought our salads. My bladder suddenly announced it needed to make an expedition. I pushed my chair back and the waiter quickly materialized and slid it out for me. My hands gripped the back of the chair as the room did a three-sixty rotation.

"Are you all right?" asked the solicitous server.

I nodded. I was fine for someone who's a lightweight

when it comes to alcohol. I negotiated my way through the restaurant, bumping into two chairs but somehow avoiding landing in anyone's chef's special.

The ladies' room was located in the back of the cocktail lounge. No sign of Jeremy anywhere in the restaurant or the bar. He probably didn't want to disturb the diners and had gone outside to make his call. It wouldn't hurt to take a quick peek. The fresh air might dispel some of the champagne bubbles that seemed to be fogging my brain. I grinned at the valet then sauntered around the side of the building.

I squinted in the direction of the river. Two men stood in the shadows along the riverbank, a hundred feet or so from the restaurant. The moonlight illuminated the back of one man's head indicating he might be bald, so that couldn't be Jeremy. The man facing him had a full head of hair and was about Jeremy's height but I couldn't be sure at that distance. The only thing I was certain of was that it was too cold to stand outside wondering.

I went inside, weaving my way around the black leather bar stools, and entered the ladies' room. After using the facilities, I tried to decide what to do next. Should I go back to the table or wait in the lounge? The beige microfiber chair in the corner of the lounge beckoned. I propped my feet up on the matching ottoman and debated what to do next.

The door burst open and I woke with a start. Two chattering women headed for the stalls. I peeked at my watch.

Good grief. Almost fifteen minutes had elapsed since I'd left the table. I stood up and smoothed my dress over my hips. Either Jeremy would be back at the table or Mr. Dom Perignon and I would become bosom buds. Although after the purchase of my dress, there wasn't enough credit left on my Visa to pay for dinner, much less the Dom.

I opened the door and stepped into the bar, which was

totally deserted. I entered the dining room and saw most of the diners lined up at the large arched windows that overlooked the river. I joined them and addressed the armpit of a navy pin-striped suit. "What's up?"

The tall gentleman glanced down at me. "There may have been an accident. A woman seated by the window thought she saw someone in the river. Several of the staff ran outside to check."

Even in my somewhat befuddled state, I knew this was a treacherous part of the river, with craggy rocks and boulders strewn everywhere. And with temperatures in the fifties, surely no one would intentionally be swimming.

Of course that was assuming the woman who spotted the person in the river wasn't imagining things. Maybe she downed most of a bottle of champagne herself. At the rate I'd been drinking, I was afraid I'd see pink elephants taking a dip. The crowd of people around the window had expanded. I was too short to see anything but I heard several people gasp.

The man next to me said, "It looks like the river rescue team has arrived. I hope they can save the poor sucker."

So did I. Unfortunately there wasn't anything I could do in the way of river rescue, so I wandered back to my romantic booth and gulped down a glass of water, hoping it would dilute some of the champagne. I spotted our server and waved. Maybe he would take pity on me and bring out my salad.

"Sorry, ma'am, I don't wish to ignore you. You heard what happened?"

"I did. Ummm, my date has disappeared. Do you know if he's helping? He's a doc—" I burped "—tor."

He looked taken aback then shook his head. "I don't recall seeing him, but a lot of the guests ran outside. Do you want to check out there? I'll bring your salad as soon as you return."

Sure. Jeremy had to be around here somewhere. I walked through the nearly deserted restaurant and stepped out onto the patio. The temperature had dropped a few more degrees but the cold air felt invigorating to my bubble befuddled brain. It looked like the majority of the restaurant patrons were milling around the outside dining area.

Much as I hated to admit I lost my date, I still needed to find out what happened to him. An El Dorado County deputy was deep in conversation with an emergency technician. I tapped the husky officer on his khaki-clad shoulder.

"Excuse me, is one of the guests at the River Inn helping your rescue team?"

"Sorry, ma'am. I can't say for sure. We've received a lot of unsolicited offers of assistance from the diners at the restaurant."

"Will the person they found in the river be okay?"

The young deputy shook his head, his red-rimmed eyes weary. "No, ma'am. The EMTs tried to resuscitate him but they weren't successful."

"How awful. Was he dining at the restaurant?"

"We assume he was. He was wearing a light gray suit." The deputy's expression was bewildered. "But no one has reported anyone missing."

My Dom Perignon addled brain produced a giggling frenzy as I visualized Jeremy jumping into the river to get away from my boring conversation. The two men appeared startled by my inappropriate outburst.

"Sorry, I've had way too much champagne. You see, my date left the table a while ago and hasn't returned."

They exchanged glances. The deputy spoke first. "We may be able to help." He pulled out a notebook and pen. "His name?"

"Jeremy Slater." My stomach growled. "Sorry. I'm in desperate need of some food."

"I'll see what I can do," he assured me. "In the meantime, why don't you go back to your table?"

The restaurant was devoid of customers with the exception of a silver-haired couple sitting at a table in the bar. They glanced my way then resumed their quiet conversation. I plopped back down in our booth in the empty dining room. I hoped the deputy had some pull. All I wanted was Jeremy and my salad, and at this point I wasn't sure in which order.

After a few minutes of waiting, my patience was maxed out. Time to track down the deputy I spoke with earlier. I slid out of the booth then realized my purse was resting under the table. My chiffon skirt shimmied up my thighs as I grabbed the leather strap. I backed up and bumped into something solid. Jeremy had finally returned.

I turned around to chastise my date but was caught off guard by the man standing in front of me. "Detective Hunter, what are you doing here?"

"I had a dinner reservation but just as we arrived someone discovered the person in the river." The detective seemed uneasy as he shifted from one leg to the other. "One of the deputies told me you were dining with a Jeremy Slater."

"Yeah, I spoke to someone a few minutes ago. Jeremy left to make a call right after we arrived and never returned. He's a physician so I thought he might be helping but no one seems to have seen him." I wrinkled my nose and frowned. "I won't be going out with *him* again."

His gaze softened as his eyes met mine. "No. I'm afraid you won't."

TEN

THE ROOM TURNED INTO A spinning kaleidoscope of colors as I pitched forward. The quick-thinking detective caught me before I connected with the floor. His arms wrapped around me and I curled into his chest as my brain absorbed the fact that Jeremy Slater was dead.

Hunter gently disengaged my limp frame from his and assisted me back to my seat. He slid across from me, not an easy task given his size and the confines of the booth.

"I know this is a huge shock for you but I have to ask a few questions." He took a familiar-looking pad and pen out of his shirt pocket. "You mentioned to one of the deputies that Dr. Slater was missing for quite some time. Was this typical behavior for him?"

"I don't know." Tears streamed down my cheeks. I grabbed a napkin and attempted to staunch the flow of hot teardrops mixed with inky rivulets of mascara. "This was only our second date. Oh, no," I moaned.

"What's the matter?"

"He didn't get to try the Dom."

"The Don?" He looked puzzled.

"The Dom," I repeated again, shaking my head. "You know, Dom Perignon. Right after we placed our dinner orders he received a page and disappeared to make a phone call. He never got to sample the champagne." I hiccupped. "It was very tasty."

"Evidently," he said, a hint of a smile crossing his face for two seconds before it disappeared. "Ms. McKay, you do realize that in the past two weeks, both men you've gone on a date with have died. Two men. Two dates. Two deaths."

I couldn't respond. I could only stare at him with tear-blurred eyes.

"I can't decide if you have an unerring ability for ending up in disastrous situations, or if I'm sitting next to a killer."

"Killer?" My flowing tears froze in shock. "Jeremy was murdered?"

He shrugged. "I don't know yet. It could have been an accidental fall into the river. But until we discover exactly what occurred this is considered a crime scene."

He paused a few seconds while he fiddled with his tie. "Since his wallet was still in his pants pocket we identified the victim as Dr. Slater, but we can make it official, if you can confirm it's his body. Do you think you're up to it?"

My eyes widened in alarm as I contemplated viewing the drowned body of my dead date.

He shook his head. "Never mind, that was a bad idea. I don't think you could handle it."

"Hey, mister. I may be a female, but I'm a mother. We do what we have to do." I stood up, placed my hands on my hips, tossed my hair and glared at the detective. "I'll do it for Jeremy."

Weak female, indeed.

He slid out of the booth, his gaze wandering down the length of my dress, slowing as he contemplated my bare legs. "Do you have a coat? It's chilly out and your dress doesn't look like it provides much warmth."

"No, I didn't bring a coat with me. I never expected to spend any time outside tonight." I shivered. "I'll manage without one."

He hesitated, then took off his sport coat and draped it slowly, almost sensually around me. I noticed his broad shoulders—the kind you wanted to lean on after your date dropped dead.

I squared my own shoulders as he escorted me toward the entrance, his hand resting lightly on my back. As we passed the lounge he halted. "Would you mind waiting here? I need to speak to the couple in the corner. I'll only be a minute."

He walked over to the elderly couple I'd noticed earlier. Could they be witnesses? He must have spoken to them previously, because they jumped right into conversation. It was fine with me if we waited before I viewed Jeremy for one last time.

As I sniffed in the woodsy scent of Detective Hunter's brown tweed jacket I briefly wondered what it would feel like to have his arms around me. Oh, dear. Not an appropriate reaction considering my date was gone. Forever. Must be the residual effects of the champagne.

The detective turned away from the table and strode over to my side. "Sorry about the wait. I needed to check with them about something."

My mind raced with possibilities. "Suspects?"

He laughed. "Hardly. They're my parents. I can personally vouch for them."

Hmm. So he was with his parents. Not a hot date.

Fewer people lingered outside than on my previous visit. The patio was cordoned off with that increasingly familiar yellow ribbon. I was running into crime scene tape far more frequently than a soccer mom should.

One of the deputies stood next to what resembled a gigantic black baggie. My heart plummeted two feet when I realized it was a body bag. The deputy nodded to us. "Evening, Tom. Is this the woman who was with the victim?"

"Yes, Sam. She's agreed to identify the body. Ms. McKay, are you sure you're ready?" Detective Hunter's palm rested on my back as he gazed sympathetically at me. Was this the same man who interrogated me less than two weeks ago? He appeared to have at least one compassionate vein running through his body.

"As ready as I'll ever be." I swallowed and braced myself for the unveiling.

Sam unzipped the bag then looked at me for confirmation.

His eyes were closed, but the pale face and damp curly silver hair were undeniably recognizable.

Omigod. I gasped and frantically looked around as the butterflies in my stomach morphed into an assault team of flying pterodactyls. Hunter took one look at my face and led me over to some shrubbery alongside the patio. A hundred dollars' worth of champagne was eliminated within seconds. The detective grabbed a clean paper napkin off one of the tables and handed it to me. I wiped my mouth and face then collapsed into one of the white plastic patio chairs. I barely knew Jeremy but to see him like that was devastating.

"I take it that was Dr. Slater?"

"Yes." I pressed my hands against my heaving stomach and tried to erase the picture of Jeremy's pallid face from my memory. "I don't know how you detectives get used to seeing dead bodies."

"Your first body is never easy."

"Well, I'm not planning on making a practice of viewing dead bodies."

"Glad to hear it. I'm not sure our sheriff's department is large enough to handle your social life."

I lasered an angry look at the detective.

"Sorry," Hunter apologized, placing his hand on my forearm. "That was uncalled for. Look, we have to complete an in-depth interview with you, but we're shorthanded and

I need to spend time with the crime techs. I hope I'm not going to regret this but I'm sending you home. I assume you drove here together."

"Yes, the valet parked his car. It's some type of large Mercedes."

"We'll need to examine his vehicle, as well. One of the police officers will have to drive you to your house."

I was about to respond when the elderly gentleman who'd been seated at the back of the bar approached and introduced himself. "Hello, I'm Bill Hunter, Tom's father." He extended his hand to me.

I checked to see if there was any icky champagne residue left on my palm before I shook his hand in response. There was a considerable resemblance between the two men. Bill Hunter's eyes were a soft faded brown and he had the same high cheekbones of his son. I detected some Native American influence in their bloodline somewhere. The senior Hunter had a very engaging smile. I recalled Detective Hunter having an equally appealing smile but it wasn't something he displayed with any frequency.

"Your mother is getting tired. Can we leave now or will you need a lift home?"

"Why don't you and Mom take off? I need to arrange transportation for Ms. McKay."

"Where do you live?" Bill Hunter asked. Detective Hunter rattled off my address.

The older Hunter looked mystified. "You two know each other? Is there something you've been keeping from me, son?" he teased.

The detective flushed. "No, Dad. I interviewed Ms. McKay a few weeks ago when her date was found…" His voice faltered.

This was the first time since I'd met Detective Hunter that he lost his composure. So he was human after all.

Maybe.

"Both of our children play soccer in the same league, on different teams. That's how we became acquainted," I explained.

"So you've met our adorable granddaughter. Isn't Kristy a sweetheart?" Bill said with pride in his voice.

"Um, yeah. A real sweetheart." I would have to see Kristy when she wasn't attacking players on the soccer field. It sounded like she had grandpa wrapped tight around her pinky finger.

"You don't live very far from us. We could drive you home. Are you having car problems?"

"Not exactly," I said, grateful for his offer. I rose from the chair then glanced at Detective Hunter. His face had reddened to a dark aubergine.

"Um, Dad, I think, it would be best if she, uh…was driven home by a deputy."

A deputy? What did that mean? Were they taking me into custody?

Bill Hunter winked at me. "I understand why you want to make sure this lovely woman gets home safe. It was nice meeting you, Laurel."

The senior Hunter walked to the back of the restaurant where he joined his wife. They waved as they exited. The detective and I stared at each other. Was this what novels describe as a palpable silence?

I was the first to break it. "Am I under arrest?" I asked, subdued, somber and one hundred percent sober.

He shook his head. "No, but it's not appropriate for my parents to drive you home. Plus I want an officer to check your house and make sure it's safe. Until I find out more about Dr. Slater's death, I still don't know if I should treat you as a suspect—or a potential victim."

Great. I didn't know whether I should be more afraid of

a murderer running amok or being arrested for a murder I didn't commit. He removed his tweed jacket from my shoulders. "I'll get a blanket from the EMTs. That should keep you warm. Let me see if Sam is free to take you home."

I nodded my assent then waited in the lounge for my official chauffeur. A guy hefting a huge video camera lumbered in and glanced around. He left when he noticed it was vacant except for the single woman at the bar. The TV crews had arrived. I hoped I'd be out of there before someone mentioned the dead man wasn't dining alone. It was horrible enough that Jeremy was dead. My children didn't need to see their mother's tear-streaked face plastered all over the eleven o'clock news.

Sam, the deputy I'd met previously, was assigned to transport me home. He handed me a navy blue fleece blanket, which I promptly turned into an oversize pashmina shawl. He escorted me to his patrol car, which was parked a short distance from the restaurant.

I wanted to interrogate my official chauffeur, but he spent most of the drive on the phone. Once we entered the house, Sam checked all the rooms, ensured that each window was locked, and waited until all the bolts were bolted before he took off.

I stared at my watch in disbelief. It felt like three in the morning but it was only ten after eleven. I was halfway up the stairs when I realized I still hadn't eaten dinner. I didn't feel tipsy any longer so my purge behind the bushes must have eliminated the champagne I'd consumed.

Comfort food was required and any form of chocolate was the obvious choice. Unfortunately I'd skipped grocery shopping in order to clean my house. The pantry was barren when it came to my favorite food group. My quick rummage through the refrigerator scored one bruised apple. A little fiber—in Jeremy's honor.

My eyes misted as my gaze drifted to the wineglasses sitting on the counter. A tragic event certainly made a person more appreciative of the simple things in life. To have your life cut short in an instant of time was heartbreaking. I reflected on the difficulties of my life. Trying to make financial ends meet. Struggling between my career and the needs of my children.

The death of my marriage.

All of those problems were mere hiccups. I was blessed with two terrific and caring children, a mother who loved me in her own peculiar fashion, and an array of wonderful and loyal friends. Who would be mourning Jeremy's tragic death tonight?

I plodded up the stairs and put on a pair of flannel jammies, which were perfect for providing the solace I needed. Soft red ones covered with cavorting puppy dogs that my mother gave me the previous Christmas. She didn't think I needed anything sexier and she was probably right. I lay there for hours in my flannel splendor pondering the tragedy of Jeremy's death. What were his last moments like? Was it an accident? Or murder?

Was I in jeopardy? Were my children?

Sometime in the wee hours of the morning, I finally fell into a troubled sleep. I dreamed I was hanging by my fingertips from a bridge over the American River. A tall man with a bald spot on the back of his head was stomping on my hand. Finger by finger, I was losing my grip on the bridge as the turbulent river crashed against the rocks below. A siren wailed in the distance, the piercing sound increasing in volume until the siren was screaming in my ear.

ELEVEN

THE SHRILL RINGING OF THE phone on my nightstand announced an unwelcome wake-up call. "Hello," I croaked as I cradled the receiver against my left ear.

"Is that you, dear?" Good question. I wasn't so sure of the answer myself. It felt like the percussion section of a drum and bugle corps was marching through my head.

"Hello, Mother, how are things?"

"How are things?" Her voice crescendoed to a high pitch. Oh, that was unpleasant.

"Things are not good, Laurel. I'm sitting in my car in the church parking lot. You were supposed to meet me for the ten-thirty service. It's ten-twenty. Are you running late?"

Not exactly. I wasn't running at all. I'd totally forgotten I was supposed to meet my parent for the late service at church, followed by brunch in Apple Hill.

"I'm sorry. I got home late last night and forgot to set my alarm. Why don't you go to church and we can get together for brunch afterward. Do you still want to meet at the Cozy Apple Café?"

"Humph. You've become very inconsiderate lately, Laurel. Your social life should not be interfering with your obligations to your church. I can't imagine what Pastor Martin will think. You've missed services several weekends in a row."

Missing church was the least of my worries. My only hope was that our minister didn't find out I was a double murder suspect. "I'll be at the café by noon."

"All right. Don't be late."

Our family has attended the same church under the leadership of Pastor Martin for the past thirty years. He's a kindly man as I'm sure all men of the cloth are. He is also a very forgiving minister. I was certain he wouldn't hold my lack of attendance against me. Although with the rate the bodies were piling up, I might need someone who had God's ear on my side.

I dragged myself down the stairs into the kitchen. Rays of sun shimmered off my bright yellow walls, which did nothing to alleviate the throbbing in my head. I eyeballed the rooster clock. Time for at least one high-octane cup of caffeine.

I swallowed four aspirin while the coffee perked. Even my automatic drip seemed noisier than usual this morning. Despite the hangover mist hovering in my brain, I couldn't forget the events of the previous evening.

I wondered how Jeremy's body ended up in the river. Could it have been an accident? And those two men I saw talking on the riverbank. If Jeremy was the gray-haired man I had seen, the other man might have left the restaurant before anything happened. He could be totally unaware of the incident. This topic needed to be discussed with Detective Hunter.

I gazed at the clock. Not enough time. The detective would have to be contacted later. It was almost eleven-thirty and I still hadn't made it into the shower. That meant arriving at the restaurant with no makeup and bed hair. I flew up the stairs into my bedroom, slipped on a pair of khaki slacks and a coral blouse that bore two tiny spots on the front, both of which my mother would undoubtedly notice.

My hair resembled Ben's, but with an additional twenty cowlicks. The silver hairs threading their way through my copper mop seemed to be cloning one another. I reached into my closet and smashed an ivory straw hat on my head. My flat hat hair couldn't be helped.

If our pastor was his usual loquacious self the service would run over. My mother normally stayed afterward to glean any new gossip such as job transfers, which could mean a potential listing. With a little luck, I would get to the Cozy Apple Café before she did.

As luck or my lack of it would have it, I hit every red light on the drive to the Apple Hill area east of Placerville. Evidently God was not happy about my missing church this morning and was punishing me accordingly. My mother's white Chrysler Le Baron, a testament to her fastidious-ness, gleamed in the parking lot. I pulled into the slot next to her car.

I jogged across the asphalt parking lot and entered the restaurant. Mother was seated in a cracked red Naugahyde booth not far from the cash register, dressed in a rose knit suit that complemented her platinum coloring. I smiled as I watched her pore over every inch of the large glossy menu, matching rose-colored reading glasses balanced on her straight nose. She was undeniably the most annoying woman on earth but…she was my mother.

"Church must have gotten out early." I air kissed her cheek then slid into the opposite side of the booth.

She looked up from the menu and frowned. "What's the matter with your hair?"

Well, hello to you, too. I chose to ignore her comment. A bad hair day was the least of my concerns.

"How was the service? Did you hear any good gossip?" That should occupy her until I decided what to order from the extensive menu. Almost twenty-four hours had passed since anything substantial entered and remained in my stomach.

Should I continue to watch my diet or just say screw it?

The café specialized in six different versions of eggs Benedict and my favorite was a poached egg sitting on a slice of tomato perched on a crab cake, drenched with a creamy hollandaise sauce. Breakfast didn't come much more fattening than that, unless I added bacon and fried potatoes on the side.

Engrossed in the bounty of Benedicts, I missed her next question.

"Laurel, did you hear me?" Her glare was magnified fourfold by the reading glasses.

"Sorry." I slapped the menu shut. "What did you say?"

"All the talk at church today was about the accident at the River Inn last night. They said a man fell in the river but he had drowned by the time the rescue workers could pull him out. The Parkers were dining there and saw the whole thing. Hugh Parker said the police roped off the patio with crime scene tape. Did you hear or see something while you were there?"

She looked at me with anticipation, probably hoping I would have firsthand knowledge she could share with her cronies.

Once she heard my "up close and personal" firsthand information, I doubted she would want to share it with anyone. Fortunately our conversation was interrupted by the arrival of the waitress with a pot of coffee. More caffeine was needed before I could deal with my mother's questions. I dumped in one packet of sugar then grabbed a second one. This breakfast required extra carbs to get me through the impending inquisition.

"Didn't you notice anything at all? And you haven't even mentioned how your date went."

I gazed at the six-tier dessert showcase displayed next to the cashier. The revolving tiers of fruit-filled cobblers and whipped cream–topped lemon and chocolate pies were spinning around and around, exactly how the carousel of my life felt right now.

"Let's place our order then I'll fill you in."

Our server materialized the minute our menus were set down. Her cheeks were as rosy as the apples dotting her crisp white apron. "Ladies, what will you have this bright sunny day?" she asked way too cheerfully.

Bet none of her dates drowned last night.

"I'll have two eggs lightly basted, with three slices of bacon, not undercooked but not burnt, and an English muffin, lightly buttered with butter, not margarine."

The waitress scribbled quickly to make sure she didn't miss any of my mother's precise order. You have to admire a woman who knows exactly what she wants. When she glanced at me I decided to go whole hog. "I'll have the crab Benedict. Lightly sauced," I added with a grin.

She winked. "Yeah, right. I'll be back with a coffee refill."

Mother folded her arms against her chest. "All right, Laurel, no more delays. Tell me about last night."

I reflected back on the previous evening, trying to decide where to begin. I commenced with Jeremy's arrival at my front door. I had just mentioned the high-end champagne when our server arrived with a huge tray loaded with our breakfast order. It looked like the eggs, bacon and muffins were all cooked to my mother's very specific directions. No wonder she kept coming back here for brunch.

"This Dr. Slater really seems like a catch. Perhaps I was too hasty in judging the Love Club." She bit into her toast. "I can't believe he ordered Dom Perignon. Did you enjoy it?"

Did I ever. I nodded, the savory hollandaise sauce dribbling down my chin.

"Did he ask you out again?" She poured some cream

into her coffee, slowly stirring it while she waited for my response. I shoveled the crab Benedict into my mouth, hoping she wouldn't expect an answer if my mouth was full.

"Slow down, dear. You're eating much too fast. Did Dr. Slater ask you to go out with him again?"

I swallowed a bite of crab. It was time to bite the bullet, as well. "No, Jeremy didn't ask me out again. He isn't going to be available for me to go out with."

"Why not? Is he going out of town?" With the skill of a surgeon she precisely cut a piece of bacon and placed it in her mouth.

"No, Jeremy is uh, uh…" I couldn't think of anything else to say so I finished with, "dead."

Her eyes bugged out and she started choking. Ever the dutiful daughter, I grabbed her water glass and handed it to her. She swallowed a few sips, eyes contemplating me as she set the glass down. "Dead?"

I winced and nodded. She picked up her fork. The utensil hovered over her plate like a helicopter, finally landing on a bite of egg. I marveled at her calm, waiting for the barrage of questions to begin.

"Am I to assume Jeremy is the man who drowned in the river?"

"Yes, Mother." I shared the details without a single interruption. She was either marvelously in control or totally in shock.

"Laurel, I must say I'm at a total loss for words." In thirty-nine years, this was the first time I could recall my mother acknowledging such an event.

"Do you see any reason why it wouldn't have been an accident?"

"I can't imagine anyone intentionally pushing Jeremy in the river. It's a good thing I was in the bathroom when this occurred or I might be considered a suspect."

She sat there shaking her head. "Laurel, Laurel, Laurel."

"Mother, Mother, Mother," I mimicked in reply.

She pursed her thin lips together. "This situation is far too serious to joke about. I hope you finally realize how foolish this Love Club idea is. Obviously they haven't screened their members. It's much too dangerous for you to go out with these strangers."

"Mother, you're making some rash assumptions. We don't know how or why Garrett was killed. And we still don't know if Jeremy drowned accidentally or not." My lips twisted as I smiled wryly. "The only danger appears to be when someone goes out with me."

Our waitress brought more coffee and inquired whether we were finished. We both seemed to have lost our appetites so I grabbed the bill and stopped at the cashier station to pay. As far as I was concerned this was enough mother-and-daughter bonding for today. As we exited the restaurant my mother halted in the middle of the pavement. Tears welled in her eyes.

"Mom, what's the matter?"

She foraged in her purse and pulled out a prepackaged tissue. She gently wiped her eyes and blew her nose before continuing. "You know how worried I am about you going out with these strange men. If anything happened to you, I don't know what I would do."

I was touched. It was so seldom my mother showed any emotion, especially in public.

"Honest, right now I have zero desire to go on another date."

"Well, don't totally give up on men. You just need to go out with someone you can trust."

We hugged and headed toward our respective vehicles. We were almost to our cars when she asked, "What kind of costume is Ben wearing for Halloween?"

Oops. Time I focused on my children instead of my primal urges. "Ben and I are going to work on his costume tonight, as soon as the kids return home from their weekend with Hank."

We parted company, she in her pristine car and I in my dusty hybrid. The kids wouldn't be home until around six so I decided some quiet time would do me some good. I drove to my favorite orchard and sat at a picnic table surrounded by apple-laden trees overlooking the farm's trout-filled pond. It felt good to relax, the sun caressing me with its warmth while I gnawed on a caramel apple. Between the sunshine and the high dosage of sugar, the tension eased out of my shoulders.

Back at the house, I decided it wouldn't hurt to emulate my mother. I not only scrubbed my car from one sparkling periwinkle end to the other, I found time to whip up some chocolate chip cookies for the kids. And possibly their father. When we were married I used to hide cookies in my lingerie drawer to keep Hank from devouring the entire batch.

One would think a man would never stray from a wife who smelled like chocolate.

My arms were elbow deep in suds when the timer beeped. I wiped my hands on a dish towel, grabbed a potholder and opened the oven door. The front door blew open and the kids serenaded me with their theme song, "Hey, Mom, where are you?"

Perfect timing. I turned to greet them, baking sheet in hand.

A furry animal scurried over my bare foot. I screamed and the metal pan flew into the air. Hot cookies rained melted chocolate on the floor.

"Kids, there's a rat in the kitchen." I opened the door

of the pantry and looked for a weapon. A can of Pringles would have to suffice.

"Mom," wailed Ben, "that's not a rat. It's our new kitten. You've probably scared her to death." Ben picked up the furry creature, which was cowering next to the stove. He cuddled her in one arm while he chomped on one of the few cookies that escaped landing on the floor.

Jenna bent over and began picking up the cookies that were splattered all over the floor.

"Mom, you need to get glasses. Can't you tell it's a kitten? Isn't she adorable?"

I took a closer look at the "adorable" kitten. She was a strange blend of orange and black hair with enormous pointed ears, definitely the homeliest cat I'd ever encountered.

"We got her at the mall and named her Pumpkin 'cause she's orange and black and it's almost Halloween. We can keep her, can't we? Dad said you wouldn't mind." Ben looked over my shoulder and I turned to glower at a sheepish Hank.

"Sure, honey, I mean, Laurel. I know you had a tough weekend, so we went to the mall to pick up a costume for Ben. He said you'd been too busy to work on one this year."

My ex. Master of the guilt trip.

"Dad bought me this terrific costume. I'm going to be Spider-Man." Ben transferred the kitten to Jenna's willing arms then proceeded to climb the cabinets in Spider-Man style, leaving chocolate imprints all over my oak paneled doors.

"We picked up cat food and a litter box. We promise to clean it every day. Honest." Jenna's eyes pleaded with me as she stroked the tiny orange-and-black critter. The odds were fifty to one that my children would remember to empty the litter box every day. But I was grateful the costume issue was resolved, so I grudgingly nodded. How much trouble could a tiny kitten be?

Hank looked relieved at my acquiescence. The four of us, plus their furry friend, trooped outside to bring in the kids' suitcases and the kitten paraphernalia. We were outside less than twenty seconds when Pumpkin leaped out of Ben's arms and decided to investigate our garden.

What I didn't anticipate was that Pumpkin would discover a butterfly and chase it. She had probably never been outside before and was now presented with the opportunity to explore the wonders of nature. Ben discovered a nine-week-old kitten could run faster than a seven-year-old boy. Pumpkin streaked across the lawn, Ben and Jenna racing after her. I was right on their heels.

We couldn't let little Pumpkin turn into pumpkin pie!

Pumpkin miraculously avoided the street. She climbed up the back tire of the Prius, jumped on the trunk, clambered up the rear window and onto the roof of the car, leaving a trail of tiny dirty paw prints for us to admire. She paused and began calmly washing her paws.

"See, Mom." Ben scooped up the kitten. "Pumpkin is smart enough to stay away from the street." Terrific. Too bad she wasn't smart enough to stay off my car. There went my plan to emulate my mother's immaculate habits. With two children and a new kitten I should concentrate on things within my control—as soon as I could think of any.

The kids hauled their stuff, including their new pet, upstairs. I offered Hank some cookies, which I knew he wouldn't refuse. I neglected to mention that his goodies adorned the floor a few minutes earlier. He inhaled them in seconds. "You still make a great chocolate chip cookie."

I narrowed my eyes. I knew when my ex was buttering me up for something.

He cleared his throat. "I need to tell you something."

"Something like you and Nadine split up?"

He stopped midchomp. "How did you find out?"

"I have my sources." I grabbed a cookie and nibbled on it. I needed chocolate—but strictly for medicinal purposes. "So what happened between the two of you?"

"I broke it off. I've missed being with you, Laurel."

I snorted. Not a wise move when your mouth is filled with cookie crumbs. I grabbed a tumbler from the cabinet and filled it with tap water. Once I stopped choking I was able to continue. "This concerns me, how?"

"Well, I…"

I thought Hank was reaching for another cookie, but he grabbed my right hand instead and pulled me close, my five foot four inches nestled against his six-foot frame. For a brief moment, I relaxed against his familiar chest. My eyes closed as he gently massaged my back in that way that had soothed me on so many nights. It felt good to be held by someone who wanted me, cared about me, desired… Hey?

I felt a movement that brought back familiar memories. I jumped back and swatted his hand. "What do you think you're doing?"

He smirked. "See, hon, you still turn me on. When Jenna told me you joined the Love Club it made me realize how much I miss you. We had twenty great years together. Don't turn your back on me. Doesn't everyone deserve a second chance?"

Evidently our definition of twenty great years differed dramatically. I wanted to kick his sorry butt through the back door but I merely shoved him in that direction. "Get out."

He snatched two more cookies and exited the kitchen with one last parting shot.

"Just remember. I love you and I want you back."

TWELVE

I DREAMED I WAS KISSING A mustached stranger. I woke up to discover a furry paw glued to my moisturized face. Blech. I pushed the kitten off my face and attempted to remove strands of her hair from my mouth. She emitted a piercing howl, ran across the bed knocking my fake Tiffany lamp to the floor, then raced down the stairs.

I finally cornered her in the kitchen where she was amenable to a bribe of roasted turkey. After I shut her in our oversize laundry room I crawled back into bed. Two o'clock. Less than four hours until my alarm went off. Hank was probably sleeping just fine tonight. Perhaps the kids should get him a kitten for Christmas so their dad could also experience the joy of owning a pet.

Seconds before I drifted back to sleep I remembered Hank's comment about my tough weekend. Was he referring to my tragic date? Or brunch with mother?

Getting the kids ready for school with the distraction of our new pet made me late to work. As I walked into the lobby, which was decorated with pumpkins and hay bales, Vivian pointed at the clock hanging over the double doors. I hustled down the corridor past two rows of cubicles, turned the corner and bumped into Stan. He was standing, newspaper in hand, undoubtedly waiting to interrogate me. He watched in silence as I hung my jacket on the coatrack and stored my purse in the bottom drawer. Then he laid the front page of the paper on my desk.

The headlines of our local newspaper, the *Mountain Democrat,* screeched at me.

DISTINGUISHED DOCTOR DIES
DURING DEADLY DINNER

That got my attention. The newspaper must be giving brownie points for excessive alliteration. I tried to read but couldn't concentrate with Stan staring at me. I pictured imaginary question marks dotting his broad forehead.

"Dare I ask about your weekend?"

"Shush." I pressed my index finger to my lips. "We'll have the whole office asking questions if they find out I was involved."

I dropped my voice and leaned across my desk. "Have you heard anything about the accident from anyone else?"

He nodded. "Rosa mentioned it this morning when we were getting coffee. She said her entire family had been going to Dr. Slater for almost ten years since he initially opened up his practice. She raved on and on about what a wonderful doctor he was, very caring and friendly. Not the kind of doctor who gives you a ninety-second exam then moves on to the next patient."

He stood and plucked at the pleats in his perfectly pressed khaki pants. "Look, I'll go back to my desk, give you time to read the article. Buzz me when you want to talk."

I read the article word for word, not skimming it like I normally would. It contained numerous glowing references to Dr. Slater, his career and contributions to local charities. His closest relative was a younger brother who also resided in El Dorado Hills. The reporter didn't mention any specifics regarding a murder investigation, just the statement that the authorities were looking into all possibilities and nothing was ruled out at this time.

My stomach knotted up as I continued reading. The last paragraph concluded: *The El Dorado County Sheriff's Department has indicated that Dr. Jeremy Slater was dining with a female companion at the River Inn the evening of his death. They are withholding her identity pending further investigation. The waiter at the River Inn described the woman as a short, middle-aged redhead.*

Middle-aged? The nerve of that waiter. He was probably upset he didn't get a tip.

Well, here was a tip. Don't expect to get tips from women you describe as middle-aged.

At least the newspaper hadn't mentioned my name. My employer was a conservative bank that catered to an equally conservative clientele. Management would not be happy if I was implicated in a criminal inquiry. But what did the sheriff's department mean when they referred to further investigation of Jeremy's dinner companion?

I wished Liz were in town to discuss the latest debacle of my brief Love Club membership, but she and Brian had gone to Monterey to scout for wedding sites. The shrill ringing of my phone disturbed my reverie. I hoped it was Liz returning one of the many messages I'd left on her home phone yesterday.

"Hi," I said.

"Ms. McKay, good morning."

I recognized the caller immediately but the formality in his voice didn't bode well. Was this what they meant by further investigation?

I decided to be equally formal. "Good morning, Detective Hunter."

"Detective Bradford and I would like to ask you some

questions. Could you set aside a few minutes this afternoon for us to come to the bank and talk?"

"Not here," I said, evidently too loudly. Mary Lou's blond waves popped over our adjoining cubicle wall. I really was going to have to get a promotion so I could get my own office. These cubes were not designed to conduct a personal conversation in private although that's probably why they were constructed that way to begin with. "I'm sorry but I doubt if my boss would appreciate having the sheriff's department interviewing me here in the bank. You would be a bit of a distraction." I wasn't sure what would create the greater distraction—the uniforms or Detective Hunter's imposing presence.

"There's a Starbucks right around the corner from the bank. Would it be possible to meet there?" I asked.

I heard him confer with someone else. "That's fine. What time?" We agreed on two-thirty for our meeting. The minute I disconnected, Stan ambled over to my desk. He must have grown tired of waiting for me to buzz him.

"C'mon, the least you can do is give your favorite personal shopper some feedback on your new dress." He eased into the chair in front of my desk. "Was the doctor so dazzled by your beauty that he fell into the river and plunged to his death?"

I frowned at Stan's warped sense of humor but realized I would never get any work done until I related what happened. Stan listened intently and only interrupted once.

"Dom? He ordered Dom Perignon for your first date? What a great catch he would have been. You need to be less careless and stop losing your dates."

"Okay, that's it. Go annoy someone else." I swiveled my chair around and watched the icons on my computer screen blur together as tears of frustration clouded my contact lenses.

The springs on the chair squeaked as Stan abruptly stood up. I immediately regretted my small outburst. "Stan, I'm sorry. I'm really shook up and your cavalier attitude was the last straw."

He walked around the desk and squeezed the back of my neck. "You're right. I was totally out of line." His gaze veered to the left. "Uh-oh. You better get back to work. I spy Earl heading this way." Stan quickly disappeared down the aisle to his own cube.

Having learned from past experience never to be empty-handed when Earl appeared, I rummaged through my file drawer, pretending to be in search of something. I felt a brief touch of a beefy palm on my shoulder and spun around, narrowly missing colliding with my boss.

"Laurel, I haven't had an opportunity to say good morning to you yet. Did you have a nice weekend?"

"Huh? Oh, yeah, fine," I mumbled and continued my drawer ravaging. Earl eased his hefty frame into the chair Stan had vacated.

"Anything new and exciting in your life?" he asked as a chorus of squeaks protested his visit.

Nope. At least nothing I planned to share with my boss.

He clasped his hands behind his neck and leaned back. "I wanted you to know how pleased the bank is with your performance. The delinquency ratio on the loans you've underwritten is the lowest in the department and I know you're handling more volume than any of the other underwriters."

Well, that was a relief. My life had been so chaotic recently I worried that I might screw up some of the loans I was underwriting. My shoulders relaxed and I blasted a broad smile at my boss. "Thanks, Earl, I appreciate the feedback."

"Just thought you should know we recognize your hard work. I was afraid you might apply for that branch manager position." He winked at me. "I wouldn't want to lose such a valuable and attractive employee."

Branch manager? How did I miss that? Well, duh, if I paid more attention to my career than my sex life I might have noticed. As soon as Earl stepped away I would check the job postings in the break room to see if it was too late to apply.

But what was this about a valuable and attractive employee?

"Anything else I can do for you, with the exception of a raise, ha-ha?"

Ha-ha. "No, Earl, everything is fine. Bye." Hopefully he would get the hint that I had work to do. Like finding out what the bank is paying branch managers these days. I could use a pay increase, especially now that there was an extra mouth to feed, albeit a very tiny mouth. Although at the rate Pumpkin was streaking through our house, our breakage costs could well exceed any salary increase.

Earl left my cube, giving me another one of those gentle pats on my shoulder.

I spent the next four hours trying to cram in a full day's work. I wasn't sure how long the meeting with the detectives would take and that branch manager posting needed to be checked out as soon as I returned.

On my way out, I stopped in the ladies' room to refresh my lipstick and peel off a few stray orange and black hairs from my teal silk blouse. I zipped through the lobby, walked outside and shivered. Although the sky was as bright as the sky-blue crayon in Ben's Crayola box, it was chilly— probably only in the mid-fifties. My jacket was still hanging in my cubicle so I increased my pace to a slow jog. I flung open the door of Starbucks and barreled straight into one massive detective.

"Whoa, little lady," he said in a fair imitation of Gary Cooper.

Little lady. How cute. Way better than the newspaper description of a short, middle-aged woman.

My nipples hardened and I drew back. Must be the brisk wind outside that produced that effect. It couldn't possibly be the proximity of my chest to his. My face flushed as I apologized. "Sorry to crash into you. It's cold outside."

"Anytime."

Anytime?

"I saved that table." He pointed to the rear of the restaurant. "A hot drink should warm you up. What can I get you?"

"I'll have a grande nonfat mocha with one Equal and two squirts of cinnamon syrup, hold the whipped cream."

He rolled his eyes. "Women. Even their drinks are complicated." He whipped out his pen and his dog-eared spiral notebook from the inside pocket of his leather jacket. The dark brown leather looked soft and touchable.

I wanted to reach out and caress him.

I mean the jacket. I wanted to caress the soft leather jacket.

"Okay, repeat that one more time. Are you sure you didn't forget anything?" His pen hovered over his pad.

I described my concept of the perfect mocha again. It was a good thing Detective Hunter kept that notepad handy to write down my order. Was that the same pad that contained his notes on the investigation?

I meandered back to the corner table in the rear of the Starbucks, the scent of freshly roasted coffee, chocolate and cinnamon permeating the room. This was one of the larger Starbucks and the store was furnished with an ample number of wooden tables and chairs, plus some seating areas with cushy deep green upholstered chairs. The only other occupants were two fortyish women at one table surrounded by shopping bags and a single man carrying on a conversation with himself. Or maybe not. A Bluetooth gadget stuck out of his ear.

A few minutes later, Detective Hunter strode toward our table with my mocha grande and what looked like a plain cup of coffee for him. Typical policeman. It was too bad Starbucks didn't sell jelly doughnuts. That might have softened him up.

The two women eyed him as he carefully wove his way down the aisle trying not to spill the drinks. They simultaneously reached into their purses, grabbed their respective compacts and applied fresh lipstick.

Interesting effect he had on women. Present company excluded, of course. Too bad his personality wasn't as agreeable as his face, and his shoulders and his...

Hunter placed the drinks on the table then hung his jacket over the chair. I couldn't help but notice how his soft tan turtleneck molded to his muscled chest. The sound of his voice interrupted my pectoral musings.

"One nonfat grande mocha with one Equal, two squirts of cinnamon, no whipped cream, and good old French roast coffee for me. How did I do?"

"Excellent," I replied. "If you ever decide to make a career change, you can always get a job here."

"Well, if I don't start making progress on both these murders, the sheriff may give me the option of being recruited by Starbucks."

"Two murders?"

"Two murder investigations with one common thread."

His dark eyes, the color of my mocha, pierced right through me as he sipped his coffee.

I gulped my mocha. Ouch. Hot. Very hot.

He lifted the notepad from his pocket and picked up his pen again.

"Talking another order?" A little levity couldn't hurt.

His brow furrowed as he contemplated his notebook, then me. Okay, maybe it could. "Ms. McKay..."

"Please call me Laurel," I interrupted. "After all, our kids play soccer together. You don't think a soccer mom could be a murderer, do you?"

"Are you kidding? I've seen soccer moms on the sidelines. They're scary." He softened his words with a slight smile. "Ms. McKay..." He hesitated then continued, "Laurel, the waiter at the River Inn stated that you disappeared from the table several minutes after Jeremy left the dining room. He said you were gone for quite a while, sufficient time to have ventured outside the restaurant and confronted Jeremy. Where did you go and why?"

I gnawed at my thumbnail, a precursor to heavy cerebellum activity for me, and reflected back on that evening. "Well, the waiter kept pouring champagne in my glass so I kept drinking it, waiting for Jeremy to return to our table. Eventually I needed to use the ladies' room. I was kind of inebriated. Wait a minute. Did the waiter say anything about those two men by the river?"

"What men?"

Now it was my turn to be frustrated. I was about to chastise him when it dawned on me that we had never discussed the mysterious strangers.

"When you were grilling me—" I paused as he frowned. Okay. Poor word choice. "When you and I discussed the incident Saturday night, I was kind of in an alcoholic haze.

Yesterday I remembered the two men. I meant to give you a call today but you beat me to it."

He picked up his coffee cup and drained it. "Tell me more."

"I wish there was more to tell. I stepped outside looking for Jeremy and noticed two men standing along the bank of the river. One man's back was to me. He was on the tall side and it looked like he was balding, although I'm not really positive because it was dark out, although the moon was shining, kind of..."

He looked confused and I didn't blame him. I backed up and tried again.

"Anyway, there were two men talking but I couldn't see them clearly, and one of them was about Jeremy's height. It was chilly out so I went back inside and went into the ladies' room. Then I sat down in this comfy lounge chair and fell asleep for about fifteen minutes."

He cocked his eyebrow at me.

"Honest." I held up my right hand. "That's the whole truth, and nothing but the truth."

He slammed the notebook shut and threw it on the table. "Laurel, this is no joking matter. Do you have any idea how serious this is?"

I slumped down in my chair. "I just can't believe I'm a suspect in both of these deaths. Who needs an alibi when she falls asleep in the ladies' room?" My face lit up as I remembered something pertinent to the investigation. "What about the fact that Garrett was killed by a blunt instrument and not from his head hitting the window when I smacked him with his cell? Doesn't that exonerate me from his murder?"

His smile evaporated in less than a second. "You know this how?"

Darn. When was I going to start engaging my brain before my lips? I needed to divert his attention from the fact that someone in the District Attorney's office might have shared some official inside information with his fiancée, who might have shared it with her best friend.

"So where's Detective Bradford?"

"He'll be joining us shortly. He was called away to look into another incident. Would you feel more comfortable if we went down to headquarters and you made a formal statement there?"

Headquarters? No, not really.

"No, um…thank you, this will do just fine. C'mon, Detective, you can't seriously think I'm some type of a Black Widow trying to knock off eligible bachelors? Trust me, there are not enough decent single men in this town as it is. Why would I want to eliminate some great candidates? Garrett wasn't much of a prospect but Jeremy was charming and generous. I think we could have developed a wonderful relationship."

He leaned back in his chair and crossed one blue-jeaned knee over the other as he stared at me.

"Really?" The intensity in his voice was surprising.

I nodded in response. "Absolutely."

Despite the clatter of cups banging against the espresso machine, the silence between us was deafening. These silences were starting to get on my nerves.

"So, what is Kristy wearing for Halloween?" Better to engage in useless drivel than sit in morbid silence.

Hunter's shoulders started shaking and the next thing I knew he was laughing. Aw, he did have a nice smile. Too bad he didn't use those facial muscles more often. "Honestly, if you are a murderer, you are the coolest, smoothest killer I have ever encountered. What is Kristy wearing for Halloween? I wish I knew what to do with you," he said, still chuckling.

"Well, for starters," I said, gazing up at him with what I hoped was a look of pure innocence. "You could share your little notebook with me."

"My notebook?" His face wore a blank look. "Did you want to review your drink order?"

"No. I want to know what you've found out. Don't you have notes on the murders in there?"

"Possibly," said my infuriating companion. He flipped the pages of the aforesaid notebook back and forth.

I forced myself to take a few calming breaths before I barreled on. Lamaze breathing comes in handy. Except for those two times I was in labor. "Okay, let me rephrase my question. Isn't it possible that I, the common thread, as you referred to me a few minutes ago, could assist you in this murder investigation? Besides, I seem to be the only link between the two murders."

"Yes, indeed. You are the only link," boomed a voice from behind my back.

Startled, I shot up and knocked my chair over backward, which resulted in Booming Voice spilling hot coffee all over his baggy brown suit. His uncensored remarks sent the barista scurrying to a room in the back of the store.

Detective Hunter attempted to stifle a smile by holding his napkin to his lips. His partner yanked a chair from the table opposite ours. He deposited himself and his nearly empty cup of coffee at our table.

Bradford was even scarier than I remembered. Still tall. Still bald. Still crabby. Detective Hunter retrieved my chair from the floor and indicated I should sit down again.

"So, Ms. McKay," growled the hulk, "you've managed to get yourself in even more hot water, haven't you? Are you ready to book her, Tom?"

Book her? Wait a minute. There were loans to review, children to pick up from soccer and Halloween cookies to bake, um…purchase. I didn't have time to be booked. I wasn't certain what booking meant, but it didn't sound like something I wanted on my agenda.

"Ms. McKay has been very cooperative," said the younger detective.

I have? I looked at him suspiciously. Was this one of those good cop–bad cop routines?

Bradford crushed his empty cardboard cup and hurled it at the garbage can. It bounced on the metal rim of the container then smacked the barista right on her pierced nose. She screamed and disappeared into the back room again. It was a good thing there were only two people waiting in line instead of the usual ten. They both graced Detective Bradford with evil looks.

"Detective Bradford, why do you refuse to believe I'm innocent?"

The broken capillaries around his nose turned an unattractive shade of magenta as he scowled at me. "Lady, you had the opportunity and the motive. We just haven't determined the means. But we will."

Huh?

He ticked them off, one meaty digit at a time.

"You had dinner with both men. And no alibi for the time either of them was killed."

Okay, but so what? That didn't prove anything.

"You have a reputation for assaulting men."

"What?" It was my turn to shout.

Hunter nodded as Bradford explained. "One of the people we interviewed said you attacked your ex-husband. You obviously have a problem with your relationships with men."

"I don't have a problem with men," I said, grinding my teeth together. "I have a problem with idiots. That is not a proper motive."

"All we're missing is the murder weapon," Bradford said. "Trust me, we will find it."

I stared at both of them. Bradford, the belligerent bull-dog, looked as pleased as if I had delivered a full confession. Hunter, the brawny bear looked...puzzled. Or could that be concern on his face.

I was frustrated and I was scared and there wasn't enough chocolate in the Starbucks to calm me down at this moment. "Detective Hunter, are we done here?"

He exchanged a look with Tall and Bald.

"Sure. We know where to find you," Bradford said, his smile even chillier than the temperature outside. "But don't leave town."

I grabbed my purse, slung it over my shoulder and strode out the door. I might as well get back to work and pursue my career options.

At least until they arrested me.

THIRTEEN

THE TEMPERATURE FELT LIKE IT had dropped a few degrees so I race-walked back to the office. How could I concentrate on work after this interrogation? I never seriously considered that the sheriff's department would consider me a suspect, but Detective Bradford made me feel like I was number one on his list. Surely there was another suspect or two or three out there.

As soon as I reached the office, I stopped in the break room to check out the branch manager posting. Hundreds of rainbow-colored flyers were thumb-tacked to the bulletin board. I located the job posting, which was dated over a week ago. Applications would be accepted through the next day. I still had time, but was it worth the effort if I was going to jail?

Stop it. I mentally slapped myself. With two children to support, there was no way I would let those overbearing detectives haul me off to jail without doing something about it first.

After work I stopped at the supermarket and bought a rotisserie chicken, fruit salad and cold broccoli salad. Then I dashed over to the soccer field. Ben was cold, dirty and sniffling. One of Jenna's friends had given her a ride home, so by the time we arrived, she was curled up in a recliner with Pumpkin perched on her shoulder, gnawing at her auburn strands. There didn't appear to be any new signs of catastrophic activity.

I left two more messages for Liz, but she and Brian must

not have returned yet. By nine, Ben and Pumpkin were tucked into their respective beds. I was tucked into my own cozy bed, boning up on some detecting techniques in a new book by my favorite mystery author. The phone rang and I shrieked, the book tumbling to the floor. That's what happens when you get too engrossed in murder.

"Hello?"

"Laurel, what's going on? You left five messages on my home phone. Why didn't you call my cell?"

"Oh, Liz. I didn't want to bother you guys on your romantic getaway. But I'm so glad you're back."

"We came home early. The District Attorney called Brian about a new case they've opened up. A doctor who drowned under suspicious circumstances."

Dead silence on each end of the phone.

"Please tell me this wasn't the doctor you had the date with."

"Okay, I won't tell you. But I met with the detectives again today. And according to Bradford, I'm their number-one suspect in both murders!"

"Wow. That is a sticky wicket."

Sticky wicket? I'd say being accused of murder was more like being sentenced to the Tower of London, waiting for the ax to fall.

"So what are we going to do?" I asked.

"We? As in the royal *we*?"

"If the *royal we* means you and I, then yes. I need help and you've got the inside track."

"Of course I'll help. But I'm not sure how much info I can wangle out of Brian."

"Visit Victoria's Secret and pick out something irresistible. Like some black feathered handcuffs."

"That would certainly get Brian's attention. But maybe you're the one who should visit Victoria's Secret. What about this Detective Hunter? Do you think he fancies you at all?"

"Fancies me as a suspect," I muttered.

"Well, that's the kind of input I may be able to get out of Brian, even without some killer lingerie."

"Back to the topic of killers, what are we going to do about finding this murderer ourselves?"

Her phone clattered to the floor. "Bloody hell. Are you off your rocker? This is not one of those mysteries you love to read. Neither you nor I are equipped to investigate a murder."

"The sheriff's department considers me the only suspect. How much time and energy do you think they're going to expend finding the actual murderer? Or murderers. They could come and arrest me any day now."

"Oh, sweetie, I wish there was something I could do to help."

I thumped my pillow in frustration. "I mean, really, what are the odds that the only two men I met from the Love Club were murdered?"

Bingo. "The Love Club!" we shouted in unison.

"Now that's something we could look into without getting into trouble," Liz said. "You're still an active member. You could talk to the staff about both men. There must be a connection between them."

"Don't you think the police would have determined if they knew each other?"

"If they think they already know who the killer is they might not waste the time. It's not like they have that big of a detective force up here. You could nose around, discover something they missed."

"I could try."

Liz must have discerned some hesitation in my voice. "Laurel, you were the one who was all fired up to investigate these murders. Now it sounds like you're getting cold feet."

"It's not that. But imagine Sunny's expression when I stop by their office. It was bad enough when she thought I killed Garrett. If she finds out I was with Jeremy the night he drowned she'll probably pass out. For all I know, they've evicted me from the club by now."

"Hey, just because you're a murderer doesn't mean you aren't entitled to meet the man of your dreams."

Liz always knew how to cheer me up.

On that note, we agreed that I would visit the Love Club as soon as possible.

The following morning I woke up at five, long before my alarm was due to go off. The night before I'd been so tired I'd forgotten to complete the job application. I tiptoed down the stairs. The children didn't need to wake up any sooner than they had to. The sound of mewling cries emanated from behind the closed door of the laundry room. I opened the door thinking Pumpkin deserved a break from her jail.

No sign of the kitten anywhere. All of a sudden a ball of fluff flew from the top of one of the cabinets, landed on all fours and skidded across the floor. I jumped back, knocked over my ironing board, which narrowly missed flattening the bundle of fur cowering at my feet.

As if I didn't have enough aggravation. I picked her up, carefully watching out for her small but deadly claws. We went into the kitchen and I sat down at the table. Pumpkin settled on my lap while I filled out the application. That lasted all of five seconds. She jumped on the paperwork, smearing the ink on the line I'd just completed.

Heaven forbid there be a piece of paper in the house unoccupied by the cat. I found some kitty treats, which must have ranked higher than the joys of reclining on my application, because I was able to finish the form without any further interruptions.

As soon as I arrived at the office, I delivered the application to the HR department then wandered into the break room for a cup of coffee. Three creams, two sugars, one squirt of Hershey's chocolate syrup, and my budget version mocha was ready. I felt a tap on my shoulder.

"Did you read this morning's newspaper?" Stan asked.

"Uh, no, was there anything important in there?" I peered over my shoulder to make sure no one could overhear us.

He dramatically flourished said paper. "There's an article on the second page of the main section. It says the doctor's death was probably not accidental and the sheriff's department is currently investigating persons of interest. The reporter asked about the mystery woman but the officer said he couldn't reveal anything."

"Whew. I sure don't need that kind of notoriety right now. I'd never get that job if the bank knew I was involved in a murder investigation."

"What job?" Stan's very broad brow wrinkled in confusion.

"Sorry, forgot to tell you. I'm applying for the branch manager position in Cameron Park. You know, the position I held before Ben was born."

"You mean you'd give up all of your wonderful friends at corporate for a measly increase in pay?"

"In a heartbeat, Stanley," I replied. "I'm tired of making life-and-death underwriting decisions. I want to work with the public again. You can come out to the branch and annoy me anytime you want. Assuming I get it. It's been six years since I held that position. I'm sure they have a lot of eligible candidates."

"Well, my vote's with you, sweetie. Hopefully this situation with your murder victims will be over before the bank ever hears about it."

"Murder victims?"

I whirled around to be confronted by the bank's receptionist. Vivian's pale moon face with its two double chins hovered inches from my face. Although I get along fine with Vivian, I'm always careful when I talk with her. Her speed of transmitting office gossip is on a par with communicating via the internet. Broadband internet.

I moved a few feet away from the pale orb of her inquisitive face. "Um, Stan and I are discussing a murder mystery we're both reading."

"Oh, I love a good mystery," she said. "What's the name of it?"

Stan and I looked at each other in dismay.

"Murder on the Orient Express," I said while Stan said at the same time, "The Drowned Man."

Vivian looked confused. "What did you say the title was?"

I jumped in before we could make that mistake again. "Uh, the title is Murder of the Drowned Man On The Orient Express. It's a s-sequel to the original m-mystery," I stammered.

Stan grabbed his coffee cup and avoiding our eyes, said a quick goodbye leaving me alone to deal with Vivian. I made a mental note to get him later.

Vivian reached into the cabinet for a mug. "Speaking of drowning, since you're so interested in murder mysteries, did you hear about that guy who drowned in the American River last weekend? Dr. Slater was my doctor. The paper said the sheriff doesn't think it was an accident."

I was anxious to move the conversation away from the murder aspect of Vivian's family physician. "Did you like him?"

Always anxious to share, Vivian didn't disappoint me. "He was terrific. You know I was upset because I gained so much weight this past year. Dr. Slater devised a diet and exercise plan to help me lose weight. He was very sympathetic about my condition."

I nodded in agreement. "He was so slim you probably just needed to follow his personal diet."

She moved closer and thrust both chins in my face. "How did you know Dr. Slater was slender?"

Note to self. Never have a conversation with Vivian before my first infusion of caffeine.

"I think someone in the office mentioned it yesterday." Who did Stan say was also a patient of Jeremy's? "Rosa."

"What about Rosa?" she asked, her eyes narrowing into a squint. Someday I would have to tell her it was not an attractive look.

"She said he was her family physician, as well. So, what was his helpful advice?" I said, hoping to distract her.

She sat down and elaborated her diet plan for me. "He prepared a chart of food groups to follow, told me to keep track of my carb and fiber grams, and recommended that I try a mild strength building exercise program. He said men are often attracted to large women. In fact, last weekend he told me he was going on a date with a woman he described as pretty but pleasingly plump."

Pleasingly plump? I hoped he was describing his date for Friday night. If Jeremy had called me that to my face, I probably *would* have pushed him in the river.

We needed to shift from the fat fighting conversation to something more constructive—like who done it.

"Can you think of a reason why anyone would want to murder him? Do you know anything about his family or friends?"

She shook her head. "I suppose I'll have to find a new

doctor now. I saw his partner, Dr. Radovich, one time when Dr. Slater was unavailable. Dr. Radovich was really abrupt with me. No bedside manner at all." She shoved back her chair and stood up.

"I've been looking for a new doctor. Maybe I should try this Dr. Radovich." It couldn't hurt to talk to Jeremy's partner.

Vivian looked at me like I'd lost even more of my marbles.

"I like doctors that are abrupt. They're much more efficient with their time, and mine."

"If you say so. Speaking of which, time to get back to work." She scurried out of the room, back on the prowl for more worthwhile sources of gossip.

Our conversation had lasted so long my coffee was now lukewarm. I placed my mug in the microwave and set the timer for thirty seconds, mulling over our recent conversation. The bell rang and I eased the cup out carefully. No point in scalding myself with overly hot coffee.

I'd already promised Liz I would visit the Love Club to see if I could find a tie between Garrett and Jeremy. My conversation with Vivian pointed me in another direction— Jeremy's medical practice. So I wasn't one of their patients. That could be rectified easily enough.

I didn't have a clue what kind of clues I would encounter at either location, but anything would be better than nothing. Especially something that would tie Garrett and Jeremy together. Something besides me.

So far all I had netted from my investigation was that Jeremy thought I was fat.

When I returned to my desk, I received a call from Anne in the HR department. We arranged for an interview on Thursday. She seemed pleased with all of my previous experience managing a branch.

My second interruption was from Mrs. Bingham, as she informed the receptionist who put through the call.

"Hello, Mother, how are you today?" I rested the receiver on my shoulder as I continued to review the loan file I was in the middle of underwriting.

"Hello, dear, I wanted to see how you were feeling after your dreadful weekend. Thank goodness your name wasn't mentioned in those newspaper articles about Dr. Slater's death. Can you imagine what would happen to my real-estate business if word went out that you were his date that night?"

I personally didn't see how having a daughter as a murder suspect would have any bearing on her ability to sell real estate, but what did I know?

"Have the police contacted you regarding that evening?" she asked.

I pondered the advisability of telling my mother that a detective by the name of Bradford had informed me that I was his chief suspect. "We chatted yesterday. Nothing to worry about."

"Well, that is good news. Are you bringing Ben here on Halloween?"

A few years ago I had taken Ben trick-or-treating in her neighborhood so she could see how cute he looked in the costume she made for him. Yes, my mother can write up a real-estate contract, cook a five-course dinner and sew a child's Halloween costume simultaneously. I still question whether I might be adopted.

"Sorry, not this year. Patti is taking Ben and Jimmy through her neighborhood then she'll drop them at my house."

Wait a minute. If his grandmother really wanted to see her grandson maybe she could pick him up from soccer practice today. I could run over to the Love Club and begin my investigation this evening.

"Mother, it would really help if I could work late tonight and catch up on my underwriting. Could you pick Ben up from practice?"

"I guess I could. But some clients are coming in to write up a contract tonight. Can you be at my office before seven?"

I eagerly assented and we said goodbye.

The majority of my workload was completed by four so I decided to devote the next half hour to perfecting my detecting. Having been an avid murder-mystery fan since my first Nancy Drew novel at age nine, I must have developed some innate investigating skills from all the mysteries I'd read in the past thirty years.

Every self-respecting amateur detective always makes a list so I wrote down the potential questions I hoped to get answered from my visit to the Love Club.

Were Garrett and Jeremy acquaintances? Did they share something in common that could be determined from their biographies?

Was someone from the Love Club out to get male clients? Was someone out to get my dates?

Was someone out to get me?

Were my children in any danger?

Those last two questions tied my stomach in multiple knots, but it only made me more determined to find the answer.

I arrived at the Love Club office shortly after five-thirty. Another young, perky blonde stood behind the front desk. We exchanged smiles as I walked past and into the main room that held all of the alphabetized member books.

An attractive brunette clad in a smart charcoal-and-pink-striped suit, and a silver-haired, silver-goateed man sat at separate tables, books and DVDs piled high in front of each of them. They were so intent on reading the profiles that neither of them looked up as I entered the room.

First I would re-examine both Garrett's and Jeremy's biographies. The book labeled *G* was available, but I couldn't find the *J* book anywhere, even misfiled among the other alphabetized books. Several black notebooks were piled in front of the brunette so one of them might have the *J* entries.

I flipped through the pages of the book until I found Garrett's biography. By now his bio should have been removed. Instead, I found a large red inactive banner stapled over his picture. When a member became seriously involved with someone else—regardless if they met them through the Love Club or not—they would notify the club and the inactive banner would be placed through their photo to discourage anyone from choosing them.

I agreed that death automatically made someone inactive, but it didn't seem like the most appropriate category to me. Maybe the police asked them to keep the profiles in the book for a while, hoping to retrieve some additional leads on the killer. Nothing startling jumped out in Garrett's biography but I wrote down his ID number—3377. What I really needed to get my hands on was the book with Jeremy's data.

I drifted over to the other woman's table to see if she had the *J* volume. She was adding a name to the selection list the club provided. The club advised its members to limit their picks to a maximum of eight at a time. Even though the odds were that less than fifty percent of your selections would respond, arranging meetings with four new members of the opposite sex could be quite time consuming, especially for a career woman.

I discreetly glanced down at her choices. I saw a James, Jared and, uh-oh, a Jeremy 4155 on the list. I couldn't remember what Jeremy Slater's ID number was but for her sake I hoped there was another current member in the book named Jeremy.

I tapped her on her shoulder. She looked at me quizzically, her brown hair swinging forward then falling back in place. Nice-looking lady. She shouldn't have a problem meeting the man of her dreams as long as she didn't pick any of the men I had chosen.

"Sorry to bother you. I need to look up one of the members I selected a few weeks ago. Would you mind if I borrowed the *J* book for a few minutes?"

"Oh, sure. I already have five candidates. That's probably enough for tonight. I usually have a one hundred percent positive response so I don't want to get too booked up."

One hundred percent response. Some women have all the luck. On second thought, it was a good thing I'd received only two positive responses. I couldn't handle any more dead bodies.

I skimmed through the pages and quickly located Jeremy. No inactive banner yet so he was still eligible from a Love Club perspective. I checked out his ID number—Jeremy, 4155.

Ms. Pin-Striped Suit wasn't going to get a perfect response rate this time.

I compared both men's bios carefully. Other than the fact that they were the same age, forty and both childless, there were no other similarities I could discern. Garrett was divorced and Jeremy never married. Of course the biographies weren't that detailed. And not particularly original—over eighty percent of the male members said their idea of a romantic evening was to take a moonlight walk on the beach. My idea of a romantic evening was dinner with someone who was still alive the next day.

Since Jeremy's number would have been issued later

than Garrett's number, Garrett could have been the one to recommend him to the Love Club. I thought of a way to find out and sauntered over to the front desk. The receptionist's name tag read Sorrento. Maybe she was conceived while her parents honeymooned in Italy.

"Sorrento, I was wondering if you could help me? I know the club pays a fee of fifty dollars for any referrals that end up joining. Is there a way to check your records that would show that my friend recommended me?"

"Oh, sure, yeah. The referrals are, like, listed by number." She chomped on a piece of gum with the vigor of a cow masticating her cud. "What's your number with the club? I can see if her name is mentioned."

I rattled off Jeremy's number with the ease of an experienced liar. My ability to tell white lies has never been my strong suit, but if I kept up this investigation I could become an expert.

"Nope, no referrals listed under your number. Wait… that number belongs to Jeremy Slater. Are you sure that's the right one?" She crinkled her pert little nose and looked baffled.

"What did you type in? Oh, sorry. My ID number is five four nine eight."

She looked confused. "I thought you said four one five five. It doesn't sound much like five four nine eight."

"Sorry, I get my ID number here confused with my bank PIN. It's so hard to keep track of all of these PINs these days," I said.

"Boy, that's for sure," she said, nodding in agreement, "I, like, have to write my PINs on stickies everywhere or I can't remember them at all. Okay, under that number it shows Liz Somerville as the referral. So I'm, like, sure she should have received a check from us by now. Do you want me to see if a check went out?"

"No, thanks for looking it up for me."

Okay. That took care of question number one. Garrett didn't refer Jeremy to the Love Club, and Jeremy couldn't have referred Garrett, since Garrett joined first. As far as question number two, unless someone was systematically removing all the forty-year-old males that enjoy taking romantic moonlight walks along the beach, there was no way I could tie their murders to the Love Club.

FOURTEEN

I ZOOMED OUT OF THE CLUB managing to arrive at the Centurion office at exactly 6:59. Punctuality is not my strong suit and my mother is not very forgiving if you screw up her carefully structured schedule.

My parent stood in the reception area conversing with a middle-aged couple. Ben sat cross-legged on the floor, racing bright metal Matchbox cars across the parquet until they crashed into an unlikely obstacle. A large tasseled black cordovan loafer. I shot a glance at Ben's oversize buddy. A thick swatch of blond hair fell over one eye. He looked up at me and winced as a cherry-red miniature fire truck rammed his knee.

"Okay, Ben. Your mother is here to pick you up." He unfurled his long legs easily. Must hit the gym more than I do. But then, who doesn't.

"Hi there, um…" I couldn't remember his name.

"Peter Tyler. We met last week."

Mother excused herself from her clients. "Laurel, you remember Peter, don't you?"

"Yes, thanks for keeping Ben occupied."

"My pleasure." A shadow crossed his face as if he were remembering something from the past. "My wife and I tried to start a family but it turned out she couldn't have kids and then we divorced and…"

He shrugged off his somber thoughts and smiled shyly at me. "I enjoyed spending time with Ben. He's a great kid."

My great kid, who seemed to have added a few fruit juice

stains to the front of his previously clean blue sweatshirt, was busy picking up his toys from the parquet.

"Ben, please thank Peter for playing with you," I said.

My son smiled his gap-toothed grin. "Thanks."

Mother chose that moment to demonstrate her match-making skills. "Laurel, maybe you can thank Peter by taking him out for a cup of coffee sometime."

My face flushed. That was so not subtle.

Peter grinned. "Sounds good to me."

I was too embarrassed to do anything but nod and grab Ben's hand. We hustled out of the office as fast as Ben's short legs could move.

"Are you going out with Peter?" Ben asked as he struggled with his seat belt.

"I don't know, honey." I waited to make sure he was securely fastened before I backed the car out of the parking space.

"Why don't you go out with Kristy's dad?"

My foot stomped on the brake pedal, causing Ben's head to whip back and forth. Thank goodness for seat belts.

Kristy's dad? Detective Hunter? I waited until I had eased out of the parking lot before I continued our conversation. "How do you know Kristy's father?"

"He came to our school last week and gave a talk about staying away from strangers. He's nice and real smart and he gets to wear that cool uniform. And he has a badge. I'm gonna be a detective when I grow up."

Ben's revelation shook me up so much I missed the Greenstone Road turnoff.

"You should go out with him, Mom. He'd keep all the bad guys away from you."

"I don't think Kristy's dad has time to go out with me. He's very busy investigating both murders right now," I said without giving any thought to my comment.

"Two murders?" squealed Ben.

Darn. When would I learn to censor my remarks in front of my impressionable young son?

"Give it up, Mom. I want to know about the other murder."

"I don't know any of the details." Well, none of the details other than the fact that I was involved in all of the murders currently being investigated in our small county.

"Bummer. I'm gonna ask Kristy tomorrow."

Now I was really confused. "There's no soccer tomorrow. It's a school day."

"Guess I didn't tell you. Kristy is in my class now. She's not so bad, for a girl. And boy, can she kick a soccer ball."

Talk about out of the mouths of babes. Not only would I be running into Detective Hunter at the soccer field, we'd see each other on Open House nights. Picturing the six-foot-three detective trying to squeeze into the miniature second-grade desks made me smile. Remembering our last meeting at Starbucks quickly erased the grin from my face.

Once we arrived home Ben disappeared into the pantry. I could hear him counting out loud. "Hey, Mom, I don't think we have enough Halloween candy."

"Of course we do. I bought twelve bags. That should be enough for this neighborhood."

He walked out of the pantry, arms laden with multicolored plastic bags filled with an assortment of miniature candy bars. He scowled at me. "We don't want to run out like we did last year."

That had been a little embarrassing. I meant to buy extra bags of candy but totally forgot and ended up handing out plastic bags filled with carrots and broccoli stalks. It was months before the neighbors let me live that down. Sometimes the benefit of living somewhere long enough that you knew all of your neighbors was offset by the fact that they knew you and all of your little foibles, as well. I had to put up with being referred to as Mrs. Broccoli for the rest of the year.

Ben was in bed by nine in preparation for his debut as Spider-Man. Jenna was singing with her high school chorale and would get a lift home from one of her friends. The phone rang and I grabbed it before it woke up Ben.

"I hope I'm not calling too late. I just finished with those clients. They went back and forth trying to decide what to offer, but we finally came to an agreement on a fair price."

"That's nice, Mother. So why are you calling me with this fascinating piece of information at this time of night?" I scanned my closet trying to decide if I should wear Halloween attire to work the next day.

"So, dear, what do you think of Peter?"

Aha. I should have known there would be a grilling once I left the office. "He seems very nice."

"He's quite a catch, you know. He's been divorced about a year now so I know he's available. He developed that Bella Lago subdivision off Salmon Falls Road. Isn't that a romantic name?"

Her voice rose to a higher pitch. "Laurel, I asked you a question."

Oops, I hadn't been listening. "Salmon, yes, that would be great for dinner."

The sound of teeth gritting echoed through the receiver. "You are hopeless. I don't know why I even attempt to introduce you to suitable men."

Okay, maybe we weren't talking about salmon.

"Mother, I don't think I should go on any more dates until these murders are solved. Peter could be putting himself in danger by going out with me."

"Nonsense. Obviously you didn't have anything to do

with the deaths of those men. Just promise me you won't go out with anyone else from the Love Club."

"You'll be pleased to know we are in total agreement there. Gotta go, big day tomorrow."

Fortunately she agreed Halloween could be considered a big day and we said goodbye.

Wednesday dawned cold but sunny, perfect weather for Halloween ghosts and goblins. I decided to forego wearing a costume but I did bring a batch of my gold nugget fudge to the office, always a surefire hit. Not surprising since anything remotely edible was welcomed with open arms and mouths. Just the mention of "free food" and seconds later a line would stretch throughout the building.

Patti had agreed to take the boys out trick-or-treating in her neighborhood until I arrived at her house. The minute I pulled up in her driveway, the two superheroes ran out of the house and hopped in my car. Once we arrived home, I walked through the kitchen door and bumped into a gruesome figure. Jenna was dressed head to toe in black, her costume topped off with a pointed witch's hat. Ben and Jimmy followed me in, engrossed in counting the candy in their bags.

"Hello, my pretties," Jenna cackled, her olive-green skin and rubber putty nose repulsive in the fluorescent lighting of my kitchen.

Jimmy, dressed in a Batman outfit, jumped two feet into the air. Ben barely glanced at his sister. "'Lo, Jenna. Cool makeup."

The doorbell rang and all three kids ran to the front door to meet, greet and scare the newcomers. It was time for Mom to transform herself into a clown. The neighborhood kids expected it. I slathered white paste all over my face, drew huge eyelashes above and below both eyes, painted two red circles on my cheeks and outlined my mouth with a bright red lipstick. A black bowler hat topped a curly red wig.

My costume included a red polka-dot blouse with puffy sleeves that my mother bought me twenty years ago. It must have been after a three-martini lunch. Red suspenders attached to a pair of baggy red shorts, knee socks covered with red polka dots, and gigantic red plastic shoes completed the outfit. My full complement of clown paraphernalia included a loud horn, buzzer hand shaker and the pièce de résistance this year, a yellow plastic flower pin that squirted water.

As my two-foot-long shoes attempted to maneuver down the stairs, the doorbell pealed. Ben opened the door but there was a noticeable absence of noise. No kids yelling trick or treat? My son stood paralyzed in the doorway so I waddled over to see what was wrong. Walking in these shoes was like being ten months pregnant.

I stepped behind Ben and stared at our visitors. No wonder he was speechless. I gazed into the mirror image of my child—or that was, the mirror image of another Spider-Man. A larger version. I wasn't surprised to see another Spider-Man costume out there but I guess Ben wasn't prepared for it. I looked at the parent accompanying the child to see if he was anyone we knew.

The boy's father was dressed in black pants, a white tuxedo-style shirt and a black cape. Half of his face was covered with a white mask. Brilliant amateur detective that I am, I recognized the Phantom of the Opera standing on my doorstep. Hmm. If this guy could sing "All I Ask Of You," he would receive all of our candy without hesitation.

"Hello there, Spider-Man. Mr. Phantom, how are things at the opera house these days?"

The phantom smiled, his one brown eye twinkling at me. That twinkling brown eye looked vaguely familiar.

My thoughts were interrupted by the annoyed voice of the Spider-Man at our door. "Trick or treat, trick or treat. Are you gonna give me any candy or what?"

The phantom finally spoke. "Kristy, that's not polite. Please apologize to Ms. McKay and Ben. I'm sure they're surprised to see us on their doorstep."

Kristy? The soccer terror was Spider-Man? What happened to little girls who dressed up like a princess or a ballerina?

Ben broke the silence. "You can't be Spider-Man, Kristy. You're a girl."

"Hey, it's a free world. I can be Spider-Man if I want. Let's go, Dad, we'll never get any candy here." She turned and trudged back down the sidewalk, her bag dragging on the ground.

"Kristy, come back," I shouted at her retreating form. "I think you make a fine Spider-Man." Okay, it was kind of a weird costume, but the poor child didn't have a mother to help her out. The phantom/detective joined his daughter and they held a brief conversation. Father and daughter walked back to the door holding hands.

"Do you really like my costume?" Kristy's voice quavered as her eyes questioned me. I could tell my opinion was important to the motherless child.

"I think it's wonderful. We girls have special powers, too." She beamed a smile so angelic St. Peter would have been proud.

I grabbed the plastic candy-filled pumpkin from Ben. Kristy's smile spread from one freckled cheekbone to the other as I dumped eight different candy bars in her bag. "Thank you for the candy, Ms. McKay. I'm sorry if I was rude before," she said without any prompting from her father.

Nice apology. Maybe she wasn't such a hellion, after all.

"You're very welcome, Kristy. But what brings you to our neighborhood tonight?"

The phantom cleared his throat. Was the detective about to burst into song?

"Kristy still doesn't know many of the kids in our subdivision. They seem kind of standoffish. She mentioned that Ben has treated her like a pal at school and she thought maybe he would trick-or-treat with her. Of course I should have realized that Ben would be going out with other friends…"

His voice trailed off as he gazed lovingly at his daughter, her tiny hand enfolded in his.

This was not the angry soccer dad I'd met across a muddy field. Nor was it the suspicious interrogator I'd encountered at Starbucks. For the first time the detective was cast in a vulnerable role. It must be terrible to be widowed, having to raise a young daughter alone. Particularly given his career choice.

I looked up into his eyes—or rather his eye. The other one was still covered by the mask.

Fortunately, my sixteen-year-old daughter who appeared to be maturing by the minute chose that moment to step in. "Detective Hunter, we'd be glad to take Kristy along with us. I was on my way out with the boys. Mom's going to remain home to hand out candy so you can stay and help her. It gets really busy with hordes of kids coming at once."

Jenna shot me a grin and I mouthed a silent thank-you. I wasn't sure that hordes of children would be congregating at my door this evening but I was thrilled at the proactive manner in which she had come to Kristy's rescue. She grabbed the young girl's hand and they walked out the door together. Kristy skipped down the sidewalk, trying to keep up with my daughter's brisk pace. Jenna paused to look back at the boys.

"Are you guys coming? If you don't hurry the neighbors will run out of candy."

That remark took care of Jimmy's and Ben's temporary paralysis. They grabbed their bags and ran after the girls, practically knocking them over in their hurry. I closed the front door and turned around. My giant red clodhoppers stomped all over the detective's shiny black shoes.

"Sorry," I apologized. "I'm not sure I'll ever get used to wearing two-foot long shoes. Can I get you something to drink?"

"No, I'm good." He hesitated, glancing down and contemplating his shoes for a few seconds. "You have no idea how much I appreciate this. It's only the second Halloween since my wife passed away. She used to make all of Kristy's costumes—Snow White, Cinderella, typical little girl clothes. I think Kristy's choosing these outlandish outfits so she won't be reminded of her mother's creations."

I nodded in sympathy. "My dad died in a car accident when I was ten. For a long time I was mad at everyone. It seemed so unfair for him to die so young. Why was I the only kid who didn't have a dad? But eventually I learned to cope. To concentrate on remembering the good times we had and appreciate what a wonderful father he was for the short time he was with us."

"It's been tough. Kristy's been so rebellious it's difficult knowing what to do. What battles to fight or when to give in. That's one of the reasons I moved to Placerville. I hoped being closer to her grandparents would help her cope. She has a hard time making friends. Even in soccer. The boys respect her for her abilities but they won't play with her because she's a girl. Ben's one of the few kids who's been kind to her."

"That's my Ben." I chuckled. "Of course he's used to

being bossed around by three generations of women so one more female in his life is no big deal."

Hunter smiled a twisted smile at me. Extremely twisted, since he was still wearing his mask. Poor guy. Having to contend with his wife's death and his daughter's emotional issues, plus attempting to solve the county's proliferating murders couldn't be easy. The unapproachable grizzly bear of a man was demonstrating some teddy-bear tendencies. He might be a detective but he was also a father, struggling with the parenting issues we all encounter on a daily basis.

The detective removed his mask, leaving his thick chestnut hair in total disarray. His hair looked like it was aching to be ruffled. Or maybe I was aching to ruffle it. My heart was beating louder than a bongo drum.

Was I the only person feeling a frenzy of pheromones floating in the air?

He stepped close just as the doorbell rang. Never had trick-or-treaters been so unwelcome. I grudgingly opened the door and mimicked a clown's squeaky voice. My shrill soprano sounded more like Truman Capote than a clown but the kids didn't seem to mind. I plopped a candy bar in each of the children's bags. The front door was almost shut when I felt something brush against my ankle. An orange-black-and-white blur streaked out the small opening.

"No!" I dropped the candy on the floor and attempted to run after Pumpkin. And no, it is not possible to run across a lawn in two-foot-long shoes. I managed three steps before my right shoe caught in one of the sprinkler heads along the edge of the sidewalk. I flew over the large azalea bush next to the sidewalk and landed a perfect face-plant in the middle of my crabgrass-filled lawn.

Detective Hunter knelt down. "Laurel, are you okay? Do you think you've broken any bones? Try moving your foot. Just a little, not too much. Lie still. Don't sit up too fast."

The nonstop litany of medical commands confused me so I chose to ignore all of them. I sat up slowly then leaned over to examine my shoeless right foot. My left foot was still encumbered by its floppy mate. My foot didn't hurt too much although my brain felt foggy.

Now why was I running?

"Pumpkin!" I grabbed the detective's arm as I attempted to stand up.

"You want a pumpkin?" A worried frown creased his forehead. "I think you have a concussion. You need to stay still." He helped me back into a sitting position.

"Pumpkin's our kitten. That's the blur of fur I was chasing. Do you see a cat anywhere?" The sensation of something sticky caressing my right hand got my attention. It didn't look like the phantom was drooling on my digits so I glanced down to find the kitten licking my fingers.

The detective stared at Pumpkin with a confused look. "There's an unusual-looking creature attached to your hand."

"Yep, that's Pumpkin. The kids surprised me with it last weekend. She's been a bundle of entertainment ever since."

"Um, she's the most unusual-looking cat I've ever seen," he tactfully replied.

Since I wasn't in the mood to discuss Pumpkin's redeeming qualities, or lack thereof, I grabbed her and attempted to get up as gracefully as I could manage. My right knee buckled and I collapsed back on the lawn. Hunter dropped down beside me. "Is it your knee? Your ankle? Hamstring?"

It looked like the detective's interrogation skills also extended into the medical arena. I held up my palm. "Slow down. Let me try to walk and we'll see what happens."

He held on to Pumpkin with one hand, keeping his other arm wrapped around my waist as I limped up the sidewalk. Once inside the house, he locked the door and the kitten

scurried off. I hobbled halfway across the living room before I stumbled on a small piece of candy that must have
fallen out of one of the boy's bags.

Once again I found myself hanging on to my rescuer. I
was about to thank him when I noticed that his eyes had
a peculiar look in them. It almost looked like, like—lust?
My heart pumped faster as he leaned toward me. I moved
closer, as well. My head swam with desire and I could feel
my chest getting wetter and wetter.

Huh?

FIFTEEN

ADVICE TO SINGLE CLOWNS everywhere. Never wear a water-squirting plastic flower if there is any chance you may be kissed by a hunky detective. And never attempt a kiss on Halloween, I thought, as the doorbell clamored yet again.

The detective strode into the foyer and yanked the door open.

Kristy's voice rang out. "What happened to your shirt, Dad?" Her question was followed by the familiar refrain of my children. "Hey, Mom, where are you?"

Two of the sugar infused miniature superheroes blasted into the room. "How come you're only wearing one shoe?" asked my pint-size Spider-Man.

"I fell down on the front lawn and hurt my knee chasing your kitten." I looked accusingly at the probable offender. "Someone forgot to close the door to the laundry room."

"Is Pumpkin okay? Did you find her?" Tears formed in Ben's eyes. Such a sensitive child. Maybe someday, he would feel the same compassion for his poor old mother.

"Hey, Mrs. McKay, your shirt's all wet. Did you guys have a water fight?"

When did Jimmy become so observant?

"I was demonstrating my plastic flower on Detective Hunter and we both got wet." I quickly changed the subject. "Are you having fun, Kristy?"

"Yeah, it's been a blast. You guys ready to go back out?"

All three of the kids ran out of the house while Jenna lingered behind.

"Thanks for taking care of the kids, honey." I put my arm around her shoulder as I leaned against one of the chairs. "Are you sure Kristy is having a good time?"

Jenna smirked. "Oh, she's having a great time, although maybe not as good as the two of you." She pointed her finger in the direction of my sopping wet shirt then sauntered out after the younger kids.

Tom closed the front door behind them then turned to me with a pensive look on his face. "We need to talk," he said abruptly. "Let's sit on the sofa."

Although the thought of sitting together on the sofa hinted at romance, the serious tone of his voice did not. He offered his arm and I hung on while I limped to the sofa and eased into the lumpy cushions. The detective grabbed a blue-fringed throw pillow and propped my leg up on the coffee table before he settled on the opposite side of the sofa.

"I better get rid of this stupid plastic flower before I douse you again." Was that subtle enough?

"Good idea. Although by the time I'm done with my explanation you may want to do something worse than soak me."

I settled into the cushions. It didn't sound like any canoodling was on his agenda. Tom was quiet for a few seconds, his index finger tracing one of the blue flowers decorating the arm of the sofa. I waited patiently. This sounded like an important discussion, a discussion that could impact me forever.

"Laurel, I haven't been in a relationship since my wife passed away. My entire existence revolves around my daughter, my parents and my job. Right now I don't have time for anyone else in my life. But the first time I saw you running to your son's rescue, racing across that soccer field in those silly blue shoes…"

"My turquoise mules aren't silly," I interrupted, "they're..."

He reached across the sofa and stopped my babbling, placing a finger on my lips. "Let me finish. Despite our hostile introduction on the soccer field, I haven't been able to stop thinking about you. And not just as a murder suspect."

He took my palm in his and stroked his thumb along my wrist. I could feel a throbbing in my body. And it wasn't my knee.

"You're the first woman I've been attracted to since my wife died. You also are the primary suspect in two murder inquiries. Do you realize what an enormous conflict of interest this is for me?"

The touch of his thumb was short-circuiting all the fuses in my body including my brain, but I still grasped what he was saying.

Tom grimaced. "I've talked to folks who have known you for a long time, like Ben's second-grade teacher, your pastor, neighbors. I told the sheriff that everyone I've interviewed says you're a great mother and all-around wonderful person. I keep hoping the favorable things I've discovered will persuade him you're innocent of either murder."

Tom had been interviewing people like my pastor? And my neighbors? I tried to digest his words but they were giving me a serious case of indigestion.

"You've been talking to my friends...about me. Without telling me first?" I yanked my hand from his grip and tried to rise. Unfortunately, I had to bend my knee in order to remove it from the top of the coffee table.

"Ouch," I whimpered as I slipped back into the cushions. Tom slid across the sofa and tried to help me.

Forget it, buddy. I struggled to get up. Detectives must be prepared to deal with criminals who resist arrest, but I doubted Tom's normal method of subduing them was to kiss them. I didn't know what his original intent was but I responded like a woman who hadn't been in a lip lock in over two years. The kiss was hot. It was so…hot. My body had never tingled this way from just a kiss.

Or was it a hot flash?

I pulled back abruptly and glanced at him. His face mirrored the surprised look on mine.

My senses were reeling but Tom's disclosure that he was investigating me behind my back ticked me off. I pushed him away and he slid back to his end of the sofa.

"I'm sorry," he said, "that never should have happened."

"You're darn right." My face was flushed and my body felt like a volcano about to explode.

Tom chuckled suddenly and I glared at him. "You might want to wipe the lipstick smudges off your face before your children come home and notice," he said, his lips curving in a smile. A smile rimmed with red lipstick. I dug into the pocket of my baggy shorts and pulled out a gigantic red-and-white-striped hankie. Clowns are always prepared. The incriminating lipstick was removed from both of our lips seconds before the kids burst through the door, their bags overflowing with candy.

Tom stood up and checked out each of the kids' booty. He pretended to sneak a piece of candy out of Kristy's bag. I remained seated, still stewing over his disclosure. He squatted down next to me, resting his hand on my injured knee. "Laurel, you should see a doctor tomorrow. You may need to be on crutches."

I folded my arms over my chest. "I don't need a…" My voice trailed off as my brain leaped a few steps ahead. Hmm. There was a doctor I'd wanted to visit. And now I had the perfect excuse.

Since I continued to glower at him, Tom astutely figured out he had overstayed his welcome. He told Kristy to gather up her stuff. She grabbed her loot, thanked Jenna and me and waved goodbye to the boys. Her father followed her out the door with a brief troubled glance at the gimpy murder suspect sulking on her sofa.

The boys probably would have stayed up all night exchanging goodies but Ben's crabby, injured mother was ready for bed. I found that if I dragged my right leg and didn't bend my knee it wasn't too painful to walk up the steps. I hoped I wouldn't need crutches. Crutches and a kitten could be a lethal combination.

After removing my smeared makeup, I put on my red puppy dog pajamas. I briefly wondered what Tom Hunter would think of my attire. If he could kiss me in clown makeup, imagine how turned on he would be by my flannel jammies.

The numbers gleaming on my alarm clock announced it was a quarter past ten. A little late, but Liz has always been a night owl. I dialed her number and listened to it ring eight times before the answering machine kicked in. She picked up just as I started to leave a message.

"Laurel, do you know what time it is?" She didn't sound thrilled to hear from her best friend. Had I interrupted some X-rated activity?

"Sorry to call so late but I need your help. I injured my leg tonight and I wondered if you could drive me to the doctor tomorrow?"

"Of course, but what happened?"

"It's a long story. I'll give you the details tomorrow."

"Call me at the office in the morning after you've made an appointment with Dr. Templeton."

Dr. Templeton was a terrific family doctor who practiced in Placerville. With years of klutziness behind me, I've visited his office so many times I could have earned frequent patient points. But I had other plans.

"There's a new doctor I want to try. I'm going to call

Dr. Slater's office and see if his partner can take a look at it. Then we can chat about Jeremy."

"Do you think that's a good idea?"

"It can't hurt to try a new doctor, someone younger than Dr. Templeton, in case my injury is a complicated one. Please don't say anything to Brian."

"Fine. I'm too tired to argue with you right now. Ring me when you want to be picked up." I winced as the phone slammed in my ear. Liz was beginning to sound a lot like my mother.

Another sleepless night followed, either due to the stimulus of the detective, the pain shooting out from my right knee every time I rolled over, or the extra caffeine from all of the candy bars I scarfed down for dinner.

By morning the throbbing ache had eased somewhat but there was no way I was going to miss an opportunity to meet Jeremy's partner. I dropped both kids at the bus stop and at nine on the dot called Dr. Radovich's office. I explained to the receptionist that I was a friend of Dr. Slater's and I wished to switch doctors since my own family physician would be retiring shortly. This was an emergency since I could barely walk. She kept putting me on hold in order to answer other incoming calls but finally agreed to squeeze me in at noon, probably so she could get me off the phone and get on with her other calls.

That gave me the morning to skim through the last two days of newspapers. Fortunately the *Mountain Democrat* focused on the upcoming election. A tiny article about Jeremy's demise was located on the back page. Politics trumped murder.

Liz picked me up promptly at eleven thirty and I wiggled into her impractical but cute red Miata. At least my small car was roomy enough for a *pleasingly plump* woman.

Yes, Jeremy's quote still rankled.

We headed down the hill to Jeremy's medical practice in El Dorado Hills. I could tell by her demeanor that Liz wasn't thrilled about spending her lunch hour sitting in a doctor's waiting room. I promised to treat her to the fast-food restaurant of her choice. As we drove to the office, I briefed her on her part of the investigation. Her initial response was somewhat less enthusiastic than I'd hoped.

"Are you out of your bloody mind? Brian will kill me or worse—he might break off our engagement if he finds out I'm mixed up in a case he might end up prosecuting. Did you suffer brain damage from your fall?"

"Hey, calm down," I said as I noticed the speedometer venturing into speeding-ticket territory. "There's no need for Brian to find out. All I want you to do is chat up the front desk staff while I'm in with the doctor. You're such a great schmoozer. Say how sorry you were to hear about Dr. Slater, blah, blah. All we need to find out is if they know of anyone who would have a reason to kill Jeremy. How hard is that?"

"I suppose I can handle it," she grumbled, "but you're going to owe me more than a lousy cheeseburger."

By the time we arrived at the doctor's office, we both had our game plans in hand. Liz was truly concerned about my knee and she carefully assisted me into the reception area. It seemed wise not to disclose that it was barely hurting. With any luck, I would trip over something and writhe with pain when the doctor examined me.

Two women were stationed behind the reception counter. An older caramel-skinned female in a lilac-flowered smock and white pants was sitting at a desk, her fingers flying over her keyboard like a skilled pianist. The other significantly younger woman, dressed in a tightly fitted version of the same uniform, was filing her nails with an emery board as she held a cell phone against her platinum buzz cut. She gave me the universal "I'll be with you when I feel like it" wave.

I waited for a few minutes then stood up and walked over to the desk, announcing that I was a new patient. When buzz cut didn't respond to my "new patient status," I raised my voice and asked whether there were any forms for me to complete. The older woman shot me a rueful look then reminded Tara, the young receptionist, that all new patients had to fill out a four-page questionnaire.

I smiled in sympathy with the older woman whose name tag read Carol. She could be a valuable ally. I filled in my medical history on the lengthy form while Liz sifted through the magazines on the coffee table. It didn't look like the office maintained a subscription to any beauty or bridal publications, the only reading material that interested her these days.

I looked up from my questionnaire, thinking how nicely furnished the office was. Old Doc Templeton still owned the original orange molded plastic chairs he'd bought forty years before. Dr. Slater and Dr. Radovich must consider the comfort of their patients a priority. Or maybe they charged more than Dr. Templeton.

Whatever the reason, the soft cushioned burgundy and navy chairs that ranged around the perimeter of the office were comfortable. Large photos of different scenes from the snowcapped Sierras and cobalt-blue Lake Tahoe lent a serene ambiance to the room.

After a wait of ten minutes, my name was called. I put down the magazine and nudged Liz. She was engrossed in an article in *Newsweek* on aging. I prodded her with the tip of my Adidas but missed, my foot connecting with her ankle.

"What's the matter with you?" She flashed me a dirty look as she reached down to rub her bruised ankle.

Some accomplice she was. I whispered to her left ear. "I'm going to try to keep this nurse occupied. You need to question the young one while I'm gone."

Carol cleared her throat. I rose and walked briskly across the room then remembered why I was in the office. I adjusted my pace and limped down a hallway lined with examination rooms. We walked into a room with light blue walls adorned with more photos depicting some beautiful views of the Sierras. I complimented the nurse on the decor.

"What a lovely room. Did you help decorate the office?" My flattery seemed to have a thawing effect. Carol produced a tentative smile as she grabbed the blood pressure thingie from a table.

"No, we had a professional decorator. Dr. Radovich didn't really care what we did to the office. He wanted to paint everything that bilious green color you find in government buildings because the paint is so cheap, but Dr. Slater insisted we have a nice ambiance for our patients." She sighed softly. "I certainly do miss Dr. Slater."

"He was very special to me, too." My sigh was so forceful it blew my patient questionnaire right off her clipboard.

Carol bent over and picked up the form. "Oh, yes, I forgot you said you were a friend of the doctor when you called. Did you know him well?"

"Well, we had been dating for a while." I guess a lunch date and an abbreviated dinner date could constitute a while. "I was very fond of Jeremy."

I sighed again but toned it down a few notches.

"Were you with him the night he died?" she asked.

Trick question. One of these days I have to buy a *Detecting for Dummies Guide*.

I debated what to disclose but decided I would get more information out of her if she didn't know I was with him the night he was murdered. "Uh, he said he was having dinner with a business associate and he would see me later. I never saw him again."

Thinking about Jeremy's bruised and battered body made me tearful and really nauseous. It was a good thing Liz and I hadn't devoured any greasy cheeseburgers before this appointment.

"Jeremy never told me who he was meeting that evening. Do you think it was Dr. Radovich?" I asked.

She shook her head. "No, it couldn't have been. He said he was at a fundraising dinner for the Boys and Girls Club that evening. The police came here to the office and questioned all of us. Don't you think it's strange they would question the staff if his death was an accident?"

"That does seem peculiar. Perhaps they suspect foul play." Foul play? Now I sounded like a character straight out of an Agatha Christie novel.

Carol wrapped the blood pressure gauge around my right arm and pumped away like she was pumping for oil. "You know, I thought it was kinda odd myself."

She hesitated then leaned closer. "Plus those articles in the paper. Do you think he coulda been…" She pumped harder until I thought my arm would explode. "Murdered?"

"Uh, Carol." I winced and pointed at my arm.

"Oh, sorry. Guess I got a mite distracted." She let the air out of the gauge, looked at the reading and seemed satisfied with the results as she marked them down on my chart.

"I'd better tell Dr. Radovich you're ready to see him." She picked up my file and walked to the door.

I hated to let her go now that she had begun opening up. "Carol, I'm sure it was murder."

Her dark eyes widened until they were almost double

in size. "What makes you think that?" she asked, her hand resting on the polished doorknob.

"I got that impression from the detective who interviewed me. He questioned me about someone that Jeremy knew, a CPA named Garrett Lindstrom. Is that the name of the accountant for this office?"

"Oh, I wouldn't know about any of that financial stuff. Dr. Slater handled all the bookkeeping. I sure don't remember a patient by that name."

The door burst open and a middle-aged man dressed in a white coat entered. Astute amateur detective that I am, I took a wild guess this was Dr. Radovich.

"Carol, is there a problem? This is my last patient before I can leave for lunch." He grabbed my chart from her hand.

"Sorry, Doctor, I was just coming to get you," she apologized and bustled out of the room.

The doctor paused to look at my medical history before he turned to me. "So, Ms. McKay, what seems to be the problem with your leg? You indicated it's difficult to put any weight on it. How did you injure it?"

I considered the question. If I told him the entire story he definitely would not have time for lunch. An abbreviated version might be in both of our interests. "My cat got loose and I tripped over her. My right knee keeps buckling when I try to get up. Last night there was some swelling although it seems to have gone down today."

I rolled my black sweat pant up over my knee to give him a better view of said injury. He sniffed then squeezed my knee. Hard. I yelped but at least I didn't scream. I am a total wimp when it comes to pain, especially my own.

"There doesn't seem to be anything seriously wrong with it. You have a little swelling but it's likely that it's merely strained. I don't think you've torn an ACL or the meniscus."

That was a good thing because I had absolutely no idea what an ABC or a missus was. A sprain or a strain I could deal with.

"Ice it every few hours, keep your physical activity to a minimum for the next couple of weeks and you'll be up skiing in no time." Obviously, he had never seen me ski—during ski season I spent more time lying spread-eagled in the snow than schussing on my skis.

He shook my hand, indicating the exam was over then walked to the door.

"Dr. Radovich, I have another question," I blurted out before he could make his exit. He turned back with an irritated look on his face. His dedication to the sick must not extend into his lunch hour.

"When you brought up the subject of skiing it reminded me of Dr. Slater. You see, the last time I saw Jeremy, he mentioned he was buying a vacation home in Lake Tahoe. He seemed concerned about the financing. Do you have any idea what he was talking about?"

A mottled red flush formed at Dr. Radovich's neck and worked its way up to his matching shaggy red brows. "Ms. McKay, I hardly think Dr. Slater's real-estate activities are any business of yours."

Considering I was the only suspect in Dr. Slater's death, I chose to differ with him. I decided to attack from another direction. "I understand you were at a Boys and Girls fundraiser the night Dr. Slater died. Where did they hold it?"

The angry vein pulsing in his temple looked like it was going to explode. I shrank back as his menacing form approached the table. "I think you'd better leave now." He snatched my file and strode out of the office without a backward look.

I caught a glimpse of the back of his head. A bald spot.

And he was about the same height as the man I saw along the river the night Jeremy was murdered. If this was an episode of *Law & Order* I'd say that was a very peculiar response to some innocent questions.

I liked him as a suspect. Now all I needed was a motive.

SIXTEEN

I WAITED A FULL MINUTE BEFORE jumping off the examining table. Purse in hand, I stepped into the corridor, cautious as I approached the reception area. Both nurses seemed enraptured by a magazine Liz had spread open on the front counter. By the time we left the office, my pal would undoubtedly have arranged a spa day for at least one of them.

Since both women were occupied, it seemed like a perfect opportunity to examine Jeremy's office. I scooted past the doorway to the reception area and race-limped to the end of the hallway. One door was closed. Probably Radovich's office. He seemed the secretive type.

Across the hall was an office furnished with a large polished mahogany desk and a navy blue leather executive chair. My head swiveled back toward the reception area. The coast was still clear.

Bookshelves lined with leather tomes covered two walls. Diplomas and licenses hung on the third wall. I remembered that Jeremy received his BS at the University of California at Davis, one of many things we had in common. I graduated from UCD a couple of years after him with a completely useless degree in history. His diploma from medical school hung on the wall. Stanford. Impressive. But not helpful.

Photos in matching silver frames rested on the shelves. One photo was of an attractive man, his arms around a pretty blonde woman and a very young girl. The man bore a slight resemblance to Jeremy. I picked up a picture of some young men dressed in caps and gowns. Could be either high school or college. I tried to locate Jeremy. There he was. The skinny kid at the end of the last row. A few of his curls had managed to escape from the tight-fitting mortarboard cap.

I turned to the scrupulously neat desk. Nothing that shouted out "clue." I left Jeremy's office and tiptoed back down the corridor. The muted sound of voices indicated that Liz and the nurses were still chatting.

I opened the closed door of the other office. Diplomas hung lopsided on the walls. Files were stacked in haphazard piles on the floor and papers were scattered all over the desk. How did a man this sloppy end up practicing medicine? I certainly wasn't coming back to him for my annual pap. Who knows what tortuous metal instruments he might leave behind?

I brushed against a stack of documents and the paper on top floated down to the floor. The sound of approaching footsteps in the corridor warned of an impending visitor. I snatched the paper and quickly glanced at it. The first page of a real-estate contract for a property on Ski Run Boulevard in Lake Tahoe. The purchaser. Jeremy Slater.

Carol walked in just as I shoved the document back on top of the messy pile. "Ms. McKay, what are you doing in here?" She gave me another one of those suspicious looks. At least I think it was a suspicious look. I had a feeling Carol used that look a lot.

"Uh, I just wanted one last memory of Jeremy. I thought there might be some photos of him in here. Is this Jeremy's office?"

She pointed in the opposite direction. "No, his office is over there."

I followed her across the hall and entered Jeremy's office once again. Carol walked around the desk and stopped in front of the framed photos. I pointed to the family picture I'd noticed in my previous foray into the office. "Is that his brother and his family?"

"Yes, that's his younger brother, Mark, and Mark's family. Since Jeremy didn't have any children of his own, he was real fond of his niece, Sammie." She leaned against the credenza, her face pensive. Once again she seemed to be missing the presence of her boss.

I lifted the group graduation photo from the bookcase. "Did Jeremy keep in contact with many of his friends from Davis?"

She shrugged. "I don't know. He went to some type of reunion last summer, but I can't remember if it was high school or college." She took the frame out of my hands and returned it to the shelf.

"Tara and I are going to lunch now. I assume you've seen enough to satisfy you?"

Not really. I wondered why the real-estate contract for the Tahoe property that Jeremy was purchasing was in Dr. Radovich's office. But I knew if I asked Carol, I would definitely get one of those "suspicious" looks.

"Yes, thanks for being so understanding." We walked down the hallway back into the reception area where Liz was still chatting with buzz cut. I thanked both women as I pushed my friend out the door. She complained as we walked across the parking lot to her car. "What's your hurry? I almost signed up Tara for my monthly microdermabrasion special. It's great for getting rid of acne."

Liz stopped in the middle of the asphalt parking lot. "How come you're not limping anymore?"

I decelerated, slowing my pace as we approached her Miata. "That Dr. Radovich is a miracle worker. So did you discover anything useful?"

She shook her head as she beeped the doors open. "I'm

not sure I'm cut out to be your Dr. Watson. Tara has only been working in the office for a couple of months, so she doesn't know anything personal about either doctor. Carol knew Dr. Slater wanted to buy a condo in Tahoe but she thought the deal had been canceled for some reason."

"This detecting isn't as easy as I thought." I mulled over everything we had discovered, which wasn't a heck of a lot. Jeremy might or might not have been in the process of purchasing a house in Tahoe.

Dr. Radovich was a pig.

A pig who possessed a copy of Jeremy's real-estate contract.

"At least I may have picked up some new clients. Feel free to take me along on your next sleuthing expedition." Liz beamed a satisfied smile at me as she shifted into Reverse. "By the way, you're looking a little pale. Have you been using that Vanilla Pumpkin enzyme masque I gave you?"

I shook my head. The only pumpkin in my life lately was the kitten that had instigated this visit.

We ate a quick lunch then Liz dropped me at my house a little after two. The answering machine indicated three messages. The first was from Tom thanking me for letting Kristy go out with the kids and hoping that my knee felt better. It was a good thing he didn't know about my detecting foray. The second was a hang-up, and the last message was from Stan informing me I'd missed my eleven o'clock interview for the branch manager position.

Darn. I had totally forgotten about the interview. These murders were a tremendous distraction. I used to be so organized.

Well, maybe not all that organized, but I still couldn't believe I'd totally blown off a job interview in my misguided attempt to solve the murders. I left a voicemail message for

Anne Lewis in the HR department, telling her about my injury and subsequent doctor's appointment, and asked if we could reschedule for the next day. Maybe if I hobbled into the office on crutches I could elicit some sympathy from Anne.

Without the kids, the house was as quiet as…as a house without kids. I grabbed a diet soda from the refrigerator and sat down at the kitchen table. I thought about my appointment this morning. It was curious how irate Dr. Radovich became when I mentioned Jeremy's real-estate deal. He obviously knew about it. What was that phrase? Follow the money.

It was also odd how upset he became when I mentioned the fundraiser he attended the night Jeremy drowned. Could the doctor have slipped out for a few minutes and killed his partner?

I debated whether or not I should attend Jeremy's memorial service. My mother would know if any of the mourners were in the real-estate industry. Maybe she could glean some tidbits about his Tahoe transaction.

Mr. Rooster clock cheeped four o'clock. Both kids would soon be arriving home via the school bus so I had to start thinking about dinner. I rummaged through the cupboards, and when I opened the lower cabinet door next to the refrigerator, I discovered Pumpkin asleep on the bottom shelf.

No wonder she hadn't been terrorizing me. The kitten stretched the full length of her tiny multicolored body. When I attempted to grab her, she evaded me and scurried out of the kitchen. Eventually something would break and I'd track her down.

I opened the freezer to see if there was anything recognizable that could be thawed in two hours. The phone rang. Another blocked call. Why I bothered with caller ID was beyond me.

"Hello," I said, distracted by the array of fuzzy frozen foods. How many years could you store ground beef in the freezer?

"Is this Laurel McKay?" asked a raspy male voice.

"Yes…" Was this a trick telemarketing question?

"Ms. McKay, my name is Neil Schwartz, a reporter from the *Mountain Democrat*. I'd like to ask you some questions about Jeremy Slater. The police report stated that you identified the body the night of his death."

Police report?

"I understand you and the doctor were dating. Would you care to tell me about your relationship? I'm sure you'd like to share your side of the story with our readers."

Relationship? Side? Readers?

A resounding crash erupted from the living room. The kitten had made her whereabouts known.

"Goodbye." I slammed the phone down and tore into the living room to assess the potential destruction. My brass floor lamp rested on the carpet, the lightbulb smashed into a gazillion glass shards. I couldn't locate Pumpkin until I lifted the lampshade and found her cowering beneath. I was relieved she wasn't hurt. Even more relieved my lamp was still intact.

"Pumpkin, thanks for the excuse to get off the phone, but let's make a smaller mess next time." The four-footed pip-squeak scampered off again.

I expected the reporter to call back, but it wasn't until several hours later when the kids and I were eating dinner that the ringing of the phone interrupted our conversation. Probably the reporter again. Or someone claiming to be conducting a survey to cover up the fact it was a telemarketer. The machine could answer for me.

The voice leaving a message got my attention. I dropped my fork and ran to grab the receiver before Detective Hunter could hang up. "Hello, Tom?" I panted like I'd walked six miles—not six feet. My breathlessness must be due to the sound of his voice. It couldn't be due to lack of exercise.

"Laurel, I was calling to see if your knee was feeling better today. I phoned your office this afternoon but they said you stayed home from work. Did you get to see your doctor?"

Trick question. Was Dr. Radovich my doctor now?

I carefully crafted my response. "The doctor said it was probably a strain. It feels fine except when I climb the stairs."

"That's good. I was worried you might be on crutches for a while. Is he taking new patients? I need to find a doctor nearby."

"Well, my family doctor wasn't available for an appointment today so I went to a physician in El Dorado Hills. But I wouldn't recommend him. His bedside manner was nonexistent."

"Really? I thought Dr. Radovich was quite personable when I interviewed him this afternoon."

I should have known better. This wasn't a social call. "Um…he was probably in a better mood after his lunch."

"I also had an interesting chat with Carol. She was surprised we hadn't spoken with Dr. Slater's girlfriend. She felt so sorry for the woman. According to her, poor Laurel didn't even have a photograph of Dr. Slater to remember him by." Tom's voice was measured. We were back in interrogation mode. "So tell me more about your relationship with Dr. Slater. I didn't realize it had progressed so far."

"Remember last night you told me to see a doctor about my knee," I said, defending my actions. "Dr. Radovich was able to squeeze me in so I took advantage of the opportunity to talk to the staff. I might have exaggerated my relationship with Jeremy when I was talking to Carol, but

I thought I could find out something useful—you know, woman-to-woman."

Tom snorted. "And what did you find out from your, ah, woman to woman discussion?"

Did I detect a hint of sarcasm in his voice? What did I find out? "Uh, Jeremy was well-liked by his staff."

"Laurel, do I have to remind you that you are still a suspect? You cannot interfere with our investigation."

"Oh. I thought we moved past that little obstacle last night." Dead silence.

"I'm sorry, I promise to stay away from your investigation," I apologized. "But I want to attend Jeremy's funeral. When are they going to release the body?"

"The family will be having a memorial service Monday evening but I'm not allowing you to attend."

"Excuse me," I said, my voice as frosty as the inside of a Ben and Jerry's carton. "I don't believe you have the authority to do that, Detective Hunter."

A mild expletive sounded in my ear. "Laurel, it's not safe. You can't just—"

I interrupted him. "I was the last person to see Jeremy alive, well, except for his murderer. You know the killer always shows up at the victim's funeral."

Everyone knows that.

"That only happens in murder mysteries." His voice crackled with anger. "If you insist on attending the service, I'll be forced to lock you up."

"On what grounds?" I was infuriated by his tone and totally irrational at this point. He probably had more grounds than I had coffee grounds in my garbage can.

"Interfering with an investigation and…" His voice trailed off and I heard some voices in the background.

The next thing I heard was a muttered "Goodbye," followed by the sound of the dial tone.

Within seconds the phone rang again. It must be Tom calling back to apologize so I gave him the full brunt of my smart-ass repertoire. "Make sure you have plenty of hot coffee for me when you haul me in."

"Hot coffee or cold chardonnay, your wish is my command," said an unfamiliar male voice.

"Who is this?"

"Peter Tyler, your mother's associate from the Centurion office. Ben's new playmate."

I laughed. "Oh, Peter, I'm sorry. I thought you were someone else."

"Someone you're not too happy with, I gather. Anything I can do to help?"

"No, although a glass of chardonnay sounds like a great idea right now." I crossed the room and opened the refrigerator. Nothing chilled except for a gallon of two percent milk.

"I'd deliver it personally if it wasn't too late. This may be short notice but I was wondering if you'd like to get together for dinner this Saturday."

I paused for a minute. After that last conversation with Tom, dinner with Peter might be just what the doctor, any doctor, ordered for me right now. And what better reference than my mother?

"I would enjoy getting together with you, but I have the kids this weekend. Does the offer hold for another time?" Was suggesting another evening a dating faux pas?

"Of course. How about next Saturday? Have you been to the River Inn recently?"

My stomach churned. "My last time there wasn't a great experience."

"No problem. I'll come up with another restaurant."

We chatted for a few more minutes then hung up. The kids had given up on me and had already gone to their respective rooms hopefully to complete their homework. I loaded their plates and glasses in the dishwasher and wondered what Tom Hunter would think of me going out with Peter.

Considering our recent phone call, it probably wouldn't bother him a bit, other than concern for Peter's safety. Maybe I should drape an orange Proceed with Caution banner across my chest. I climbed the stairs then stopped abruptly when I reached the landing. What if something terrible happened to Peter? Maybe Bradford was right. I could be the common link.

It hadn't crossed my mind that these men were murdered because they went out with me. Honestly, who would be interested in hurting the men I was dating? I plopped down on the carpeted step as I remembered Hank's comments the previous weekend. Was his recent ardor because Nadine kicked him out? Or was he jealous of the guys I went out with?

All this detecting was driving me nuts. The thought of the father of my children committing murder was unthinkable. And the thought of him eliminating my dates in order to get me back was as likely as me dropping down to a size two.

The next morning I dressed in a navy suit, hoping Anne had rescheduled my interview. When I arrived at the office my red voicemail light was blinking rapidly. My conservative suit would be wasted. The Human Resources department was booked solid with appointments all day. The official cutoff for interviews was today, but Anne said she would try to squeeze me in sometime Monday.

She didn't sound overjoyed with the idea of postponing the meeting but at least she didn't say no. I called her back and left another voicemail thanking her for making an exception for me. By Monday, I wouldn't have to pretend my leg was still injured, so that was one less obstacle.

I was reviewing a file when I felt a tap on my shoulder. I spun my chair around, practically knocking Stan off his feet. He jumped back just in time. "How's your knee feeling? Were you were able to reschedule?"

"Anne postponed it until Monday. My knee feels a lot better, though. The doctor said it was just a strain so I'll be as good as new by then."

"You know, you never told me how you hurt it. Did you go out trick-or-treating?" He paused. "Or trip-or-treating?" He slapped his knee and howled at his wit. It was going to be a long morning.

I peeked over the wall of the adjoining cubicle to see if Mary Lou was at her desk, but her chair was empty. I gave Stan an abbreviated version of Halloween evening and my subsequent visit to the medical office.

"So they're sure Jeremy was murdered. Can't I help you and Liz investigate? I haven't seen the dear girl in ages."

I pacified Stan by promising I would include him in my next snooping expedition. He wandered back to his own cube and I grabbed a file to underwrite. Immersed in my work, I started when I felt a light tap on my shoulder. I swiveled slowly, a wise move, since this visitor was my boss. "Hey, Earl, what's new?"

My boss looked like he had just lost his best friend. "Laurel, how could you do this to me?" he moaned.

What did I do now? Did Dr. Radovich call and tell him I didn't really need to miss work yesterday? Or did I make a mistake that cost the bank millions of dollars?

SEVENTEEN

I RESPONDED WITH MY USUAL KEEN insight. "Huh?"

Earl's agitated hands ruffled the few remaining strands of hair intricately placed in his comb-over. "Anne said you want to leave me. I mean, this department. I never thought you would apply for that position, even if it is a bigger salary."

"Earl, I have two growing children to feed. There isn't much opportunity for advancement here."

His mouth dropped open, reminding me to get him some Crest Whitestrips for our Christmas gift exchange.

"No opportunity for advancement? Why, I was planning on promoting you to Operations Manager." He laid his hand on my shoulder and winked. "We'd be a great team."

A wave of nausea followed his declaration. Did my boss have designs on me that were other than professional? Time to deflect the conversation. "Earl, did you ever meet Garrett Lindstrom, a local CPA? I think he might be a member of the Rotary. Aren't you a Rotarian?"

Earl jumped back. His face bore the same expression as Ben's, whenever I caught him sneaking cookies. "He's not a friend," he yelled, shoving his hands in the pockets of his rumpled brown suit.

What?

"So you do know him? Have you seen him recently?"

"No, and I'm not planning to." His face darkened and he thrust his pudgy chin toward me. "Do you need more loans to underwrite?"

Nope. No shortage of loans on my desk. I shook my head and he strode down the corridor toward his office.

What was Earl's problem? One minute he was ogling me. The next minute he was yelling at me. Why couldn't I have a normal boss? Earl had been single for quite a while. Maybe he just needed to get laid, although not by one of his "team" members. It might be time to have the HR department send him a reminder of the bank's sexual harassment policy.

My extension rang. I hoped it was Anne calling about a cancellation so I could interview today. It was time to get out of this department.

"Laurel, I met the most extraordinary person." Mother sounded breathless, quite unlike her usual self-possessed self.

Not again. "Are you trying to set me up with someone else? I already have a date with Peter next weekend." One fix-up was quite sufficient for this week.

"No, dear. A representative from the sheriff's department showed up at the office today. I've never met anyone quite like him."

That wasn't surprising. I had never met anyone as masculine and virile as Detective Hunter, either. Or anyone so annoying. But showing up at her office without a prior phone call? That wasn't playing fair. He should have warned me he was going to interview her.

"What did he say?" I asked.

"He was so charming. We compared notes about raising our daughters, you know, what a trial they can be—especially when they make poor decisions about their relationships with the opposite sex."

They compared issues Kristy and I had with the opposite sex? What issues did Kristy have other than making sure she didn't squash any of the boys during her soccer games?

This conversation was not improving my bad mood. "I don't get it. Why were you and Tom talking about Kristy and me?"

"Tom who?"

"Tom Hunter. Detective Hunter. Isn't that who you met?" Was my mother showing early signs of senile dementia?

"No, his name isn't Hunter. It's Bradford, Detective Robert Bradford. Quite an unusual man." She emphasized the word *unusual*.

"You met Tall, Bald and Homely!" The thought of Detective Bradford interrogating my mother sent shivers from my bangs down to my bunions. But she didn't sound nervous, or even annoyed.

"Tall, Bald and Homely. Oh, my. That's funny." She giggled like a schoolgirl. "I'll have to tell Robert what you said the next time I see him."

See who? Robert? This conversation was getting loonier and loonier. Was my mother consorting with the enemy?

"Why are you seeing Detective Bradford again? You do realize he thinks I killed Jeremy. He's using you to get incriminating evidence on me."

She giggled again. The last time I heard Barbara Bingham giggle was…well, I had never heard my mother giggle. "Don't be silly. I told him there was no way you could have killed Dr. Slater. You're not organized enough to pull off a murder."

Thanks, Mother. Remind me never to call you as a witness for my defense.

"I appreciate your help, I think. But why are you meeting him again? Does he still think I'm guilty?"

This conversation was making me so crazy I had managed to turn an entire box of rainbow-colored paper clips into mangled metal squares. I shoved them into the wastebasket while I listened to her response.

"We're going to look at some houses next week on his day off. He just went through a very painful divorce and has been living in an apartment for the last year. I told him buying a house would help the healing process. Don't you agree?"

My mother is a firm believer that home ownership can solve all of life's problems. But if she could distract Detective Bradford from concentrating on yours truly as a murder suspect she would help solve one of my current problems.

"Good luck selling him a house. But don't let him trick you into disclosing anything that would reflect badly on me. I don't trust him. At all."

"I have everything under control." She hung up, sounding more like the woman I had known for the past thirty-nine years than the giddy girl of the past five minutes.

I replaced my own receiver, stood up and managed one step before it rang again. "What now, Mother?"

"Is this Laurel McKay?" said a slightly familiar male voice.

"Yes. Who is this?"

"It's Neil Schwartz from the *Mountain Democrat*. Please don't hang up again," he said with a rush, "I may have some information for you."

The reporter was either intuitive or accustomed to hang-ups, because that was my initial response. "Yes, Mr. Schwartz." I wasn't going to put my foot or even my little toe in my mouth if I could help it.

"I appreciate that you may be reluctant to speak to a reporter." He chuckled. At least I thought it was a chuckle. It resembled the sound of Draino gurgling down the pipes, which didn't do anything to relieve my anxiety. He burbled on, "I would hate to write a story portraying you as a murder suspect without presenting your point of view. And of course, we'll want comments from your family."

No way. The last thing the *Mountain Democrat* needed was comments from my mother. I was still ticked off by her remark that I was too disorganized to be a murderer.

Okay, getting a little off track here. What was the reporter saying?

"…and give us your side of the story," he said.

"Mr. Schwartz, I don't have a side to my story. Dr. Slater and I only had one date. Okay one dinner date plus a lunch date, but I don't think that counts—you might have to read *Cosmo* to find out—and I didn't actually get to eat dinner, because he drowned, but first he was hit, but of course I didn't know that because I was drunk, well, not really drunk, just mildly tipsy—have you ever had Dom Perignon?"

"Um, no, I haven't. I'm not sure I got all of that, could you repeat what you just said?"

Not in a million years.

"I need to get back to work. You said you had information for me so it's your turn to share."

His phone clattered and the sound of raised voices filtered back to me. "Sorry," he said, sounding rushed. "I have to call you back. A truck overturned on Highway 50 and I need to cover it. I wanted you to know that when I was researching your story I came across something you might find interesting. I'll call you as soon as I'm free."

Don't hurry on my account. I doubted if he had any information I would find useful. It was probably a reporter's ploy to get me to spill my guts. Speaking of which, I hadn't had any lunch yet. I managed to get to the break room without any further interruptions, bought a candy bar and a diet soda from the vending machines and headed back to my desk.

I arrived home in time to catch the six o'clock news. I was pleased to see that the overturned truck and closure of the main highway from Lake Tahoe was still the main story. Not that I wanted to deprive anyone of a trip to the mountains, but at least it should keep Mr. Schwartz out of my hair for a while.

The three of us enjoyed an old family favorite, *National Lampoon's Vacation*. That movie almost made my life seem sane by comparison. Almost.

Rain pummeling my bedroom window woke me early Saturday morning. Based on past history, nothing less than a flash flood would cause a soccer game to be canceled. I filled thermos bottles full of hot chocolate for the two of us. Ben wasn't any more excited than me about going out in the driving rain. With multiple turtlenecks under his soccer jersey, he looked more like a waddling duck than a speedy halfback, but I doubted if any of the kids would be at their best today.

I sat in my car sipping from my thermos, waiting for the teams to head out on the field. Even the thought of bumping into Detective Hunter wasn't incentive enough to make me venture out of my toasty car into the pulsing rain.

Hard to believe it was only three weeks ago that I'd first met Tom. I smiled thinking of our first meeting. What a grump he was. And still was, I thought, as my smile reversed into a frown. After our last conversation when he forbade me from attending Jeremy's memorial service, I wasn't sure I wanted to run into him anyway.

Although maybe the reason he yelled at me wasn't just because I was messing up their investigation. He might care about me a little. Enough to not want anything to happen to me.

Whether it was the mini Niagara Falls pouring down my windshield or my eyes misting, it was becoming impossible to discern anyone on the field. I thought I saw Ben talking to one of the soccer players who had walked off the field. His friend wasn't recognizable since he was covered in brown muck from the top of his head to the spikes on his shoes.

As the kids drew closer to the car, I realized Ben's companion was Kristy. He pounded on my window so I rolled it down.

"Hi, Kristy," I said, addressing the four-and-a-half-foot-tall glop of mud. "How was your game?"

Her eyes sparkled, shining through her mud-flecked face. "We won, and I scored a goal."

I smiled back. "That's terrific." I tried to think of a subtle way to ask if her father was around.

"They called my game off 'cause of the mud," Ben explained. "Three players on Kristy's team got hurt and they don't want no more injuries. Her grandpa brought her 'cause her dad has to work. Can she come over to our house? Her grandpa's waiting for her in that car over there."

Ben pointed to a large charcoal sedan parked five slots down from mine. "Go ask if she can come home with us, Mom. We'll wait in the car."

They clambered into the backseat before I could lay down some of the towels I had brought. Oh, well, the backseat could use a good hosing anyway. I reluctantly stepped out of the car and hustled through the rain, which was now attacking me horizontally. I tapped on the window of Mr. Hunter's car.

He looked puzzled, then his face cleared as he recognized me. "Hello there. You're that friend of Tom's we met at the River Inn last Saturday."

Was it only last weekend that Jeremy had died? It seemed like a month, so much had occurred in the interim. "Yes, Mr. Hunter, I'm Laurel McKay. Kristy is friends with my son, Ben, and she wondered if she could play at our house this afternoon. Is Tom working today?"

He nodded. "Tom hated to miss out on Kristy's game but some new evidence came up on a big murder case he's working on. I watched the game for a while then gave up and decided to wait it out in the car." He chuckled as he rubbed his gloved hands together. "My old bones can't take this cold like they used to."

New evidence. That sounded intriguing. I was curious to know what Tom was checking out, but it was unlikely he had shared any information with his father. Still, it was worth a try.

"Did Tom say anything about the new evidence he discovered?"

"Nope, I only know that he's really frustrated with this particular case. Between you and me, I think the woman did it."

I stood there in the pouring rain, nodding back at Mr. Hunter. I supposed there might be another case that involved a woman as a suspect, but I doubted it. I wondered if Kristy's grandfather would have agreed to let her come to our house if he knew I was the woman.

We said goodbye and I sloshed back to the car. These soccer games were destroying my shoes. My water-soaked loafers would need to be retired after today's outing. Ben and Kristy were having a great time together, sharing knock-knock jokes ad nauseam. The smell of sweat and wet socks mingled with the aroma of hot chocolate added to my nauseum.

As soon as we arrived home, both kids hit the showers. Kristy was too tall to wear Ben's sweats, so she put on a pair of mine and we rolled up the cuffs. Her muddy soccer clothes went into the washing machine. If her father was chasing down a hot lead, the least I could do was relieve him of one domestic duty.

Kristy's grandfather had driven off so quickly I wasn't

sure how long she would be at our house. Hopefully he knew where we lived. The kids spent the afternoon teaching the kitten how to play soccer. First they threw the ball and she ran to it. Eventually Pumpkin learned how to bat the ball with her paws. Ben thought Pumpkin should be on television, but I had no intention of becoming an agent for a cat.

I was in the laundry room folding Kristy's clean clothes when I heard the doorbell ring. It was probably her grandfather so I figured the kids could get the door. Seconds later Tom walked into the room.

His dark hair was plastered to his drawn face. He had the look of a man who would welcome a comforting hug, but after our last conversation I wasn't sure where we stood. I held on to the white plastic laundry basket with a death grip. As he approached, I stepped back, bumping into the churning washing machine. His face somber, Tom silently removed the laundry basket from my arms, placing it on top of the dryer. He lifted me up on top of the machine.

Was he about to read me my rights?

EIGHTEEN

TOM PLACED HIS HAND ON THE back of my neck and drew me close. My head spun, my heart palpitated and my body pulsated.

Okay, part of the pulsating might have been due to the spin cycle. The rest of my reaction was due to the close proximity of a man who could turn my body into a fiery inferno. A loud bell suddenly pierced the air. Tom jumped back three feet and I almost tumbled off the machine.

Jenna appeared in the doorway with an armful of dirty laundry. She narrowed her eyes at her mother perched on top of a washing machine. I could hear the thud of her eyes rolling. She turned her back on both of us and retraced her steps back down the hallway.

I hopped down and began moving the towels from the washer to the dryer. Tom remained silent as I completed the transfer.

"I guess you're here to pick up Kristy." I held the laundry basket containing her clean soccer clothes as I rambled on, "I washed her stuff. She was really a mud pie after today's game."

"That doesn't surprise me." He lifted the basket out of my arms and set it on the dryer. "Kristy takes every opportunity to create as many loads of wash for me as she can. Thanks for doing her laundry and letting her come over here. My parents are wonderful about babysitting but she usually wears them out within minutes."

"Your father said some new evidence came up today.

Anything that will remove me from the list of suspects?"
Which as I recalled, was a list of one.

"You're still numero uno." He stuck his hands in his
pockets and rocked back and forth. "Laurel, how well did
you know Garrett Lindstrom?"

"The only time I met him was that evening at Leonardo's. Why? What happened? Did any new evidence show
up?"

Tom placed a finger on my lips then wrapped his muscular arms around me. I rested my head against his broad
chest. It was like being comforted by a grizzly bear, but I
liked it. A lot.

"This might be the only way to stop you from asking
questions."

I smiled a sweet smile at him. My body might be occupied, but that didn't stop my brain from working, especially
where murder was concerned.

Jenna appeared once again with her armload of clothes.

"Are you guys through doing whatever it is you're doing
in here?" She tapped her left foot, her ponytail swinging
to and fro. "Melissa is coming by in less than an hour and
I don't have anything to wear."

"Well, excuse us," I said to my long-suffering teenager.
"C'mon, Tom, let's go see what Ben and Kristy are up to.
The house seems much too quiet." I was worried the two
seven-year-olds had been up to no good, but both of them
were sprawled asleep on the floor of the family room in
front of the television set. A sleeping Pumpkin was cuddled
between them, the Wiffle ball secured in her front paws.

Tom followed me as I walked into the kitchen. Mr.
Rooster clock said it wasn't too early for a glass of wine.
"Do you want anything to eat or drink? I have wine, soda,
peanut butter and jelly?"

"A glass of merlot with a PB and J sounds particularly

enticing," he said as he settled into one of the oak chairs, "but I'll stick with a cola for now. I need to go back out with the crime scene techs."

I poured sodas for both of us then sat next to him, our toes within touching range. Tom's expression was reflective as he sipped his drink. I noticed threads of silver in his thick brown hair. Were those gray hairs there three weeks ago? Before I became a presence in his life? Since he wasn't interrogating me for a change, I decided to switch roles. "So what was the new evidence you mentioned? Something to do with Garrett?"

He nodded. "I've been doing everything I can to find a motive for his murder. You wouldn't believe how many Love Club women I had to interview."

I hazarded a guess. "Twenty?"

"Lucky guess?" He frowned. "Or some amateur sleuthing?"

"Neither. Sunny mentioned it when I told her about our altercation." I was curious to know if Garrett had attacked any other women. "Were there any other assault victims?"

He sipped his soda. "Nope. No one else was stu…um… no one else was invited to sit in his car."

It didn't surprise me that no one else was stupid enough to get in Garrett's car. Or leave their keys in the ignition. Or their phone in the charger. Or become a murder suspect.

"Okay, so I was the only woman dumb enough to get entangled in his front seat acrobatics. And to smack him. That still shouldn't qualify me as a suspect."

"Did you ever go to his house?"

I shook my head.

"Let me rephrase that. Did you happen to drive past his house in a periwinkle Prius, license plate LAUREL M, on the day the body was discovered?"

My face colored. "It was just a drive-by. The afternoon

Sunny told me he was found dead. I had to confirm it with my own eyes. There's no law against driving past a victim's house, is there?"

"No, but in your case there probably should be." He drained his glass. I stood up to refill it but he waved me back into my chair.

"Ever visit his office?" he asked.

Darn. Why didn't I think of that? I shook my head. "Why?"

"Due to the financial nature of his business, we wanted a forensic accountant to look through his files, but we had to wait for someone to come up from Sacramento. They finally made it there yesterday. No files. Not a one. The place was empty except for some miscellaneous junk in his desk drawers."

"Someone broke in?" I asked.

He nodded. "It wouldn't have taken much to get in. They could have used a credit card to unlock the office. Anyone could have done it."

"Anyone?" Even a lock challenged mother of two?

"Yep. The only thing left behind was one significant piece of evidence."

Our eyes locked. I had a feeling I wasn't going to be happy with his response.

"A business card from Hangtown Bank. One Laurel McKay, underwriter."

I walked over to the pantry and grabbed a bag of Oreos. I ripped opened the bag, threw it on the table, grabbed a Double Stuf cookie and took a bite. Then another. My blood pressure dropped as the chocolate worked its McKay magic.

"You're awfully quiet," he said, reaching for a cookie.

"I'm thinking. I don't remember giving Garrett my card, although it could have fallen out of the side pocket of my purse and landed in the backseat of his car. But I don't know how it would have ended up in his office. Jeremy asked me for my card when we met so he'd have my office number. Tons of people have my card."

Well, not exactly tons. But certainly more than the two men.

I offered Tom more cookies. He grabbed a couple and put the bag on the table. Looks like we had something else in common besides dead bodies.

"Just because my business card is in his desk doesn't mean anything," I mumbled through chocolate crumbed lips.

He sighed. "Let's just say it's highly suspicious that all of his files are gone. But I must admit, your card in the drawer seems way too obvious to me. I told Bradford I think you're being set up by the real murderer."

"How did Tall, Bald and Homely respond to that?"

"Who?" He looked puzzled then chuckled. "Oh, Bradford. As far as he's concerned you're the one. Especially now that Garrett's and Jeremy's deaths may have been linked with the same murder weapon."

"What?"

I saw the "oops" flicker across his face.

"I hope I don't regret this. And you cannot share what I tell you with anyone, not your mother, not Liz."

I lifted my right hand. "Scout's honor." Did you actually have to be a Girl Scout to utter those words?

"If you hadn't been with him when he died, it's unlikely Slater's death would have been pronounced anything more than an accidental drowning. There were bruises on the back of his head. Lacerations and contusions all over his body, mainly from the battering he took from the rocks in the river. Since his lungs were full of water, the official cause of his death was drowning."

Okay, that made sense.

"Since both men were members of the Love Club, and both dined with you shortly before they died, the medical examiner intentionally looked for similarities between the two deaths. Lindstrom had an unusual indentation on the back of his head but the back of Slater's head was a mess."

I grimaced and pressed my hands against my stomach.

"Sorry, didn't mean to be so graphic. Let's just say that during the autopsy of both men, minute flecks of red paint were found embedded in their skulls."

"Okay, I watch *CSI* but what the heck does that mean?"

"It means both men could have been bludgeoned with the same instrument. It's just far more difficult to ascertain in Jeremy's situation. But that's why I'm meeting with the crime techs later. They should have their analysis completed by then."

"So what kind of weapon are you talking about?"

"It's hard to say at this point. I'll know more after our meeting. Some kind of tool, maybe a hammer or wrench with a red handle, assuming the paint flecks match."

"So, since it looks like the same weapon was used both times, Bradford is even more certain that I'm responsible?" I wrinkled my nose in frustration. "It's not like I carry hammers and wrenches in my purse."

He grinned. "I've seen your purse. You could carry a chain saw in there."

"Well, I think the evidence is lame," I muttered.

Tom shook his head. "Opportunity, weapon. All he needs is a motive. And as far as Bradford is concerned he has a motive for both deaths."

What? My eyes opened wide and my lips opened wider as I stuffed another medicinal Oreo in my mouth.

"Here's the deal with Robert. His thirty-five-year marriage ended in an acrimonious divorce a year ago. A couple of months after that, he was forced to release a suspect accused of killing her husband because he didn't have enough evidence. She ended up murdering her in-laws a few days later."

I remembered that case. It was nasty.

Tom grabbed a cookie, rolling it around the table as he selected his words. "It's not that Bradford is biased against women, but because of his history, he may be overly suspicious of women in general. According to him, between the evidence we've discovered and his gut feeling, you're the killer."

We sat there eating cookies and contemplating one another. A detective and his suspect.

The sound of giggling children echoed from the family room. Tom went in and carried his daughter back to the kitchen table.

She rested her head on his broad chest as she settled in his lap. "Daddy, did Laurel tell you about my game? I made a goal."

Oops, I was so distracted by the murders and damaging new evidence that I forgot to report on today's game.

Tom hugged her tight. "That's wonderful, honey."

"Are we going home now?"

"No, I need to go back to work. You'll have to spend the night at Grandma and Grandpa's."

"Again?" She sighed with the gusto of a daughter trying to squeeze her father's tender heart.

"Can I stay here tonight? Would that be okay with you, Laurel?" she asked, her eyes hopeful.

As far as I was concerned she could stay, but Tom shook his head no. "Sorry, sweetie. I don't know when I'll be done and we don't want to disturb Ms. McKay in the middle of the night."

Why don't we ask Ms. McKay if she would like Detective Hunter to disturb her in the middle of the night? Heck, yes, but probably not with his young daughter in tow. I went into the laundry room, gathered Kristy's soccer clothing, put it in a bag and met Tom in the foyer. He still held Kristy, her arms wrapped around his neck. No wonder his biceps were so well developed. She was one big little girl.

He lingered for a minute to say goodbye. "Thanks for watching Kristy."

"Sure. Anytime. Provided I'm not in jail."

"I'm doing everything I can," he promised.

"I know. Maybe I'll discover something at Jeremy's memorial service."

His face closed up faster than the ticket window for a Rolling Stones concert.

"You're still planning on attending?" His eyes turned harder than granite and his voice dropped thirty decibels. How quickly he could revert to his official capacity.

"I don't have a choice. I was the last person to see…" My voice faltered when I realized Kristy was listening to our conversation.

Tom set Kristy down and told her to go play with Ben for a minute. She looked puzzled but evidently recognized his official tone, too. She was certainly better at obeying him than I was.

Tom waited until his daughter was out of the room before he lashed out at me. "Laurel, there is a killer out there." His face grew more purple with each overly enunciated word. "He has already murdered two people. Do you want to be the next victim?"

"No, but…"

"Laurel, there are no buts. No buts whatsoever. Can't you see how dangerous this amateur detecting is? What about your kids?"

"What am I supposed to do? Sit here until Bradford arrests me? Then who will take care of my children?"

He didn't answer. How could he?

NINETEEN

THE NEXT MORNING THE KIDS AND I finally made it to church. With ten minutes to spare. Mother showed up shortly thereafter, dressed in an orange knit suit, a perfect Creamsicle confection.

Every time I belted out a "Hallelujah," my thoughts returned to my encounter in the laundry room the previous afternoon, and it was difficult to keep a grin off my face. *Thank you, Lord, for the health of my family, and for providing me with that very healthy specimen, Tom Hunter. Now if I could ask one tiny favor like providing the detectives with another suspect, I would be eternally grateful.*

I reviewed the information Tom had shared about the murderer possibly using the same weapon on both men. Visions of tools as potential murder weapons danced in my head. Suddenly, I dropped the hymnal splat on the floor. That didn't get me any brownie points with Mother or Pastor Martin, who was right in the middle of his sermon. His sweet blue eyes didn't look all that sweet as he zeroed in on the source of the disruption.

I dropped my gaze and folded my hands together while my brain considered various options. Hammers, wrenches—my ex-husband had all of those items on his tool belt. But any normal male would have access to those tools. Even I possessed a tool kit, albeit in plastic. And in Ben's toy chest.

As soon as I arrived home, I changed into my navy blue sweats. My culinary skills are adequate but something inevitably spills when I cook. It was best not to tempt fate with one of my better outfits. Mother arrived about twenty minutes later.

"Laurel, you'll never guess who I was speaking with," she said as she entered the kitchen.

"Lay it on me." I bent down to reach inside the cupboard that held my odd assortment of baking pans. I pulled my head and arm back out of the cabinet. Success at last, one slightly bent and corroded baking dish. A bacon-scented kitchen was only minutes away. I heard the tail end of her sentence.

"…don't you agree with me?" Like I would dare to disagree with my mother. Maybe by the time I turned sixty.

"Yes, absolutely." I would agree with anything if I could entice her to attend Jeremy's memorial service with me.

It turned out that the wife of the new young couple from church was the granddaughter of one of my mother's former clients. The couple was looking for a new house in the area and my mother was going to help them. The real-estate queen was never happier than when she had three generations of loyal customers.

The kids inhaled their bacon, avocado and mushroom omelets within seconds. They loaded their plates in the dishwasher and politely excused themselves, giving me an opportunity to discuss what had been foremost on my mind throughout the meal.

As I walked into the pantry to grab some more coffee beans, I tried to think of a scintillating lead into the conversation that would involve Jeremy. Before I could open my mouth, my mother brought the subject up herself.

"Have you heard anything further about Dr. Slater's death? I didn't realize what a well-respected man he was. Even though his practice was in El Dorado Hills, several of the real-estate agents in our office said he was their personal physician. Detective Bradford told me his memorial service would be held on Monday."

"Really?" I said with an attempt to look surprised. Unfortunately, the surprise was on me. The lid on the coffee grinder must not have been clamped down because beans skittered across the tile counter. I glanced at Mother to see if she had noticed the wayward beans, but she was in the pantry rearranging cans and boxes.

She popped out of the pantry, arms laden with boxes. "These have all expired."

I had lived with the pantry queen's invasions for twenty years so her latest mission didn't even faze me.

"Um, speaking of expired..."

"Yes, what a shame Dr. Slater died so suddenly." She proceeded to dump half my food staples in the trash. "He would have been quite a catch for you. Maybe you should attend the service since you were the last person to see him alive."

There are times when I love my mother, pantry invasions and all.

"What a wonderful idea. I wish I had thought of that." I could sense my nose growing as I continued my lie. "I should go to the service, out of respect to Jeremy and his family. But I'd feel funny going by myself. Would you come with me? At least you'll know some of the people there."

She thought it over, nodded and patted my hand. "Of course I'll go with you, dear. You've had a tough few weeks and I'm sure attending this memorial service is the last thing you want to do."

Right.

"Do you think that intriguing Detective Bradford will go?" she mused out loud as she completed one more sortie into my pantry.

I almost gagged up my omelet imagining a potential

coupling of the ornery detective and my mother, but decided to keep mum for now. My mum was needed for my next detecting expedition.

Since the service was scheduled for three, we agreed to meet at two-thirty at the Starbucks that was a few blocks away from Fullers Memorial Home in El Dorado Hills. I don't know where people had meetings before Starbucks appeared on every corner.

She thanked me for brunch, but of course couldn't walk out the door without a typical maternal parting shot. "Be sure to wear a nice dark suit for the service."

"Oh, I was planning on wearing a red polka-dot dress. I thought it would liven things up a little." Fortunately, looks can't kill. She shook her head and walked out the door.

The next morning I wore my best black wool suit to work. As I stored my purse under my desk, I glanced at the desk calendar. My agenda was clear so I wouldn't have any difficulty leaving at two. Earl probably wouldn't mind if I left a few hours early, especially when he was bent on enticing me to stay in the department.

The phone rang and I grabbed it. "Laurel speaking."

"It's Anne Lewis. We managed to squeeze in an opening for you today but it wasn't easy. Bill Becker wanted to make a decision over the weekend because he needs to fill the position, but I talked him into waiting until he met with you. Your interview is scheduled for four."

Darn and double darn. How could I attend both the service and the interview at the same time? Talk about prioritizing.

"Um, Anne, a dear friend passed away and I have to attend the memorial service at three. Is there any way you can squeeze me in this morning?"

"You are not making my job any easier, Laurel," she

responded in a clipped tone. "I doubt if Bill can change his plans again. Was this a very close friend?"

"Very, very close." I sighed an Oscar-worthy sigh. "We were romantically involved and I'm devastated by his death."

"I'm so sorry," she said apologetically. "I didn't realize you had a boyfriend. What was his name?"

"Jeremy Slater," I blurted out without thinking.

"The doctor who drowned in the American River? I thought he was murdered by the woman he was dating."

A few seconds elapsed while Anne and I both contemplated her comment.

She cleared her throat. "Laurel, maybe this position isn't a good career move for you. There's a tremendous amount of customer service involved, plus considerable contact with the community. You wouldn't want the public worrying about your reputation."

"You aren't insinuating I had anything to do with Jeremy's death, are you?"

"No, of course not. I'll get back to you if Bill says we can move up the interview." The phone slammed in my ear. Evidently being considered a murder suspect was not an ideal career path. But was it sufficient grounds for termination?

As I mulled over my future employment prospects, Stan slid into the chair in front of my desk. I noticed that he, too, was dressed in a very conservative charcoal suit and subdued burgundy tie, quite unlike his normal fashion plate *Queer Eye* wardrobe.

"You look like you're going to a funeral, Stan."

"I am, sweetheart. We're going together, remember?" Shoot. I'd forgotten Stan volunteered to attend the memorial service with me.

"Thanks, but you don't need to go. Mother is coming with me now. You look very nice, though." I hoped that would appease him. After all, he had dressed for the occasion.

"C'mon, you said I could help you look for the culprit." He pouted as only Stan could pout. "You know I watch *CSI* every week. I'm sure I can discover some clues. Plus it can't hurt to have another set of eyes and ears."

"What do you think you're going to find? Are you going to climb on top of the casket looking for clues?"

"Puleeze. You know what a good judge of character I am. I have an intuitive sense when it comes to people." He crossed his legs, pursed his lips and looked down his nose at me. "It's a gay thing, you know."

I wasn't sure how useful gaydar would be in finding a murderer, but I decided to acquiesce. As he walked out of my cube, the phone rang again. I thought it might be Anne calling back to reschedule my appointment but I was greeted by a British accent.

"Hi, Liz. What's up?"

"Today's paper said that Dr. Slater's memorial service is this afternoon. I thought we should go together and do some more investigating. Isn't that an excellent idea?"

Apparently everyone I knew thought it was a great idea to accompany me to the funeral. So much for discreetly sneaking into the service.

"I'm already going with my mother and Stan. There's no need for you to come, too."

"Are you sure? It never hurts to have another set of eyes and ears."

Great. Now my dysfunctional detective team was starting to sound alike. Liz agreed to meet us at Starbucks. If nothing else, that particular Starbucks was going to have a profitable afternoon.

By the time I had to leave the office, I still had not heard back from Anne about rescheduling. I decided to focus on the memorial service and, to paraphrase a few friends, keep my eyes and ears open.

Liz and Mother, dressed in nearly identical black pin-striped designer suits, were chatting over a couple of lattes when I arrived. I cast lustful eyes at the Frappuccino menu but decided to forego my favorite treat. Stan arrived right behind me. He and my mother argued over who would chauffeur our foursome. Even though Liz wanted to ride in Stan's new Beemer, we decided my mother's car was the largest and most suitable for our entourage.

When we arrived at Fullers Mortuary and Chapel, the parking lot was full of BMWs, Mercedes and Lexuses, or was it Lexi? It made sense since many of the mourners were probably doctors.

I pulled my team aside. "Now remember, I'm hoping to find that man I saw talking to Jeremy along the river-bank the night he died. He's tall and balding. If we sit in the rear of the chapel, it'll be easier to notice someone with a bald spot."

All three agreed it was an excellent plan. We walked through the nine-foot double doors into a large foyer of wall-to-wall plush cream-colored carpeting. The overpowering floral mix of gardenias, gladioli and lilies made me gag. A gangly man with a prominent nose and an Adam's apple the size of a cantaloupe ushered us into the chapel. A substantial number of people were already seated, but fortunately there were enough chairs in the next to last row to accommodate the four of us.

Perfect. I sat down and looked around to see if I could find a man with a bald spot.

Whoa. The late-afternoon sun slanting through the arched stained-glass windows of the chapel cast jewel-toned motes of light throughout the room. The sun glistened on the backs of the people seated in the fifteen rows in front of us. And in those rows was a sea of shimmering, balding heads, ranging from small glowing bald spots to round gleaming domes.

I gasped and turned to Stan and Liz. When they saw my consternation they both convulsed with silent laughter. Shoot. We had at least sixty suspects with glow-in-the-dark bald spots.

Liz whispered to Stan and pointed toward the front of the room. A man with salt-and-pepper hair. No bald spot that I could see. When he shifted to speak to the man seated next to him, I saw his profile. Brian. He must be here on behalf of the District Attorney. Brian said something to the man at his side, who nodded in response.

A big man with thick chestnut-brown hair. And broad shoulders.

I slunk down in my seat, hoping Tom wouldn't turn around. The next thing I knew, Liz was waving at Brian and blowing him a kiss. He looked surprised to see her then he nudged Tom.

I couldn't make myself any smaller unless I crawled under my chair. Tom's stare burned through me. Fortunately, a tall middle-aged man with a full head of wavy white hair walked up to the podium and began addressing the crowd. Tom turned to face the speaker.

The service lasted well over an hour. Between the music and the glowing oratory extolling the nurturing character of Dr. Jeremy Slater, I was highly depressed. The sound of muffled weeping and sniffling almost drowned out the speakers.

How ironic that someone so health conscious should be cut down in the prime of his life. I began to feel like it was my fault Jeremy had died. I had lured him to dinner at the River Inn and it resulted in his death. The fact that he landed in the river without any help from me seemed irrelevant at this point.

Hushed sobs emanated from my right. I glanced at Stan. He, too, had a tissue pressed against his nose.

"What's wrong?" I whispered.

He leaned closer. "Jeremy was such a wonderful man," he said, a tear running down his cheek. "His loss is so tragic."

I always knew Stan was compassionate but he hadn't even met the man.

The seemingly endless service finally came to an end. The gray-haired man turned out to be the minister from the Methodist church that Jeremy's brother and his family attended. He announced that guests were welcome to come back to Mark Slater's house afterward to mingle and mourn together.

Since we were seated in the back of the chapel, we waited for the rows of mourners to leave before we stood up. I held an impromptu consultation with the others to decide if we should go over to Mark Slater's house.

Stan was all for going to the reception. "I haven't had an opportunity to use my investigative prowess. Plus, there are a couple of men I want to check out," he said with a smirk.

Mother chimed in, "I recognized several of the physicians. I'd like to make sure they have my business card. Doctors are excellent real-estate prospects." She nudged my arm. "Did you see Detective Bradford anywhere?"

"I need to talk to Brian," Liz said. "I've barely seen him in the past two days."

Someone needed to talk to my team about priorities.

We moved into the foyer that was now filled with wall-to-wall dark suits. Even though my shoes had three-inch heels, there were bald men towering over me as well as a few at eye level. The crush of people made mingling difficult and detecting impossible.

Liz, Stan and my mother were swallowed up in the crowd. I was ready to climb up on one of the blue brocade Louis XV chairs in the foyer to see if I could locate any of them when a hand gripped my elbow and hauled me back into the chapel.

TWENTY

THE CHAPEL WAS AS DARK AS THE inside of a coffin. The hand clasping mine was too strong and I couldn't break away. Was my assailant the killer? Which bald man would it turn out to be?

No big bad baldies here. Just one angry detective.

"Tom," I said in relief, my heart still beating like a bongo drum on speed.

"I thought I ordered you not to come," he growled.

I yanked my hand from his and folded my arms over my chest. "Who do you think you are ordering me not to attend the memorial service of a man who was the kindest, most compassionate and intelligent man I've ever met, present company included? His loss is incredibly tragic, and the least I can do is share memories of the last moments of his life with his family."

I turned on my heel, but my dramatic exit was stymied because it was too dark to see the door. All of a sudden both doors flung open. A familiar profile appeared in a beam of light.

Hank.

My ex rushed to my side, fist raised, ready to come to my rescue. Tom glared at him then stomped out without another word.

"What the hell are you doing here?" I asked, frustrated with all of the men in my life.

"I was talking to some friends when I saw that man grab you and pull you in here." Hank put his arm around my shoulder and drew me close. "Are you okay? Who was that guy? You know I'd do anything to keep you safe."

I took a long hard look at Hank. He seemed sincere, but an ex-husband's sincerity was questionable on the best of days. I brushed his arm away, opened the massive door and reentered the lobby. "I didn't expect to see you here. How do you know Jeremy?"

"We ran into each other at a Sig Ep fraternity reunion last August," he replied. "Jeremy was a year ahead of me and we didn't hang out that much during college. He wasn't much of a partier."

Spoken by the Panty Raid Prince of Sigma Phi Epsilon.

"When I found out he was practicing medicine I asked for his business card. Remember a couple of months ago when I hurt my back? I haven't had any medical insurance since our divorce, so he was willing to give me a break on his fees."

Hmm. Did Jeremy discuss any of his financial issues with his former frat buddy? "So did you guys chat about anything other than your injury?" I asked.

"We talked about the construction business, how it's really been in the tank. I sort of hinted maybe he'd like to hire me to build him a house. He's a doctor. He must have tons of cash."

I had visions of Hank running around the frat house wearing a pair of tightie-whities over his head. Just the kind of guy I'd hire to build a custom home. "Any luck with that?"

"Nah, he wasn't interested. He did say he was having some loan issues and wondered if I could help him out. I told him that was your area of expertise. In fact, I gave him your card."

Hank moved closer, mere inches from me. "So is that how the two of you ended up dating?"

I moved back, stumbling as my foot caught in the carpet. Hank caught me. He was so close I could taste the onions on his breath. Before I could respond, Liz appeared at my side. "Bugger off, Hank," she said with a look so scathing even my ex could get the hint. Liz had always intimidated Hank and apparently she still did. He quickly melted into the crowd.

She curled an arm around my waist. "Are you okay, luv? Did Hank say something to upset you?"

"No, but I was surprised to see him here. I didn't realize he knew Jeremy from college. Hank said he gave him my card but Jeremy didn't mention the connection when we first met."

"Jeremy probably thought you wouldn't go out with him if you knew he and Hank were acquainted," Liz said.

"Good point. Did Brian say anything to you about us being here? Tom went ballistic. I sort of intimated he couldn't touch Jeremy when it came to intelligence and compassion." I reached into my purse, grabbed a tissue and blew my nose. "But he's absolutely right. We don't have any business being here."

"Bollocks. These men are all alike. Brian wasn't happy I was here, either, even after I told him your theory of finding the bald-headed guy. It would serve them right if we discover something."

"Absolutely," I replied, feeling somewhat mollified. "It's not like Tom's been able to discover the murderer. And look what happened when Anne in HR found out about my relationship with Jeremy. Now my career is on the line, as well as my reputation."

"Let me say goodbye to my honey. I'm sure I can get him to come around to my point of view when he comes home tonight," she said with a lascivious wink at me. She flicked her hand through her bronzed curls and sauntered over to

Brian. Even in a suit, Liz could make her curvaceous hips swing seductively. The man didn't stand a chance.

I looked around for the rest of my retinue. Stan was conversing with a thirtyish man of average height and build. I scrutinized the back of his head—good, at least one baldy was being investigated. Of course, knowing Stan, he was trying to determine which team the guy was slugging for.

Mother was chatting with a heavyset woman in a tweed suit, and a tall man with a full head of hair. As I walked up, I overheard her say, "Laurel thinks she saw the murderer. That's why we came here tonight. To see if she could recognize him."

Some detective she was turning out to be. Before the end of the evening, she would probably tell every bald man at the service that we were in the process of investigating him. Fortunately, the man she spoke to was Peter Tyler. The woman I recognized as Penny, the longtime receptionist from the Centurion office.

"Shh," I hissed in Mother's ear. She looked confused so I moved closer and whispered, "You're not supposed to tell everyone what we're doing. You might tip off the murderer."

"Don't be silly, Laurel. They won't tell anyone about our detecting, will you?"

Penny's eyes sparkled as she responded. "Are you kidding? This is great stuff. I'm gonna get me a magnifying glass and a deerstalker hat and help. Big bad bald-headed guys, ha, ha, ha." She whacked me on the back and strode off chuckling.

Mother looked miffed as she stared at the departing receptionist. I wagered Penny wouldn't be laughing in the morning. The last thing an employee wanted to do was get on the wrong side of Barbara Bingham's desk.

Peter was busy placating my mother. "I'll keep everything you've said confidential. But don't you think this could be dangerous?"

"Trust me. If we find out anything we'll immediately share it with the police. I don't want to be a hero. I just want my life to return to normal. I'm tired of being a suspect in two murders."

"You're involved in two different murders?" Peter's eyebrows jumped a couple of inches and his voice ratcheted up to a tenor.

"Um." I was trying to figure out how to respond when Liz and Stan appeared, rescuing me from having to go into any further detail. Peter said goodbye without mentioning anything about dinner the following week. Did that mean our date was off? A woman suspected of two murders probably wasn't considered a social asset in the top producer circle.

The four of us climbed into the car and headed for Mark Slater's house.

"This investigating is way more difficult than I thought it would be," Liz said. "I asked two couples what they were doing the Saturday night Jeremy was killed and they both walked away. Do you think I insulted them? Maybe I need to be a little more subtle."

"You think?" Stan mocked her. "You know, the sheriff's department may be able to use the storm-trooper approach, but we civilians need to be more discreet."

"So what did you find out, Mr. Discreet?" Liz punched Stan in the shoulder.

"Hey. Watch it. I found out one of Jeremy's neighbors is gay and we're meeting for a drink tomorrow night." Stan grinned. "His name is Barry and he's been single for a while, too."

"Terrific," Liz said. "What if he's the killer? Did he have a bald spot?"

"Practically every man attending the service was balding somewhere on his cranium, including Jeremy's brother. We need to check him out, too," Stan said. "You know, in ninety percent of murders, it's a close friend or relative."

"True," Mother replied, "but don't forget they also say to follow the money."

"Exactly what we're going to do," I announced. Someone had to take charge of this group. "The one thing we know for certain is that Jeremy was about to buy a house in Lake Tahoe. But he had some concerns about the purchase."

"What kind of concerns?" Stan asked.

"He never had a chance to tell me. But if anybody can squeeze information out of a bereaved mourner, you guys can."

Liz and Stan exchanged glances. Okay, as pep talks went, it kind of sucked.

"We're here," announced Mother as she maneuvered the car into a parallel parking space. Parking skills are obviously not a genetic trait. The last time I parallel parked, I ended up on the sidewalk, less than an inch from a fire hydrant.

The Slaters' house was located in the country-club side of Serrano, an area of huge homes fronting the Robert Trent Jones–designed golf course. I stopped to confirm the address, but by the time we climbed the limestone steps of the imposing French Manor–style mansion, there wasn't much doubt this was the Slater residence. Lights blazed out of every gabled window.

It took all four of us to push open the massive paneled front door. As we stepped on the ivory marble floor, Mother nudged me, and pointed to the enormous chandelier hanging twenty feet over our heads, shooting out aurora borealis rays of light.

"Waterford."

Wow. Knowing what one Waterford crystal wineglass cost, I couldn't imagine the dollars invested in that light fixture. I bet they didn't get it at Home Depot.

We followed other dark suits into the living room, which was close to the size of my entire house. The two spotless ivory sofas flanking the fireplace would never have survived a day around my kids. The perfectly coordinated yellow-and-blue chairs and matching draperies and rugs looked like something out of *Architectural Digest*. I was both impressed and disappointed. Mark Slater certainly didn't need any of Jeremy's money, unless they were mortgaged to the hilt.

I glanced at some of the paintings hanging on the walls. Original works of art including some early-twentieth-century artists. Definitely not the thirty-nine-dollar landscapes I've bought at weekend sales at the Holiday Inn.

Many of the guests seemed to be acquainted with each other, probably relatives or friends and neighbors. A petite woman with spiked blond hair, dressed in a clingy black Lycra spandex dress more suitable for clubbing than mourning, waved at us. I didn't recognize her but Liz waved back.

"Who's that?" I asked.

"That's Tara. Don't you remember her from Jeremy's office? She's the receptionist with the acne issue."

Liz swirled her head to the left and the right. "Lots of good spa candidates here. I should have brought more business cards."

"You're going to market at a memorial service?"

My brash friend chuckled. "Hey, with my health and beauty tips, these women can live ten years longer. Didn't you hear that collagen loss is approaching epidemic proportions? They need me." With that remark, she crossed the room and greeted Tara.

Stan noticed his new acquaintance, Barry, standing by the enormous limestone fireplace, so he wandered over to expand on their friendship. The next thing I knew, my mother was striding across the room, smiling animatedly as she joined two elderly couples.

So much for my team.

My stomach gurgled. It had been eight hours since my last meal. Even Nancy Drew didn't look for clues on an empty stomach. The best place to start was obviously wherever the food was being served.

I maneuvered through the crowd in the living room and across the entry into an equally enormous dining room. The glossy mahogany table, which could have been Sheraton or Chippendale, but definitely not Ikea, was covered from one end to the other with plates of colorful pungent food. The aromas of garlic, onion and chocolate perked up my salivary glands.

I contemplated getting two plates, to keep myself balanced, but decided it would be difficult to shake hands with potential suspects. There was only one other couple in the room. The man's bald dome was almost as bright as the highly polished table. He was in his late sixties or early seventies, tall and stooped. I couldn't imagine anyone that age being able to knock Jeremy into the river. But timing was everything. If he surprised Jeremy and pushed him just the right way, it might have worked. I would begin with them.

I sidled closer to the elderly couple and extended my right hand. "I'm Laurel McKay, a close friend of Jeremy's. Are you members of the family?"

"Oh, hello there," the man responded, setting down his wineglass in order to shake my hand. "Yes, Jeremy is, or rather was, my nephew. I'm Henry Slater and this is my wife, Bonnie." Bonnie nodded at me with red-rimmed eyes as she stared at her plate of hors d'oeuvres.

"I'm so sorry for your loss." I always feel inept talking to relatives of the deceased. "I will truly miss Jeremy."

Henry Slater focused his watery blue eyes on me. "How were you acquainted with my nephew, my dear?"

"We were friends, um, social acquaintances." No point in going into more detail. I tried to think of something relevant to ask them. Interrogating required far more tactical skills than I seemed to possess.

"This is a lovely home. Mark must be very successful in his line of work." I grabbed a piece of bruschetta and bit into it. Yum. Great caterer.

"Yes, he is." Henry answered my implied question. "Mark is an attorney. He works with me in my law firm. In fact, the whole family consists of lawyers, with the exception of Jeremy. I guess you could call him an ambulance receiver, not an ambulance chaser, as my profession is often derided."

All attorneys. So money probably wouldn't be a motive among this family. Not unless someone was a really lousy lawyer.

"I wonder who the beneficiaries are in Jeremy's will," I said, as I crunched on the bruschetta. Unfortunately my mouth and brain were not working in tandem. Henry seemed taken aback by my lack of tact and stepped away from me.

He placed his arm around his wife's waist. "Let's go, Bonnie. It was nice meeting you, I suppose," he added under his breath, as they left the room with disgusted looks on their faces.

I didn't blame them. I was disgusted with myself. I had absolutely zero skill in conducting a discreet inquiry. The senior Slaters left their plates behind on the table. They probably lost their appetite after speaking with me. I wish I had the same problem. My stomach was carrying on a conversation with itself and it didn't sound happy.

Maybe the reason my questioning was so incompetent was that my brain had been deprived of carbohydrates. I contemplated the gold-rimmed platters of desserts, torn between a piece of chocolate mousse cake and an apple crumble. Someone tapped me on my arm and I dragged my gaze from the delectable desserts to the new arrival.

"Hi, Peter. You disappeared so quickly from the service I didn't think you were coming to the reception."

"Sorry," he said with a sheepish look. "I admit I was a little freaked out when you said you're now a suspect in two murders. I've got to admit it really takes guts to look for a killer."

Guts? Or stupidity?

I swallowed the piece of rumaki I'd been chewing. Peter could be a useful ally from a real-estate standpoint. Not to mention the rest of my team had deserted me.

"When Jeremy and I were at dinner, he seemed concerned about the purchase of a vacation home in Tahoe. Did you handle his real-estate transactions?" I tried to talk and eat a mini quiche at the same time. "By the way, how did you know him?"

"Jeremy is, I mean, he was my doctor." Peter looked thoughtful as he gnawed on a carrot stick. "It was kind of surprising how many Centurion agents were his patients, but he really was an excellent physician. I'm not sure whom he worked with in our office. He never called me for any real-estate advice, if that's what you're asking." He pushed his plate away. "I still can't believe his drowning wasn't an accident. You're certain the sheriff's department thinks he was murdered?"

"Absolutely. I have it right from the horse's mouth." Although it was more like a horse's ass, as far as I was concerned.

"So, what's the next step in your investigation?" asked Peter.

"Yes, Nancy Drew, what is the next step?"

Busted.

TWENTY-ONE

"HI, TOM," I MUTTERED. "Have you met Peter Tyler? He works at Centurion with my mother."

Tom shook Peter's hand then turned to me. "Peter, would you excuse us? I need to discuss something with Laurel."

"Certainly," Peter said. "I'll see you next week, Laurel."

"Can't wait."

Tom grabbed my elbow, and I relinquished my plate of goodies as he led me into the living room, which appeared even more crowded than before.

I scowled at him, not sure if I was more annoyed that he had removed me from Peter's company, or that I'd had to leave my plate of appetizers behind. He glowered at me as a few people walked past, giving us curious looks.

"Now what? Can't I have a conversation with a handsome cultured man without you dragging me away?" I said.

"Why won't you let me do my job without interfering? Don't you realize any one of these people could be the killer?" Frustration lined his face as he worried about dead bodies, dangerous murderers and one stubborn female.

The hunk of my dreams stood in front of me. Begging me to stop meddling in his murder investigation. What indeed was my problem?

Stubbornness. Stupidity. I didn't even know the answer. All I knew was that this attractive and occasionally sensitive man was pleading with me to stop looking for a killer. Was there any other option than to acquiesce to his wishes?

Tom moved closer. My antenna quivered but not due

to his presence. My gang of detectives had surrounded us en masse.

"Laurel." Mother folded her arms across her chest. "Would you care to introduce us?"

My cheeks flushed. "This is Detective Hunter. He's in charge of the investigation into Jeremy's death. Tom, this is my mother, Barbara Bingham."

"I'm pleased to meet you." Tom offered his hand and bestowed his high voltage smile on her.

Mother smiled back and kept his hand clasped in her own. "Detective Hunter, how nice to meet you." She lowered her voice and I couldn't make out her next few words.

Tom shook his head. "I'm sorry but I'm not authorized to share that information. It's confidential police business."

She gave him the look that had terrified hundreds of her competitors. "Then I guess I'll have to ask Detective Bradford. I'm sure he'll accommodate me. Let's go, Laurel."

I looked sheepishly at Tom, but with my team surrounding me, there wasn't much I could do or say other than goodbye. He looked relieved that I was leaving. One less amateur detective to worry about, I guess.

Our group filed out the front door and down the steps. I was lagging behind the others when a heavyset man bolted out the front door and crashed into my shoulder. I lost my balance and grabbed hold of the first thing I could find, which happened to be the man's arm. Our eyes locked.

"Dr. Radovich!" I hadn't noticed him earlier at the reception. I wasn't sure if he would remember me from my brief visit to his office. He stared at me as if trying to recall my name. All of a sudden, recognition dawned.

"Ms. McKay," he said, in that same brusque tone I remembered. "How is your leg feeling now?"

It felt fine before he crashed into me and almost pushed me down the stairs, but that didn't seem the most tactful response. "It's much better. You seem to be in a hurry this evening." I jogged alongside as I attempted to keep up with his brisk pace down the sidewalk.

He raised his shaggy brows, muttered something under his breath, and proceeded to rush down the street in the opposite direction from my mother's car. The chirp of a remote entry key signaled he had reached his destination, a gas-guzzling black Hummer parked at the end of the block.

"Laurel, let's go," Liz called out, motioning to me from next to the Chrysler. I hurried down the pavement.

"Follow that car."

My quick-witted detective trio responded in unison. "Huh?"

Luckily, my mother has excellent reflexes for a senior citizen. She jumped in the driver's seat, turned the key in the ignition and had her right foot hovering over the accelerator by the time Liz, Stan and I were belted in.

We briefly lost sight of our prey, but caught up to him as he waited for the entrance gate to open.

"Don't get too close," I said as Mother's front grille hovered a few inches from his rear bumper. My plan did not include plowing into the car of a murder suspect.

Liz peered over Mother's head. "Who are we following?"

"Dr. Radovich. He was acting in very suspicious manner."

"How do you know what's suspicious behavior for the doctor?" Stan asked.

"Um…"

We followed the SUV as it turned left onto El Dorado Hills Boulevard. The doctor drove up the Highway 50 on-ramp and headed east toward Placerville and the Sierras.

Mother sped up, remaining a few car lengths behind him. "What should I do? Do you have any idea where he's going? Where does he live?"

Three excellent questions. Too bad I didn't have answers for any of them.

"His practice is nearby. He must live around here somewhere."

"It better be close. I don't have time for a wild-goose chase."

Like I did?

Three exits later, the Hummer moved into the right lane. We were right behind him. He turned on his signal and exited the freeway at an off-ramp that dead-ended at one location.

The Goldenwing Casino.

The doctor pulled the super-size SUV into a parking stall and jumped out, heading straight for the casino entrance. We parked in a stall a few cars down from his.

"It's somewhat unusual to go directly from the memorial service of your partner to a casino, isn't it?" Mother asked.

Liz bounced in her seat. "I forgot to tell you. Tara, their receptionist, mentioned two creepy guys stopped in the office the day after we did. That would have been Friday. They didn't have an appointment but they insisted on speaking with Dr. Radovich. She said the guys could have starred in the Sopranos. After they left, Radovich canceled all his appointments for the rest of the week. Tonight he told her he's going on vacation for a couple of weeks."

"I bet the doctor owes the casino tons of markers and they sent their goons after him," Stan said.

I turned around and shot him my "puleeze" look.

"It could happen. Don't you know there's mafiosi everywhere?"

"You have got to stop watching all those crime shows," I said.

"Hey, just 'cause I'm gay doesn't mean I spend my evenings watching the Home and Garden network," Stan replied. "Although, did you see *Design on a Dime* last night?"

"Amazing ideas for staging houses. Did you see the one the week before—'Don't Break your Budget on your Bedroom'?" Mother asked.

"I really liked the segment they did on 'Having Fun with your Futon,'" Liz said.

"Guys," I said. "Can you switch from designing mode back to detective mode?"

"What do you suggest, Miss Drew?" Stan asked.

I shrugged. I was running out of clever ideas. Not that I'd had any to begin with.

"Laurel, it's six forty-five. I told Brian I'd meet him at seven," Liz said.

"Okay. I need to get home, too. There probably isn't anything further we can do here anyway," I said.

"Hey, do you want me to come back and spy on the doc? See if he's a high roller?" Stan asked.

I hesitated. "Don't do anything that could be dangerous."

"Oh, c'mon. Tonight has been the most fun I've had since we went shopping together. I need a little excitement in my life."

"Okay. But be careful. I don't want him to suspect anything."

"I'll go home first and change into something more suitable. Maybe a tux—you know, the James Bond look. So I'll fit in at the casino."

I pictured my slight friend dressed in a black tux, playing roulette, surrounded by senior citizens in pastel sweat suits, the mainstay of the Indian casino.

Mother spoke up. "You know, it's hard to believe that two men so different could be partners in a medical practice."

I compared the charming, handsome Dr. Slater to his surly and somewhat scary partner. Not exactly two peas in a pod. I twisted around and looked at my two best friends. No one would put us in the same pea pod, either.

We pulled into the parking lot in front of the Starbucks. Liz started to climb out of the backseat then stopped. "Laurel, you know that bald man you saw with Jeremy the night he was murdered? What if the bald man left the River Inn after their conversation was over and someone else pushed Jeremy in the river?"

All eyes turned to the team leader. Master Detective McKay.

I slumped down in my seat. Liz had a point. Did the suspect list just increase by thousands of people who weren't bald?

Stan shoved Liz out of the car. "C'mon, sweetie, I've got a stakeout at the casino. Don't worry, Laurel. You'll figure it out."

Liz and Stan exchanged farewells and I hugged my mother goodbye. "Thanks. You were a big help tonight." I pulled on the door handle.

"Of course I was, dear. You children would have been lost without me." I eased my leg out of the car as she imparted her standard maternal reminder.

"Don't forget your purse."

"I've never forgotten it. Yet. Good night." I slammed the door shut then stomped over to my own car. Mothers!

Speaking of which, it was time this mother checked in with her offspring. I called the kids as I drove out of the parking lot. The phone rang five times before Jenna picked up.

"Hi, honey, everything okay?"

"Yeah, we're fine, but I'm on the phone with Katie. What time will you be home? Some guy has called you three times but he won't leave his name."

That was odd. It seemed like every male I knew had been at the service this evening.

"I'll be there in twenty minutes." I heard my son hollering in the background. "Why is Ben yelling?"

"Oh, you know how Ben is, always whining. C'mon, Mom, Katie's still holding for me."

"Tell her you'll call her back. Put your brother on the phone."

Ben's shrill voice blasted out of the phone. "Mom, Mom, when are you coming home? Jenna is making me play with my Legos. I don't want to play with my Legos. She says I have to do whatever she says."

Honestly. I told Ben to put Jenna back on the line.

"What?"

"Ben said you're making him play with his Legos even though he doesn't want to play with them."

"I'm in charge so he has to do what I tell him." I heard the implied "Duh" in her voice. It was obvious my daughter needed a few lessons in leadership training.

"Jenna, you can't dictate what toys he should be playing with."

"Why not?"

I counted to five. "As long as he isn't doing anything wrong, he can play with whatever toy he wants."

"Fine, whatever. Can I go now? I promised to call Katie back." She sounded anxious to appease me and get on with her busy social life. I made a mental note to mentor her on her management skills.

The discussion about Legos reminded me that Garrett had lived just a few blocks away. He was single and childless so I had no idea who his beneficiaries were, but it was possible his home might be listed for sale. I couldn't remember his exact address but if I could get in the entrance gate, I was certain I could find it again and see if there was a for-sale sign on the lawn.

Sneaking into the subdivision proved to be a simple task. Someone must have crashed into the gate because it was propped wide-open. I missed Garrett's street on my first attempt. If the roads all looked alike in the daytime, the starless sky certainly didn't enhance my ability to find his house. I finally turned onto his street and located his residence. The crime scene tape had been removed and a green for-sale sign was posted on the front lawn. I grabbed a pen and paper and stopped to write down the agent's name and phone number. It wouldn't be difficult for Mother to arrange for us to look inside.

I made it back to the entrance without any unwanted detours. I turned right, heading east on Serrano Parkway. Once the tree-lined parkway ended I turned left on Bass Lake Road. It should take me less than fifteen minutes to get home to Greenhills.

I drove down the two-lane road, my brain contemplating the tidbits of information we'd pulled together. None of which made much sense. Suddenly two beams of light radiating from a vehicle behind mine blinded me with their brilliance. The high beams of the truck or SUV flooded my car with enough megawatts to light up Arco Arena.

The vehicle moved closer and closer until it was inches from my bumper. I accelerated but it stuck to me like glue. I slammed the gas pedal all the way to the floor and my car shimmied to the left. I yanked the steering wheel in the same direction and my tires skidded on the gravel alongside the road. We were approaching a ninety-degree curve with a posted speed of forty miles per hour. My eyes flashed to the speedometer.

Crap. I was doing seventy. My hands were cemented to the steering wheel. If I didn't slow down, my car would never make the curve. I glanced in the rearview mirror to see how close my tailgater was.

I barely had time to scream when the tank riding my bumper slammed into me.

TWENTY-TWO

I ALWAYS WONDERED WHAT THE phrase "your life flashing before your eyes" meant. In my case it meant a whirling kaleidoscope composed of the faces of my loved ones superimposed over the oak trees whizzing past the windows of my car.

Bam. The Prius landed on a rutted dirt track. My first thought was if I survived this ordeal I would finally break down and replace the shocks. My hands were frozen to the steering wheel, stuck in the official ten and two position.

The screech of the brakes, which I had the foresight to recently replace and which I now had the foresight to utilize, announced the end of our jarring journey. The car landed with a thud and a groan, the front bumper face-to-face with the massive trunk of one of those great old dowagers—the California oak tree.

Either my air bag was broken or it wasn't set to go off midflight. I sat there for a few minutes with my head pressed against the steering wheel. A pair of headlights approached from the opposite direction. The noise of the engine indicated the car was slowing. I prayed it wasn't the lunatic who had rammed me coming back to finish the job.

Neither a lunatic nor a Good Samaritan. The car rounded the curve and proceeded on its way.

I opened my door and eased out of the car. The midnight-blue sky made it too difficult to assess the damage, but if there was any, it was minimal. I breathed in the pungent night air. A few deep breaths and I started to calm down although my chest felt like a small elephant had careened over me. At least my back and neck seemed to have handled the impact okay.

This spot was way too dark and isolated to be hanging around so I climbed back in my sturdy little car, backed down the muddy path and headed north once again. My eyes remained superglued to the rearview mirror all the way home. Once I was safely in my subdivision, I breathed a sigh of relief. I pulled into the garage, entered the house and to my amazement found Ben engrossed in his Legos.

Kids.

The next morning my chest still ached but that seemed to be the only side effect from the previous night's encounter. The rear bumper was slightly dented and there were some scratches on the front bumper from the tree I'd nudged, but the Prius had proven to be surprisingly durable.

The big question was obviously whether there was a connection between the SUV ramming my car and our detecting last night. Someone might have followed us from the casino. Or followed me home from Garrett's house.

Or it could have been a teenager out for a joyride. I debated whether to call Tom to tell him about the incident but decided to wait until later in the day. It was too early for another one of his lectures on the perils of amateur detecting.

When I arrived at the office the first thing I did was stop to see how Stan's investigating went. His cubicle was empty. No sign of him anywhere.

Omigod. If something happened to Stan at the casino I would never forgive myself.

I was ready to report a missing underwriting assistant when I walked by Earl's office. Stan was sitting in front of our boss's desk. He didn't look happy. Neither did Earl. I was relieved to see that my buddy was safe, but what was going on?

The phone rang and I grabbed the receiver. "Laurel. Come to my office. Now." Earl's voice was curt. Not at all like the smitten boss who'd been hanging around my desk lately.

"Yes, sir." I would have to find out about Stan's meeting after my own. I grabbed a yellow legal pad, turned right, left then right again, arriving at the door of Earl's office just as Stan rose, indicating their conversation was over. Stan averted his gaze as he exited the office.

My chest constricted but I summoned up a fake smile. "Hi, Earl. I'm almost finished with yesterday's submissions."

Earl stood up, walked to the door and closed it. Loudly. One might even suggest that he slammed it. I surmised this would not be a social visit. He lowered himself into his ergonomically correct leather chair, which groaned in response, then waved at me to sit in one of the visitor chairs.

"Laurel, I'm not going to waste your time or mine. It appears you haven't been honest with me." He grabbed a forest-green Mont Blanc pen and rolled the slim cylinder back and forth over his desk blotter, the only uncluttered area on his desk.

"I don't know what you're talking about." I perched on the edge of my chair. That was no lie.

Earl took a break from staring at the rolling pen. He looked tense and...mad. "It's come to the bank's attention that you're being investigated by the sheriff's department for the murder of a respected member of our medical community."

My stomach clenched as my mind raced. Could Stan have told Earl? I was sure Tom would forewarn me if they were going to question anyone at the bank about me. Who else did that leave?

I grabbed the arms of my chair for support. "I don't know where you could have received your information."

"From you—" He glared at me. "You told Anne Lewis about your involvement with Dr. Slater when you canceled your interview yesterday. She followed up by calling a friend of hers in the sheriff's department."

Rats. I squirmed in my seat, crossing and uncrossing my bare legs, trying to get comfortable. "Anne doesn't have all of the facts. Yes, I did go out on a date with Jeremy Slater. Yes, he did fall into the river. Yes, he did drown that evening. And yes, he was murdered."

Hmm. So far my defense was somewhat lacking in inspiration. I decided to go on the offensive. "I can't believe you would question my innocence. I barely knew Dr. Slater. Plus the sheriff's department doesn't consider me a suspect." Or at least I didn't think Tom did. As far as Bradford, all bets were off. Actually, all bets were probably on me.

"Even worse," Earl continued, his expression still morose, "a reporter from the *Mountain Democrat* has been hounding the president of the bank for a comment. Ask me how happy Mr. Chandler was about that."

I suspected Mr. Chandler, the bank president, wasn't pleased about having a murder suspect working for the bank. Was the reporter that guy with the Draino chuckle? I had to get him off my back.

"You should have mentioned this situation to me. Not only is the bank's reputation at stake but Dr. Slater was one of our best customers."

Great. Now I wasn't merely losing dates, I was also responsible for losing deposits.

"Earl, I'm sorry. Since I had nothing to do with Jeremy's death, I didn't think it was important for anyone at the bank to know about it. I promise I'll keep you informed about anything else I hear about the case."

"Make sure you do that."

His pen fidgeting was driving me crazy. I was about to grab it out of his hand when he dropped another bombshell. "You know if you hadn't joined the Love Club we wouldn't be in this situation."

Interesting segue from death to dating. "Um, I've only gone on two dates so far."

"Yes, but look what happened each time." His gaze started at my chest and drifted down to my crossed ankles. "There are eligible bachelors here in this office. Stick with people you know rather than this dating service."

Since I couldn't think of any bachelors at the bank that I personally considered eligible I needed to direct the conversation elsewhere. "Did Anne say anything further about rescheduling my interview?"

"The HR department decided they had sufficient candidates to choose from. Between missing your appointment and your involvement in a murder, they selected someone else."

My face fell at the news. This was turning out to be one crapola day.

"Looks like you're fated to stay in this department." Earl ran a hand over his balding pate, his smile so satisfied you'd think he'd won the lottery. "I promise to assign you additional responsibilities. It'll give us an opportunity to work closer together."

Oh, goody. At least I was still employed although I would have preferred a position where my boss wasn't hitting on me, harmless as Earl was.

I left his office and went straight, well, left, right, left, down to Stan's cube. I parked myself in the chair beside his desk. "Stanley, why the long face when you came out of Earl's office?"

He took off his glasses, rubbed his bloodshot eyes then

pushed the wire rims back on his pointed nose. "I should have told you before. When you applied for the branch manager posting, I assumed you would get it, so I asked Earl if I could move up to a full underwriter. He said I could, provided you got the position. I guess they won't promote you, right?"

I nodded glumly. "Evidently they prefer their managers not be murder suspects. I'm afraid if we don't solve the murders I'm going to be fired."

Stan's frown reversed into a grin. "Hey, wait until you hear what Stan Spade discovered last night."

"Really? At the casino?"

He nodded. "It took me a while to track Radovich down. That place is huge." Stan sent me a sheepish look. "And I got a little distracted by the dollar slots. But I won eighty bucks."

"Swell. So…"

"So, after that I wandered everywhere and finally spotted him in a private room in the back. Texas Hold 'Em poker. Five thousand minimum."

"Five thousand dollars?"

"Yup, five thousand minimum to get in the room. Just one table with six guys. One guy had a ton of chips in front of him. Our doctor did not. He must have lost big and lost fast. I tell you, this guy definitely has a gambling problem."

"How long did you stay?"

"Not long. Once his chips were gone he left the table so I left the casino. My eighty bucks was starting to burn a hole and I didn't want to leave it behind in the slots."

"Excellent work. Are you ready for more?"

"Yeah, baby," he said, rubbing his palms together in the worst Austin Powers imitation I'd ever heard. I mentally rolled my eyes.

"Remember that first guy I went out with who was murdered?" I said.

"Sure. Garrett somebody. Why?"

"After we left the funeral home last night, I drove by his house. It's listed for sale so if my mother can get us in, we might find something the detectives missed. What do you think?"

"Are you kidding?" He flashed me a brilliant smile. "I'm in."

I went back to my desk and called Mother's office. Penny, the receptionist, said she was on a call and asked me to hold. Penny also asked if I'd eliminated any more dates.

Everyone's a comedian.

As I waited on the line, I tried to recall my conversation with Earl. Something he'd mentioned didn't make sense. Mother's abrupt greeting interrupted my thought process. "What do you want, Laurel?"

"Oh, hi. I was wondering if you could get me into Garrett Lindstrom's house in Serrano. I drove by last night and it's listed for sale. Can you show it to Stan and me this afternoon?"

There was a slight delay and I heard her punching some device. "I'm booked almost all day, but I could probably squeeze you in between one and three. I need to call the listing agent but since the house must be vacant I should be able to use my lockbox key."

"Perfect. We'll meet you there at two."

My observant mother would no doubt notice my crumpled hybrid. If she suspected my car crash was due to our investigating, she'd have that key back in the lockbox faster than I could say Prius. I told Stan about the accident and asked if he could drive.

"You were rammed from behind? After we split up?" His jaw dropped so low it almost touched his loafers.

I nodded. "I'm amazed the car got away with only a small scratch. Probably some kids driving too fast."

The freckles on his nose popped out as his face paled a few shades. "I think we may be asking the right questions. Someone is scared and they tried to stop you. Permanently."

Much as I was starting to agree with Stan, I wasn't ready to give up. I had too much at stake. "We just need to be more cautious from now on."

That was something we both agreed on. We took Stan's car and arrived at Garrett's house a couple of minutes late after making two wrong turns, both of which Stan blamed on my poor directions. Evidently gay men don't have any better navigational skills than straight men.

Mother's gleaming Chrysler was parked in the driveway. She stood on the front porch, arms crossed over her chest, the right foot of her Prada pump tapping her noticeable displeasure.

"You're late and you have lettuce on your blouse." She picked the offensive piece of foliage off my chest and flicked it on the front lawn.

"At least I'm wearing healthy food these days." I took a deep breath and tried to maintain my cool.

"The agent won't be meeting us so we can go inside. Hopefully this won't be another wild-goose chase," she said as she inserted the key in the lock.

Wild-goose chase? We'd been collecting clues by the dozens. Not to mention the high probability someone had attempted to murder me last night. Not something I needed to share with the woman who'd brought me into this world.

The three of us entered the great room. All leather and glass-topped tables. Garrett was one of those white freaks. White leather sofa, white walls, a few abstract paintings in shades of white and gray. Slate floors throughout the house.

Mother and Stan wandered down a long hallway to the

left. I went the opposite direction into the kitchen, which followed the same theme, white cabinets with uncluttered black granite countertops. Chrome appliances. I opened a few doors but except for one cabinet filled with plates and glasses, the cabinets were empty.

Laughter radiated from the other end of the house. I followed the sound of their voices into the master suite, entering a replica of Hugh Hefner's bedroom straight out of the Playboy mansion. A leopard-printed furry thing covered the king-size bed. Mirrors lined most of the walls.

They both chuckled at the ceiling. Yuck. An enormous oval mirror hung over the bed.

Stereo equipment and a huge flat-screen television comprised the rest of the furnishings. Garrett probably had a collection of porn for late-night screenings. Other than the adult fantasy motif, the room was fairly sparse. I was certain the police would have removed personal items of any significance but calling Tom was not an option.

Stan opened a drawer in the black lacquer dresser before I could stop him. After looking at the decor, I had no desire to learn anything further about Garrett, like the style of his underwear. Or size.

Ick. Too late. Stan held up a teeny-weeny zebra-print thong.

I peeked in the bathroom, which continued the jungle theme with leopard-print wallpaper and matching towels. Where on earth did he find this stuff? There was a large Jacuzzi tub, enormous dual-head shower stall, and dark brown oversize wicker hamper. Mother and Stan walked up and peered over my shoulder.

"I would kill for a bathtub that size," I mused. My companions stared at me. Guess I could have phrased that better.

The room down the hall from the master bedroom was

probably a guest room, very plain and furnished in beige on beige. The last room appeared to be Garrett's office. Now this was more like it. Garrett must have been a golfer because he had a multitude of golf related souvenirs decorating the top of a large glossy ebony desk. It sure beat the animal safari theme in his bedroom. Framed prints of what I gathered were various famous golf courses hung next to a wall that was lined with matching polished black bookcases and file cabinets. Stan wandered over to examine the prints.

I opened a few of the file drawers but as I suspected they were empty. Either cleaned out by Garrett or the sheriff's department.

"Anything in there?" Mother asked.

I sighed and slammed another drawer shut. "No. I don't know what I was thinking. I guess I'm just desperate to find something that would point to a suspect other than me."

"If you'd only listened to me and not joined that stupid Love Club."

"Hey, what's done is done. You don't need to air our dirty laundry in front of Stan."

Stan's face lit up. "Dirty laundry. *CSI* always goes through the laundry hamper."

"Ick." Mother and I responded in unison. At least we agreed on something.

Stan wandered off to emulate his favorite investigators. I opened the rest of the desk drawers. Nada.

"Oh, girls," trilled my buddy from the master bedroom.

After accidentally viewing Garrett's zebra-print thong, I didn't need to learn anything further about his personal habits, but his office wasn't providing anything useful. We returned to the master bath.

"Voila," Stan said, pointing to the opened wicker hamper with the panache of Vanna White. The hamper was full of teeny animal-print bikinis, T-shirts and dirty socks. No vowels or consonants that I could see.

"Stick your hand in all the way to the bottom," he instructed.

It was a very big hamper full of dirty laundry. Double ick.

"Stan, you have five seconds to reveal the secret in the bottom."

He smirked.

"Wait a minute. That's the secret, right? A false bottom?"

"That's my girl detective."

I knocked the hamper over. Not subtle but effective. Dirty disgusting smelly underwear, tube socks, T-shirts and...

Tax returns?

TWENTY-THREE

I GRABBED THE STAPLED RETURNS off the floor. "Interesting choice of filing cabinet."

"He must have been afraid someone would go through his files in the office and the house. Who would think to look in his dirty laundry?" Stan's smile was as wide as the double sink vanity.

Underwriters reviewed tax returns all day long so it only took me a couple of minutes to riffle through the pages. Nothing jumped out other than the fact that all six returns showed excellent income, in the hundreds of thousands. Maybe Garrett kept them in a special place because they were his best clients. He was definitely a weirdo. Just because the returns were filed in his dirty laundry didn't mean there was anything dirty about them.

We debated what to do with the papers. Since I was a prime suspect, I couldn't keep them. Mother didn't want anything to do with them, so I turned them over to Stan Spade's safekeeping until I figured out a way to tell Tom what we'd uncovered. We locked up the house and Stan and I hurried back to the office, hoping Earl wouldn't notice we'd been gone for over an hour.

I plowed through my loan files to make up for the time I'd spent out of the office then left a little after five to pick up my son. Soccer practice went into overtime. Although I'd planned on cooking a homemade meal for a change, the unhappy duet of Ben's and my growling stomachs left me no choice. I was forced to buy a home-cooked Chinese dinner from Lotus Garden, the closest takeout to our house.

The phone rang as I cleared the dishes—okay the cartons—from the table. Jenna grabbed it. She spoke briefly then handed it to me.

"Who is it?" I mouthed. She shrugged and walked out of the kitchen.

"Hello," I said, my voice husky, expecting to hear Tom's voice.

"Hi, Laurel. It's Peter."

"Oh, hi."

"We're still on for this weekend, I hope. I thought we'd try a new restaurant in Placerville called the Sequoia. It's received some excellent reviews."

"Sounds good."

We agreed he would pick me up at seven on Friday. We chatted for a few minutes until I begged off saying I had to help Ben with his homework. After my car crash, I was having reservations about going out with Peter. What if something happened to my mother's colleague while he was out with me?

Maybe I should start doling out pepper spray to my dates. Just in case.

The phone trilled again as I mulled over my situation. Probably Mother trying to make sure I hadn't screwed up her matchmaking efforts.

"Yes, Mother, Peter and I are still going out Friday night." I grabbed a sponge and started cleaning the kitchen counters.

"Well, that's disappointing news," said a deep familiar voice. Startled, I knocked over Ben's unfinished glass of milk. White liquid spurted all over my lactose intolerant silk blouse.

"You are so lame," I muttered as I dabbed at the spots with a wet towel.

"Excuse me?"

I apologized for my lame remark. I hoped Tom wouldn't remember my earlier comment.

"So, about this dinner date Friday night," he said. I swear the man has a memory like an elephant. Of course that could be the reason he made detective.

"Just dinner at the Sequoia with a friend of my mother's. You know how that goes."

"Sure. My parents have fixed me up a few times. They feel I've been a grieving widower long enough. They think Kristy needs a mother."

"A little feminine influence couldn't hurt," I agreed, envisioning the muddy tomboy as she attacked the boys on the soccer field.

"It's hard to be both a mother and father at the same time. I guess you can relate to that firsthand."

"Definitely." There was a lull in the conversation. Should I tell him about our discovery today or wait to see why he was calling?

"Uh, Laurel, I've been thinking that I was sort of off base last night, you know, at the memorial service. I realize you and your friends are only trying to clear your name and since you don't know what you're doing, you can't really interfere with our investigation."

Humph. If this was Tom's definition of an apology, it wasn't working.

"Great. I've managed to put my size twelve in it again."

I dropped into the nearest chair. This could be a lengthy phone call. "Would you like to start over?"

"First I want to apologize for my behavior the other night. It was absolutely inexcusable." He paused. "By the way, do you really think it's safe to go to dinner on Friday?"

"Safe for me or my date? My mother would kill me if I canceled."

"Okay, but try to stay out of trouble."

"Trouble? Me?" I laughed. "I don't suppose there's anything new with my case."

"One dead end after another. No pun intended. Add to that a fatal motorcycle accident off Salmon Falls Road late last night. You didn't crash into any bikes on your way home, did you?"

"No, but something crashed into me," I mumbled.

"What?" His shout was so loud I thought my receiver would explode.

"I was rear-ended last night. I just missed colliding with a tree."

"Are you okay? Did you report it?"

"No. I mean, I'm okay but I didn't report it. The car or truck that hit me just kept on going."

"Jesus H.," he swore. "Laurel, why didn't you call me? Where did it happen?"

"On Bass Lake Road. I was on my way home after driving by Garrett Lindstrom's house."

Uh-oh. TMI. Too much information.

"You just happened to drive by Lindstrom's house last night?" His tone of voice had ventured back into frostbite territory.

"Um, kind of. I was checking to see if the house was listed for sale."

"And?"

"It is. So Stan, my mother and I sort of looked at it today."

His voice softened, something I'd noted didn't usually bode well for me.

"So now your fingerprints are all over the house, correct?"

Fingerprints. That was dumb. Next time I'd bring latex gloves with me.

"Um, well, sure, but my mother and Stan's prints are there, too."

"Your mother and Stan are not murder suspects."

Right. "We found some clues." He'd be happy about that.

"Clues we missed." His sigh was so forceful I felt it through my receiver. "Sure."

"Did your guys find the tax returns in the laundry hamper?"

"What?"

I spent the next five minutes explaining Stan's unusual but effective foray into Garrett's dirty laundry.

"I'll get someone over to Garrett's house right away," he said.

"Um, there's a strong possibility they aren't there anymore."

I held the phone away from my ear while he ranted. When the decibels diminished to a moderate level, I jumped back in.

"We were afraid the killer might come back to the house and discover them. There has to be a reason why Garrett hid the returns in the hamper. Anyway, I assumed you wouldn't want me to hang on to them since I'm your number-one suspect, so Stan took them home. He's going to bring them to the office tomorrow."

"Fine, just fine," he replied.

Funny, he didn't sound fine.

"Would you like to know what we found out when we followed Dr. Radovich?" Maybe that would put him in a better mood.

"You followed Dr. Radovich? When?"

"Oh, we sort of ended up behind his car after Jeremy's memorial service," I muttered.

The sound of garbled conversation in the background came over the phone.

"I need to go. I'll come to the bank tomorrow to pick up those tax papers. But listen to me. No more following suspects, no more attending memorial services, no more visiting dead guy's houses. My job is difficult enough without worrying about you all the time."

"But—"

"Goodbye." The phone slammed in my ear.

Alrighty then.

TWENTY-FOUR

I HAD BARELY SETTLED INTO MY office routine Wednesday morning when the phone rang.

"Laurel, it's Liz. Guess what I discovered?"

"What?"

"Something dodgy is going on at Slater and Radovich's medical practice."

I closed my loan file. Detecting definitely trumped underwriting. Even though it meant putting aside the credit file of a well-known Hollywood personality buying a mega mansion in Lake Tahoe. Yes, a little glamour occasionally wanders into the life of a mortgage underwriter.

"What did you find out?" I asked.

"I stopped at their office yesterday to drop off some brochures for Tara. That kid may dress like a bimbo, but she's a brainy bimbo. After we chatted at the service, she decided to do a little investigating herself. Neither she nor Carol have anything to do with the books, so she had to wade through a ton of clutter in Radovich's office before she found something."

Liz paused for effect. Why did my detectives have to be so dramatic?

"Tara eventually found the checkbook for the practice in his miscellaneous file. She has no idea how much money they normally keep in the account but Dr. Radovich has been writing checks to himself every week for several months. For thousands of dollars."

"Wow. That ties in to the losses Stan noticed at the

casino Monday night. I wonder if Jeremy realized what Radovich was doing."

"Should we follow him again?"

"No, I think we're supposed to leave that to the sheriff's department. When I spoke with Tom last night he was adamant that we stay away from the doctor."

"Any new developments I should know about?" She giggled. "Either from a criminal or a sexual perspective?"

"Very funny. Most of our conversation consisted of him yelling. Although he did say he was worried about me."

"Worried about you getting hurt? Or worried he might have to arrest you?"

"Thanks, Liz. You really know how to boost a girl's spirits. Oh, dear. Stan Spade just appeared with our latest evidence. Call you later."

I hung up to greet my assistant. Clad in a belted beige trench coat and plaid fedora, Stan looked more like a pervert than a detective.

"Nice duds," I remarked.

He tipped his hat to me before he plunked it down on my desk. The tax returns were clasped to his chest. "I swear I couldn't sleep a wink last night worrying someone might break in and steal these. I made an extra copy just to be on the safe side." He thrust the originals and the copies into my waiting arms.

"Did you look at them?" I asked.

"Nah. I figured my job was to discover the evidence. Your job is to evaluate it." The sound of approaching footsteps got our attention. Stan grabbed his hat and slunk away while I quickly stashed the purloined papers in a drawer.

Carl King, manager of the loan-servicing department, paused in front of my desk. He was dressed in his standard navy blue suit, crisp white shirt and red-and-navy-striped tie. He handed two fat manila files to me. "Laurel, I'd like you to review these delinquent loans. They're ready to go into foreclosure."

I grabbed the files and blinked at him in surprise. Despite other banks' issues, conservative Hangtown Bank hadn't foreclosed on a property in over twenty-five years.

"Did I approve them?"

"No. Mary Lou underwrote both of them and Earl countersigned since both loans are over a million. That's why I want you to examine them. Just to make sure..." He hesitated, obviously not wanting to cast aspersions on my coworkers. "Let's just say I'd like another set of eyes to check over the paperwork."

"Sure. I'll get right on it."

Carl smiled in appreciation. "Then I'll leave them in your capable hands."

I appreciated Carl's confidence and opened up the first file. The Carters, a wealthy couple, had purchased a two-million-dollar house. The six-thousand-square-foot Tuscan-style home was situated on a two-acre lot with magnificent views of Folsom Lake. Based on their assets, income and credit scores, the underwriter had approved a loan for $1.4 million, 70 percent of the sale price. According to the notes from the loan-servicing clerk, the borrowers had not returned any phone calls.

I flipped through the file. Just because our bank hadn't previously encountered any fraud didn't mean it was impossible. Technology had provided even more creative tools for those with a criminal bent. It didn't take that much brainpower to produce false documentation.

The monthly bank statements appeared authentic. Our funding clerk had verbally verified with their banks that their assets existed. The Carters' tax return, which showed sufficient dividends, interest and pension income to make the house payment looked legit. I compared the borrowers' signatures on the tax return to the loan documents. Everything looked okay.

Wait a minute. Whose signature was in the spot reserved for the tax preparer?

Garrett Lindstrom, CPA.

Interesting. But not particularly relevant. Garrett had owned his CPA practice for almost ten years. He probably did taxes for tons of our bank customers. Was the Carters' return included in the group we had taken from Garrett's house last night?

I reached into my drawer and removed the stashed returns. Herman and Glenda Carter. Hmm. Would I find the other delinquent borrowers' return in there, as well?

Bingo. Darren and Margie Andrews. Their return was also in the pile. I flipped open their loan file with increased interest. Another well-to-do retired couple buying a $2.2 million dollar home, this time with a $1.5 million loan.

Two delinquent borrowers who used the same CPA.

A clue? Or a coincidence?

My deductive processes needed a caffeine infusion. I headed toward the break room, stopping at Stan's cube on the way. I was relieved to see he'd hung up his trench coat and fedora.

"Any luck with the returns?" he asked.

"I'm not sure, come grab a cup of coffee with me." The smell of scorched popcorn filtered into the hallway. "Hey, who burned the…" My voice faltered when I saw Earl removing a blackened bag of popcorn from the microwave. He turned around with a sheepish look.

"Guess I stunk up the office, huh? I can never get the hang of this microwave popcorn. I thought I would have time to take a phone call but…" His voice trailed off as he ruefully looked at the charred mess in his hand.

My brain did a quick calculation. Four, maybe five minutes to microwave one of the large bags of popcorn I store in the cupboard. That would occupy Earl while I checked out his office. As the manager of the mortgage division with full signing authority, Earl could have been involved in some type of scam. It was a lot easier to commit fraud when you have an inside source.

"You know, that popcorn is really unreliable so I use this brand." I bent down and grabbed some of the stash I'd hidden in the back of the cupboard. When I straightened up I noticed Earl's eyes glued to the back of my thighs. He had a hungry look on his face but I couldn't tell if it was directed at the popcorn or me.

I handed the canary-yellow bag to my boss. "Make sure you don't leave the break room while it's cooking or you'll burn it. Stan, while he waits, tell Earl about that problem file we were working on."

Stan started to protest but I stared him down. If anyone could drag out five minutes with useless chatter, Stan could. I strode down the hallway to Earl's office, checking out the other cubicles to make sure a gallery full of viewers wasn't watching. Most of the staff appeared to be out to lunch. Or rather, out at lunch. Only a few of them were really out to lunch.

I slipped into Earl's office and plunked down in his chair, keeping an eye out for any employees passing by the door. I peeked through the mess on the desk. A few candy wrappers. A bowl of dried-up instant oatmeal and a half-eaten granola bar. A stack of loan files with familiar borrower names waiting for his review. As an underwriter I had the authority to approve or reject a loan, but all rejected loans were given a second review by management, which in this office was Earl.

I opened the top drawer. Messy, messy boy. Earl's desk

made my cubicle look like Martha Stewart's by comparison. Napkins dotted with multicolored stains of dubious origin were interspersed with the usual office supplies. A trillion paper clips in every shade of the rainbow were scattered everywhere. I poked through the debris with a pencil—no telling what viral germs lurked in his desk.

My attention shifted to Earl's credenza. I squatted with my knees locked together, slid open the doors and shuffled through the folders. I glanced through a couple of files before I struck gold—Slater, Jeremy, typed on the label.

Male voices reverberated from outside the office. I thrust the files back in the credenza and ducked down. I peeked over the desk. Stan was attempting to block Earl from entering the office. I lowered my head just as a muffled crash sounded, followed by a loud expletive.

I couldn't resist looking. Stan must have run out of stalling tactics and decided to knock over the bowl of popcorn. White kernels mixed with shards of blue ceramic covered the floor. Both guys had disappeared.

I grabbed the Slater file, stood up and stretched, both knees creaking in harmony. I definitely needed to get to the gym. A tiny scrap of paper the size of a fortune from a cookie flipped out of the folder. I shoved it in my jacket pocket and streaked through the door, seconds before the guys returned, a broom and dustpan in Stan's hands.

"Hey, guys, do you want me to clean that up for you?" Normally I balk at performing the menial tasks assigned to women for the past couple of hundred years, but in this case, it would provide an excellent distraction.

"Here." Stan handed the broom to me. I grabbed it, tucking the pilfered file under my arm.

"Thanks, Laurel." Earl smiled slyly. "Like I said, I don't know what I would do without you. You don't mind if I have some more of that popcorn, do you?" Without waiting for an affirmative from me, he ambled in the direction of the break room.

"What were you doing in there?" Stan said.

"I wanted to go through Earl's files and I figured this might be my only opportunity. Guess what? I found one with Slater written on the label. Unfortunately, you guys showed up and I didn't get to finish going through the stuff in his credenza."

Out of frustration, I walloped one of Stan's Ferragamo loafers with the broom then shoved it into his more than capable hands. I headed back to my cubicle to review my purloined file.

Mary Lou popped her head over our adjoining wall. Today she was attired in a lime-green suede jacket, matching turtleneck and black leather miniskirt. It didn't take much analysis to deduce that another meet and greet with a member of the opposite sex must be on her schedule.

"Did you go out to lunch?" she asked.

"Nope. Just the break room. Why?"

"Some big guy stopped by your cubicle. I told him you were probably at lunch." She giggled nervously. "He was kind of scary-looking."

So was she in her glow-in-the-dark outfit, but who was I to hand out fashion tips?

Hmm. Was he one of those goons who visited Dr. Radovich's office? Or worse. Detective Bradford coming to arrest me. That man could frighten the Sopranos into becoming model citizens.

Her eyes veered in the direction of the reception area. "He's back. Good luck." She ducked back down.

I took a sip of cold coffee and turned to meet the big scary-looking guy.

TWENTY-FIVE

WITH AN EXPRESSION SO STERN HE could scare the panties off a suspect, an angry Tom towered over my desk. "Hand them over."

I didn't waste time pretending I didn't know what he was talking about. I grabbed the original returns and handed them to him.

"Is this all of them? Did you make any copies?"

Did I personally make any copies? I chose to go with a literal translation and shook my head.

He thumped the pages against his hand. "Anything new in your investigation?"

Hey, that was my line. Did I detect a hint of sarcasm?

"Nope. No investigating. Just underwriting." The fact that two of the six sets of tax returns found in Garrett's laundry hamper belonged to two of the bank's delinquent borrowers was curious, but at this point it was a foreclosure problem for the bank, not a homicide issue.

"Good. I'll call you at home tonight. I expect you to be there."

He strode down the hallway, leaving me alone with his ultimatum. This detective was starting to tick me off. It was a good thing we hadn't become involved. He was bossier than my mother.

Time to review the Jeremy Slater file I'd grabbed from Earl's credenza before he noticed its absence. The property was located on Ski Run Boulevard in South Lake Tahoe. Since the sales contract I'd discovered on Radovich's desk was for a condo on Ski Run this must be the same purchase. His application indicated he owned only one piece of property, his residence in El Dorado Hills, valued at $700,000 with a mortgage of $300,000. He had several substantial bank accounts and made several hundred thousand a year from his medical practice.

I glanced at his credit report. Two credit cards with balances under a thousand dollars on each. He had a mortgage with our bank with a balance just under $300,000 and another mortgage with Worldwide Bank for $1.2 million.

Huh? Where did that come from?

I went through his file again. His application clearly stated he owned only one piece of property, his home. So why did the credit report show an additional loan in the amount of $1.2 million? That's not a dollar amount someone forgets to mention.

According to the credit report, the jumbo mortgage was originated in June, only five months earlier so there wouldn't be a record of it on his tax return. And it was ninety days delinquent. Jeremy was the last person I would expect to be behind on his mortgage payments. Just out of curiosity, I looked to see if he did his own taxes.

Son of a CPA. Garrett Lindstrom had prepared the return.

We had a dead accountant who stored tax returns in his dirty laundry and a dead doctor with a delinquent loan. If I were Columbo I'd be in detecting heaven.

Me. I was just confused. Why was this file in Earl's credenza?

Time to use my detecting skills for my job. I went on the internet and within seconds I was searching an El Dorado County Assessor's website. All I had to do was type in Jeremy's last name, and it listed all of the properties owned by a Jeremy Slater in the county. According to the tax rolls, he owned two properties, both in El Dorado Hills.

The first property was the residence he listed on his loan application. The other property had an assessed value of $1.8 million sold to Jeremy Slater on June 22. That meant that the $1.2-million-dollar loan must be on this property.

Big house. Big loan. Big problem if he couldn't make the payments. Was he delinquent because Dr. Radovich had cleaned out the funds in their business account?

With the parcel number, I was able to retrieve the street address from another website, 124 Via del Lago. Builders in El Dorado Hills are big on using Italian names for their subdivisions. I had to admit Via del Lago sounded way better than Street by the Lake.

Much as I hated to put a halt to my investigation, it would have to wait until tomorrow. Time for this detective to turn back into a mom. Since the school district had scheduled teacher meetings for the Friday before the Veterans Day weekend, Hank informed me he would take the kids to Tahoe for all four days. The weather in November could be iffy, meaning two feet of snow was as likely as sixty-degree temps.

The odds of Hank planning ahead for inclement weather were as likely as the Easter Bunny showing up on Thanksgiving. That meant I needed to make sure Ben had snow gear that fit.

Supposedly they were staying at some big fancy resort. Knowing Hank's ability to wheel and deal, he probably lined up a free stay that would involve sitting through a ninety-minute timeshare presentation. Jenna was excited about using her empirical skills to calculate the most likely candidates to win horse races. With her assistance Hank could clean up at the casino Sports Book. Why couldn't I have a normal daughter who wanted to shop and hang out at the spa?

I picked up Ben from soccer practice then drove down to Budget Mart, the area big-box store. Two hours and one hundred dollars later, Ben had the latest in waterproof snow gear in a mottled green-and-brown camouflage pattern. The good news was that it was affordable. Hopefully by the time he grew out of it, his taste in clothing would have improved.

The phone rang seconds after we walked into the house. My arms were loaded with parcels so Ben raced into the kitchen to answer it. I plopped the packages on a chair and waited for him to hand the receiver to me.

Strange. He wandered into the living room chatting away. Must be his father on the line. A few minutes later he ambled into the kitchen, his rounded cheeks as rosy as if he had been playing in the snow.

He handed the phone to me. "It's for you."

"What do you want?" I asked Hank, annoyed that I was a hundred dollars poorer due to his winter expedition.

"I want to talk to the most beautiful murder suspect in the county," said my favorite baritone.

I flushed. "Oh, I thought Ben was talking to his dad. How did you get on the line?"

"Kristy called Ben so I thought I'd touch base with you after they were finished."

So that was the reason for my son's inflamed cheeks. I hoped he was more successful with his budding romance than I'd been so far.

"I'm trying to decide if being called the most beautiful murder suspect in the county is a compliment. Although I suppose it's better than being known as the hottie in the Hangtown hoosegow." My attempt at frontier humor ended in a whimper.

"You know I've tried to be brave about this situation but you guys don't seem to be getting anywhere," I blubbered. "Anytime now Bradford is going to show up on my doorstep, arrest warrant in hand. I don't want to be Miranda-ized."

Tom waited until my outburst was over and my sniffling had subsided.

"So are you checking to make sure I'm staying out of trouble?"

"I'm not sure that's possible. Is it?"

I wasn't in the mood for sarcasm. "Did you make any progress with those tax returns?"

"We reached a couple of his clients but all we've learned so far is that Garrett had been their CPA for years. None of them had any complaints about his tax work. Why he chose to store those particular returns in a clothes hamper is beyond me. Do you have any ideas?"

"*Moi?* My job is to provide the evidence, not evaluate it."

He grunted. "Well, just in case you happen to run across an extra copy of those returns and after looking through them, happen to discover something we've missed, you will report back to me, right?"

Did I hear him correctly? Did Tom officially promote me to unofficial underwriting detective?

"Of course. Don't I always?"

"Yeah," he replied, not bothering to hide the sarcasm in his voice. "Listen, I'm about to share some critical information with you. Remember that motorcycle accident I mentioned last night? The one off of Salmon Falls Road?"

"Yes. What about it?"

"The victim was a guy named Mike Clark. Does the name ring any bells?"

"No. Should it?"

"Not necessarily." He sounded relieved for some reason. "He's a part-time real-estate appraiser. That's why I thought you might know him."

"Are you kidding? Every Tom, Dick and Mike became licensed appraisers in that last refinance boom. They made a fortune doing eight to ten appraisals a day. Half the time they didn't even bother getting out of their cars."

"Interesting, but not relevant," he replied.

"So what exactly is relevant?" I asked.

"Give me a minute. Originally we thought the victim took the curve too fast and then crashed down into this steep canyon. The rear of his bike is bashed, which could have occurred when it rolled down the hill. His body probably wouldn't have been discovered for days if some teenagers hadn't been wandering around looking for a private spot to do something they shouldn't be doing."

I chuckled. "You'll have to give them a medal."

"Yeah. Anyway when the guys examined the body, they found an unusual wound on the back of his head that seemed inconsistent with the fact he was wearing a helmet. We think someone rammed his bike then went back and finished the job."

"What does that have to do with me?"

"The crime scene guys think there may be a similarity between Lindstrom's head injury and this one."

"Tom. You can't possibly think I had anything to do with this incident. Just because the guy is an appraiser."

His sigh reverberated over the phone line. "Let's just say I'm not the detective you need to convince. But as far as I'm concerned you're still the most beautiful murder suspect in the county."

TWENTY-SIX

BEING TOLD I WAS THE MOST beautiful murder suspect in El Dorado County may have boosted my self-esteem, but it certainly did nothing for my peace of mind. Tom's remark just reinforced my belief that I would have to solve these murders before they hauled me off to jail.

Four new loans requiring a rush underwriting decision were perched on the corner of my desk when I arrived at work the next morning, so I wasn't able to look at the delinquent loans until late afternoon. I finally had time to open both files and compare them, line item by line item.

The Carters were moving from a half-million-dollar house to the two-million-dollar residence on Vista del Monte. The Andrews lived in Placerville and planned on moving down the hill to their multimillion-dollar purchase.

After reviewing both files I couldn't fault Mary Lou for approving the loans. The borrowers were strong from both an income and asset standpoint and everything looked in order. The loans funded a month apart. So far the only commonality was that Garrett had prepared both tax returns.

I flipped to the appraisals. Both of the Mediterranean-style houses were gorgeous. For two million plus they should be. I drooled over the exterior and interior photos, which revealed one mouthwatering custom feature after another. Granite counters, slate floors, Brazilian cherry built-in cabinets throughout the house, shower stalls as big as my bedroom.

I would kill to…

I would love to have a house like that.

After flipping back to page two of the appraisal I finally had an Aha! moment.

It's standard procedure for an appraiser to use at least three recent sales to determine the value of a property. Each of these appraisals used identical comparable sales. It could be a coincidence. Or merely the fact that there were limited sales in the two-million-plus range the appraiser could use. The distance between the properties was less than a quarter of a mile. They were probably all from the same subdivision.

My eyes dropped down to the signature line.

Get out of town.

The appraiser was Mike Clark. I pulled open the other loan file and flipped to the back page. Mike Clark again.

The man who prepared the tax returns for the Andrews and Carter loans had been murdered.

The man who appraised both properties was dead. Possibly murdered.

The woman who underwrote both loan files was alive and…

I screamed, dropping one of the files on the floor, as Mary Lou popped her overpermed blond head over our adjoining wall. She shot me a curious look. "Laurel, are you okay?"

"Yeah, fine, just immersed in some loans." I bent over and rescued the file before glancing up at my cubicle mate. Could the beautiful blue-eyed blonde be a killer?

We must have been on the same wavelength. "Have you heard anything new about those murders?" she asked.

I dropped the folder again but at least this time it landed on my desk. "No, nothing recent." Was this the time to mention that two of the loans she underwrote were about to go into foreclosure?

"So do you have any more Love Club dates this week-end? I'm still waiting to see how that works out for you," she said.

At the rate the bodies were piling up, it would be a very long wait.

"No dates in the near future. Say, have you ever met Mike Clark? One of the bank's approved appraisers."

Her face clouded up and her smile turned into a snarl. "Stay away from him, Laurel. He's bad news." She grabbed her purse and sailed out of her cube.

What did she mean by that remark? I looked at my watch. Darn. Clues galore but no time to pursue them. The delinquent loans would have to wait until tomorrow. I needed to sneak out a few minutes early so I could say goodbye to the kids before they disappeared for four days.

When I arrived home, Hank's black Ford truck was parked in the driveway. Two battered navy suitcases, two backpacks, and a shopping bag full of boys' toys were scattered on the wood planked entry. The squeak of a faulty piece of plywood resonated as one, two, then three bodies clambered down the stairs.

"Mom," hollered both kids, making me feel warm and fuzzy, as welcome as Norm when he entered the bar in *Cheers*.

"Hi, honey," greeted Hank. The fuzzy feeling vanished when I realized my ex had been wandering through my home. For some reason, maybe because he designed and built the house himself, Hank still felt he had some owner-ship in it. As far as I was concerned, the only ownership he possessed was providing the child support for me to make the mortgage payments.

I scowled at him. "What were you doing upstairs?"

"It's okay, Mom." Jenna laid her palm on my arm in an

attempt to placate me. "The upstairs sink was dripping and I asked Dad to fix it."

Hank smiled. "If it needs fixing then I'm your man."

Okay. I could be a grown-up, too. "Thanks. I appreciate it. Are you guys ready to go?"

Ben threw his arms around my waist. "Dad says we can go sledding if it gets cold enough."

I raised my eyebrows at their father.

"Yep. If it drops below freezing, they're going to make snow at Sugar Bowl."

Brr. Snow in November wasn't my cup of hot chocolate, but I knew they'd have fun whatever they did. I hugged the kids until they complained I was squeezing them to death. Hank was halfway out the door when I had a thought.

"Hank, you probably know a lot of appraisers, don't you?"

"Yeah, I've bumped into quite a few of them when they were making their final inspections on the houses I built. Why?"

"Do you know a guy named Mike Clark?"

That Mike Clark sure didn't have much of a fan base. Hank's face turned darker than snow clouds over the Sierra. He clenched and unclenched his jaw then shook his head. "Nope."

I was stunned by his reaction, and so stupefied by his obvious lie that I stood there while he kissed my cheek and sauntered out to the truck.

I mulled over Hank's surprising response as I waved goodbye to the kids. He backed the truck down the driveway then turned right, passing a car approaching from the opposite direction. A mud-speckled white sedan with big brown letters on its side and a bar of red, white and blue on its roof. The phone rang and I slammed the front door shut, racing into the kitchen before the caller could hang up.

"Laurel, it's Tom."

"Hi. Hey, do you…" My words were interrupted by the sound of the doorbell ringing. "Someone's at the door. Can you wait a minute?"

"Yeah, about that. I'll call you later." He hung up on me.

He hung up on me?

I was not in the mood to greet whatever maniac was ringing the bell so incessantly. I peered through the narrow window next to the front door. What was Tall, Bald and Homely doing here this time of night, a nervous deputy shifting restlessly by his side? I flung open the door to be greeted by an official-looking document covered with the tiniest font I'd ever attempted to read.

"Ms. McKay, I have a warrant to search your house." Not waiting for a reply, Detective Bradford strode through the entry, followed by the deputy who bore a strong resemblance to a sad-eyed spaniel trotting after a St. Bernard.

Make that a rottweiler. A St. Bernard would at least have brought me a keg of brandy.

TWENTY-SEVEN

"You can't do this," I stuttered.

Bradford blasted me with his razorlike gaze. The burly detective might be old, crotchety and biased against women, but I had a feeling his mental agility hadn't diminished with the years.

"We most certainly can," he sneered. "It will be less painful for you if you cooperate with us."

Who, me? Just call me Miss Cooperation. "Fine. May I ask what you're looking for?"

"Let's start with where you keep your tools."

They must be looking for the murder weapon. It certainly wasn't in my house so I didn't have anything to worry about. Except I had no idea where my tools were. I vaguely remembered Jenna using the hammer to hang a picture in her room. And years ago my screwdriver had grown legs, occasionally appearing in the most unlikely places.

Tall and Bald noticed my hesitation. He smiled, but it was the smile of a cat, after he'd feasted on a canary for dinner. "If you can't direct us to your tool drawer or tool chest, we'll have to examine every inch of your house." He looked around the cluttered room. "Inch by inch."

"Hey," I protested. "I'm not reluctant to help but I don't know where all my tools are. It's not like I'm a contractor. Or a guy. Just do whatever you need to do, but please make as little of a mess as possible."

Detective Bradford and Deputy Spaniel—I still didn't know his name—conferred for a minute then split up. The younger deputy headed toward the kitchen and Bradford went into the garage. Good luck finding anything in there. In fact, the garage might look even better after he scavenged through it than it did right now.

I settled into the sofa and switched on the television to the early-evening news. The camera zeroed in on a reporter from Channel Two reporting live from the side of some road. He pointed down a rocky treed hillside to a spot far below. I hit the volume button on the remote.

"I'm standing at the site on Salmon Falls Road where a deadly accident occurred three nights ago," announced the reporter. "Or was it murder?"

Uh-oh.

"The sheriff has been unavailable for comment. It's difficult to believe that three murders have occurred in this small county in less than a month. Our sources claim there are distinct similarities in each incident. Can these lovely Sierra foothills be harboring a serial killer?"

The reporter shivered. I shivered along with him.

"This is Chuck Basso, reporting live from…"

Bang. The door into the kitchen slammed shut and I missed the last thing the reporter said. I jumped up from the sofa as Bradford entered the room. He grunted but didn't stop. The sound of his heavy feet clumping up the stairs alerted me to his current mission. I saw no reason to stay behind so I followed him. He crossed the threshold into Ben's room then hesitated. Since I was directly behind him, I plowed right into his back. Ouch. He was solid.

Ben's room already looked like it had been ransacked but that was due to my son's packing technique, which consisted of emptying every drawer on his bed. It was one way of ensuring he didn't forget anything. Bradford shrugged his shoulders and moved on to the next room. My bedroom.

He walked over to my armoire then yanked on the handles of the top drawer.

I screamed and slammed the drawer shut, managing to nick the raised surface of the detective's hairy knuckles. His eyebrows drew together in one furry unattractive line. "So this is where you hide your tools."

No. This is where I hide my white cotton granny panties. I did not want that getting back to Tom Hunter. That was a mental image he might never be able to erase.

We were in the middle of a glaring duel when the squeak of footsteps on the stairs got my attention. The young deputy stepped into the bedroom. He shifted from one foot to the next.

"Get on with it, Mengelkoch," barked Bradford.

He hesitated then asked me, "Would you mind if I use your bathroom?" He blushed as he looked at his superior officer.

"Of course not." I smiled sweetly at Deputy Mengelkoch as I reverted back to Miss Cooperation. "The kids' bathroom is right across the hall."

He ducked his head at me then disappeared. We returned to exchanging baleful glances. I was wondering when our stalemate would end when Bradford growled again.

"What now, Matt?" he said, looking over my shoulder.

I turned around to see the deputy beckoning to Bradford. The senior officer rolled his eyes then followed the deputy. I was tempted to use the opportunity to relocate my undesirable underwear but I was also curious what the deputy had discovered. I followed the curmudgeonly detective across the hall and into the bathroom.

Matching schisms appeared on both sides of the detective's craggy face as he broke into a broad grin. Was he admiring the rainbow-colored tropical fish decor, which dated back to Jenna's toddler days?

Or was he looking at…

What was that strange thing sitting on the vanity? It was almost a foot long. Funny-shaped metal on the top with a chipped red wood handle.

"Ms. McKay, thank you for making our job so easy," he said. "I never expected the murder weapon to be out in full view."

"Look, I don't know what that, that—" I waved my hand at the offending tool "—that doohickey is."

Bradford snickered. "You know, I was beginning to think you were one of the smartest criminals I've ever encountered. But it looks like Detective Hunter was finally successful in getting you to let your guard down. Imagine having the nerve to use the same pipe wrench not only as a murder weapon, but to fix a leaky pipe." He pointed to the wet spot under the sink.

The leak my ex-husband had fixed minutes before.

TWENTY-EIGHT

TWO HOURS LATER I WAS CURLED in a fetal position on the sofa, dressed in my red Betty Boop flannel pajamas and fleece robe. Multicolored candy wrappers littered the coffee table as I attempted to distract myself by watching a mindless reality show.

The detective and his deputy had packaged the evidence, Hank's pipe wrench, which they were rushing to the crime lab to determine if the red paint on the handle matched the paint flecks discovered in the victims' wounds.

I half expected Bradford to cuff me and take me down to headquarters. Fortunately my fingerprints weren't on the tool or I would have received an official invitation to a sleepover at the jail. With my luck I'd be bunking with Burly Bertha, one of the Hangtown jailhouse locals.

Bradford repeated his previous warning not to leave town then he and Mengelkoch pulled out of my driveway, tires squealing. I called Tom on his cell and we conversed briefly.

I accused him of pretending to fall for me in order to get me to confess to a crime I didn't commit. I waited for his response but he didn't deny anything.

So I hung up on him.

As far as the pipe wrench, what could I say? It was Hank's. But did that make him the murderer? I clutched the remote to my chest, massive hiccupping sobs racking my body as I contemplated the duplicity of the men in my life. A bundle of fur jumped on my lap, and a pair of sympathetic green eyes stared into mine as a tiny sandpaper tongue licked salty tears from my cheeks.

Pumpkin and I cuddled together watching TV until the late news came on. The two anchors greeted their audience and immediately launched into the lead story: the unsolved murders of El Dorado County.

I bolted up, disturbing the sleeping kitten. Pumpkin squawked as she tumbled off the sofa, landing on all fours. I grabbed my furry friend and she settled next to me. Two pairs of eyes glued to the news.

Camera shots veered from the River Inn to the hilly shot they had shown on the earlier broadcast. Someone in the sheriff's department had leaked the surprising fact that the same weapon might have been responsible for the deaths of three prominent residents of El Dorado County—a CPA, a doctor and a real-estate appraiser.

The reporter interviewed several locals, all of whom demanded that additional resources be brought in from the FBI to solve these horrible crimes. The camera switched back to the reporter on his hillside perch. His expression was grave as he spoke into the mike. "Chuck Basso, signing off from El Dorado County."

With this kind of media publicity it could be mere hours before they hauled me in. What would I use for my defense? Tell them the father of my children owned the pipe wrench?

"Pumpkin, what should I do?" I moaned to the kitten. She stared at me with unblinking eyes then proceeded to clean her privates.

We all have different ways of dealing with stress.

I dealt with my own stress by watching *I Love Lucy* reruns into the wee hours of the morning. I woke at six, bleary eyed, bushy haired and with a crick in my neck, but bound and determined to prove my innocence. Without the kids to slow me down I arrived at the office a half hour early.

I vaguely recalled reading about a famous philosopher who declared there were only six degrees of separation between each person and everyone else on the planet. Or maybe it was Kevin Bacon.

Regardless, in our small foothills community, the number must be even less. Just how many degrees separated my field of suspects from the victims?

Dr. Radovich—he had massive gambling losses and was stealing money from his partner. Was Garrett his CPA? If so he might have killed both Jeremy and Garrett to cover up the theft.

Earl Fisher—Jeremy's loan file was in Earl's credenza. Mike Clark did appraisals for the bank. Earl knew Garrett, even though he wouldn't admit how. Was my boss getting paid under the table to approve fraudulent loans?

Mary Lou—she underwrote both delinquent loans. She didn't like Mike. Was she part of a financial scheme involving Mike, Garrett and Jeremy?

Hank—Jeremy was his doctor. He disliked Mike Clark. He hated the thought I was dating again. He owned a pipe wrench. Did he own *the* pipe wrench?

Detective Bradford—he suspected me of killing off my dates. I suspected him of trying to date my mother. That was a crime in itself.

Okay, Bradford wasn't a suspect but any of the other four could have committed the murders. Would my ex-husband intentionally plan the trip to Tahoe, leaving behind the weapon that would implicate me in the murders he committed?

Omigod. Were my children at risk? I dialed Jenna's cell. No answer. I started to freak out but then remembered that cell service in Tahoe was erratic. I hated to involve my mother but it was time for some maternal advice. I phoned the Centurion office.

"Centurion Realty, Peter Tyler speaking."

"Peter, it's Laurel. Is my mother in yet?"

"No, amazingly enough. Sometimes I think she lives here."

His comment made me laugh. "Yeah, there's a reason why she's the top producer."

"Well, I'm going to give her a run for the money this month. Anyway I'm glad you called. I'm looking forward to dinner tonight."

Oh, yeah. It was amazing how murder could distract a person from their social engagements. I doubted if I would be very entertaining as a dinner companion, but with Peter's knowledge of the local real-estate market, I might be able to get some of my questions answered for the bank.

Tom was definitely out of the picture now that his underhanded scheme to trap me had been revealed. I still couldn't believe how he'd lured me into believing he cared about me.

We confirmed that Peter would pick me up at the house at seven. Mary Lou approached my cubicle so I said goodbye and hung up. "Sorry I jumped all over you when you mentioned Mike Clark yesterday," she apologized.

I flapped my hand at her. "Don't worry about it. You know he's dead, right?"

She nodded as she slumped in the chair. "I read about it in the paper this morning." Her baby blues widened as she met my gaze. "You don't think I had anything to do with it, do you?"

I shrugged and attempted to look nonaccusatory. She contemplated the ceiling for a minute. "Okay, promise not to tell anyone what I'm about to tell you. Especially Earl."

I wasn't sure I should promise in case she revealed anything criminal, but I nodded.

"Mike and I lived together briefly five years ago. At the time I was working at another bank. One day I was underwriting a loan and the information on the appraisal didn't make sense. Mike was the appraiser so I asked him about it at dinner that night. It turned out the builder bribed him and he falsified some information stating that the house was worth more than it really was. He promised me it only happened the one time and he would never do anything like that again. When I told him I would still have to report it to my boss at the bank, he hit me. I chickened out and never told my boss." Tears welled in her eyes. "I moved out the next day."

Her face turned a sickly shade of green, which did not blend well with the tangerine angora sweater and skirt ensemble she was wearing. She rubbed her palm over her forehead. "I feel a migraine coming on. I think I better go home."

She grabbed her purse and raced down the hallway in her four-inch stilettos. I stared after her, mulling over her rapid departure, as well as her comments about the fraudulent appraisal Mike produced five years ago. Could there be an issue with the appraised values of the two delinquent files?

In most fraud situations the borrowers were the beneficiaries. In this case, if the loans went into foreclosure they would lose their custom homes. And their big down payments. It was odd they would purchase such beautiful houses and then not make any payments, unless both families had encountered some recent financial reverses.

I flipped opened the preliminary title reports to find out the name of the seller. The owner of record for both houses was TLC Partners.

According to the legal description, both lots were part of a subdivision called Bella Lago. The words evoked images of a beautiful lake setting. In El Dorado Hills, faux Tuscan architecture was prevalent, so the more expensive the subdivision, the more Italian the name.

I lifted Jeremy Slater's vacation home loan file from my three-tiered tray and placed it on my desk. The $1.2-million-dollar loan that appeared delinquent on his credit report was on a property located on Via del Lago, the same property used as a comparable sale for the Andrews and Carter files. I did a search on Google for the address. Just as the appraisal stated, the property was within a quarter mile of the Andrews and Carter houses.

Which proved nothing.

I tried Jenna on her cell. Nothing.

I called Liz. Voicemail.

I wandered down to Stan's cube. It was trench coat and fedora free. Where was my team when I needed them? I passed Earl's office. My boss was seated at his desk reading the funnies. He read the *Dilbert* comic strip daily, assuming it was a guide to good management skills. I heard him chuckling. If he was in a good mood, it might be an excellent time to ask about Jeremy's loan.

"Hi, Earl."

His face creased into a welcoming smile, which resembled a leer, but at least it appeared friendly. He waved me into the office.

I settled into a chair and leaned forward. "You remember Jeremy Slater, right?"

He nodded. "Of course, one of the bank's best clients who died on your watch."

I wished people would stop thinking it was my responsibility to keep my dates alive. I was never going out with a large depositor again.

"Yeah, about that. Jeremy mentioned he was concerned about a mortgage he was trying to get on a vacation home in Tahoe. Did you help him with a loan?"

He reached into a jar of miniature candies, unwrapped the gold paper and stuffed the candy into his mouth. No invitation for me to do the same, so I tapped my foot and counted to ten while he chewed.

"We started processing an application for him on a condo but when we ran his credit it showed a ninety-day delinquency on a mortgage with another bank. We denied his loan but he claimed the delinquent loan wasn't his. Since he is, or rather was, such a good client of the bank, I told him I would research it. Once he died there didn't seem to be much point in pursuing it."

Earl swiveled around and opened the credenza. He sifted through a stack of files, looking perplexed. It wasn't easy maintaining an innocent expression when I knew the missing Slater file was currently in my possession.

"I must have mislaid the file." He reached for another shiny gold-wrapped candy. "So how's that Love Club thing going for you?"

The last thing I wanted to do was discuss my social life with Earl. "I've given up on the Love Club."

He cocked his finger at me. "Wise decision."

I agreed. No more men from the agency. No more detectives from the sheriff's department. I was sticking with referrals from now on. Speaking of which, I needed to see if my mother had returned my call.

I returned to my desk, checked both my office phone and my cell. No messages from Liz, my mother or Jenna. I dialed Stan's cell. "Where are you?" I whined.

"I'm home sick," he sniffled, sounding equally whiny. "What do you want?"

"I need you. Are you on your deathbed or just lying in bed watching your soaps?" Stan was an *All My Children* addict, recording the program daily and catching up on the weekends.

He sneezed in response. "Don't you have anyone else to pester?"

Not really. Everyone had disappeared. Stan was it.

"I have some detecting for you." That would be the true measure of determining how sick Stan really was.

"Can it wait? I've hung up my trench coat this week."

Okay, he definitely was ill. "I suppose, but…"

He sighed, sniffled, wheezed then sneezed. "Tell me what you want me to do."

I proceeded to explain about the multimillion-dollar delinquent loans and the coincidence that they were all located in the same subdivision. Stan lived in El Dorado Hills so he could drive by the houses, see if the borrowers were home, and hopefully find out why they weren't making their payments. He reluctantly agreed to complete the task sometime over the weekend.

By Monday we might discover something that would help the bank deal with the delinquent loans. And maybe make them appreciate what a great employee I am. Just in case they were starting to doubt the wisdom of having a murder suspect in their employ.

I left the office promptly at five. Threatening rain clouds made the sky appear darker than usual for that time of day. It looked like the kids might get the snow they wanted.

The phone rang as I was zipping up my date night black skirt. "Hello, may I please speak with Laurel," said a familiar masculine voice, but one that I couldn't place at the moment.

"This is she."

I ran through my database of male callers. It wasn't that large of a database.

"Um, Laurel, it's Earl, you know Earl Fisher—from the office," he added, as if there could be more than one Earl Fisher.

"Hi, Earl, what's up?" Earl had never called me at home

before. Did he discover the missing Slater file in my desk drawer? I knew I should have put it back in his credenza.

He cleared his throat. "I was wondering if you'd like to go to dinner with me tonight."

Over my dead body was my first thought as I attempted to jab my pearl earring stud into place.

"I don't think that would be appropriate, Earl. Besides I already have a date tonight."

"Oh? You gave me the impression you were done with the Love Club. Wouldn't you be more comfortable going out with someone from the office? Someone safe?"

Safe? I wasn't sure Earl qualified for that category. But this was the perfect opportunity to grill him.

"Before I could even think of going out with you, I need to know more about your relationship with Garrett Lindstrom. Were you and he involved in a scheme to defraud the bank?"

"What?" he yelled. "Are you drunk?"

Not yet but the way my week had been going it sounded kind of tempting. I looked at the clock. Peter would be arriving shortly. Time to play hardball.

"Earl, my contacts at the sheriff's department informed me you're the number-one suspect in Garrett's death."

Okay, I was stretching the truth a little. But it might shake him up and get him talking.

I must have sounded more threatening than I intended. A crash followed by a scream assaulted my ear.

TWENTY-NINE

"Earl, are you all right? What happened?"

"I dropped my glass," Earl responded, his voice quivering. "What do you mean I'm a suspect in Garrett's death? Garrett's dead?"

"He died a few weeks ago. You didn't know that?"

"No. I haven't seen him in several years. He used to live a couple of blocks away from us. Garrett and my wife became romantically involved after they both joined the neighborhood watch committee. I guess they decided it was more fun to watch each other."

"I'm so sorry. I had no idea." Poor guy. I could certainly empathize with the torment of a wayward spouse.

"The four years since our divorce haven't been easy. I know you can't tell, but I don't date very often."

I didn't have the heart to tell Earl it was fairly obvious he didn't get out much.

"You didn't hear about Garrett's death on the news last night? Or read about it in the obituaries?"

"I don't watch the news. Too depressing. And who reads the obituaries?"

A few of my single girlfriends read them daily hoping to find eligible widowers to date, but that probably wasn't relevant to our current conversation.

"I had no idea he was dead." Earl paused and his voice reflected his terror. "Oh, jeez, you killed him, didn't you?"

"Me?"

"Yeah, I heard you telling the staff you whacked him

with a cell phone. You're a murderer. I'm calling the cops," he shouted.

"I didn't kill—"

The dial tone buzzing in my ear was accompanied by the pealing of the doorbell.

Great. Now Earl and I suspected each other of murder. That reminded me. I never got around to reading that slip of paper that fell out of Jeremy's file when I removed it from Earl's credenza. It must still be in my jacket pocket. Could a fortune from a cookie contain a clue?

The doorbell continued its relentless ringing. Too many suspects. Too little time. The scrap of paper would have to wait until I returned home. I ran down the stairs, opened the front door and was greeted by a smiling Peter dressed in a black turtleneck, charcoal blazer and slacks. He held out a spray of multicolored fall flowers. The last bouquet I'd received was from Hank on our first wedding anniversary. Seventeen years ago.

I was touched by Peter's thoughtfulness. Although knowing my interfering mother, she probably gave him a list of the top-ten ways to woo her daughter. Peter followed me into the kitchen. His six foot two inches came in handy retrieving my one and only crystal vase from the top shelf of my cabinet.

"How long have you lived here?" he asked while I attempted to arrange the yellow, orange and purple flowers. I vaguely remembered learning how to do this at some point in my life, but never had any occasion to practice.

"Since Jenna was a toddler, almost fourteen years now." I finally gave up my power struggle with the flowers and jammed the stalks in the vase.

"That's right. Ben said he had an older sister." Peter chuckled. "I bet he keeps you on your toes. Are Ben and I going to have a Matchbox matchup before we go?"

"No, he won't be smashing any miniature cars into your wing tips this time." I smiled, remembering the two of them playing on the floor at the Centurion real-estate office. "Both kids are spending the weekend with their father in Tahoe. So you have me all to yourself."

Peter took my hand in his. "I'm looking forward to that."

I pulled my hand free. I liked Peter but I wasn't ready for any kind of intimacy just yet. I grabbed my black leather coat and he courteously helped me with it. We were almost out the door when the phone rang.

"I'd better answer it. I've been trying to get hold of the kids all day." I ran into the kitchen and lifted up the receiver before the answering machine could kick in.

"Hi, Laurel," said that familiar husky voice.

"Oh, it's you."

"Am I interrupting anything?"

"Yes, a dinner date, so if you'll excuse me." I waved at Peter who was leaning against the door.

"Where are you going?"

"Why. Are you joining us? Bringing some matching metal jewelry for my wrists?"

"That's not necessary, Laurel. Besides..."

I heard voices shouting in the background. I glanced over at Peter. He was frowning and pointing at his watch.

"Let me call you back in a few."

The dial tone came on and I banged the phone down. Peter gave me a curious look. "Well, that conversation sounded intriguing," he said. "Was that one of your amateur detective buddies?"

"No. Just some jerk."

We almost made it to the front door when the phone trilled again. I flashed Peter an apologetic look and raced back into the kitchen, skidding across the wood floor.

"Hello," I gasped, winded from my twenty-foot run. No doubt about it. It was time to enroll in a gym.

"Ms. McKay, Neil Schwartz from the *Mountain Democrat*," gurgled the Draino voice of the reporter. "I'm glad I caught you. We never finished our conversation the other day."

"Mr. Schwartz, I have a dinner date. Can't you find someone else to annoy?" I wanted to hang up but was afraid if I upset the reporter I would end up as a headline on the front page of the paper. *Murder suspect seeking new victims to date.*

"Trust me, I have information you'll want to hear. Did you know the sheriff's department has identified the murder weapon? The killer used a pipe wrench."

Peter cleared his throat. So far this conversation with the reporter had yielded nothing I hadn't already learned from my own official sources. "Yes, I'm aware of the weapon that was used. I really need to leave now."

"How about giving us a statement regarding the fact that your ex-husband has been hired by the largest plumbing company in Sacramento?" No comment other than the fact that maybe I would receive my child support payments on time.

The reporter zeroed in for the kill. "Your ex has been reported as saying he would kill any man that got near you. Any comment now?"

THIRTY

I HUNG UP ON THE NOSY REPORTER and we made it out the front door without any further interruptions. Peter held on to my elbow as he guided me to his luxurious British racing–green Jaguar parked in the driveway. Two more things in his favor—a well-mannered gentleman and financially stable.

I was seething over the reporter's remarks. It took more than motive and a weapon to make a murderer. It took planning as well as guts, both of which Hank had in short supply. But he did have a temper. Could the breakup with Nadine have sent him over the edge?

Although Peter attempted to entertain me by sharing humorous real-estate anecdotes during the ten-minute trip into Placerville, I couldn't stop replaying the reporter's implied accusation in my head. I'd read too many stories about husbands killing their wives and children when they cracked.

I fumbled in my purse for my cell phone. Shoot. We were in one of the hilly no-service zones. I'd try again after we reached the restaurant.

The Sequoia House had been renovated from a decaying clapboard Victorian mansion into a spectacular first-class restaurant. It was obviously a popular dining spot since we pulled into the last vacant parking space. The massive stained-glass embossed doors opened into the beautifully remodeled entry. I stepped onto a gorgeous carpet, either Aubusson or Chinese, I never could keep them straight. Rose-colored velvet chairs lined the wall for guests who had to wait for a table. Fortunately that did not include us. We were immediately ushered into the Verandah dining room.

With its stained-glass windows, patterned tin ceiling and plantation fans, I felt like I had been transported back to a more tranquil time period—the Victorian era. A nice respite from the crazy life I called my own. The hostess led us past a room full of antiques to our table. Once we sat down I realized the velvet chairs were designed for the sole purpose of promoting good posture. Our silver-haired waiter approached dressed in a burgundy jacket and black trousers. He brandished two dinner menus along with a wine list.

"Would you prefer a white or red wine?" Peter peered at me over the large red-and-gold embossed menu. "Or maybe some champagne to celebrate our first date?"

My face colored slightly at the thought of my last date when I swigged almost an entire bottle of champagne.

"I think I'll stick to water for now."

He returned the wine list to the waiter with his request. "We'll have a bottle of Syrah. I might be able to talk her into sharing some of it later on."

After the wine was delivered and our dinners were ordered, rare steak and a baked potato for Peter, and blackened salmon accompanied by pesto mashed potatoes and haricots verts—aka teeny-weeny green beans—for me, we settled back in our chairs.

Peter rested his elbows on the table and leaned in. "You look so stressed. I hoped this would be a nice break from your troubles."

"That's very sweet of you. I wish I could forget my problems but I'm worried about my kids and concerned my ex-husband is involved in the murders."

Peter looked puzzled. "Why would you suspect your ex?"

"Well, for one thing, he's jealous of the men I've dated. I think that gives him a motive."

Peter smiled. "I'd be jealous too if my beautiful ex-wife were dating other men." His compliment momentarily bolstered my spirits.

The waiter chose that moment to deliver our entrées. My cell buzzed just as he set down my plate. I rifled through my purse and located my phone. The call had come from Jenna's cell.

"Peter, would you excuse me. I need to call my daughter." I streaked out of the dining room before he could respond. The lobby was packed and noisy so I went into the ladies' room, which was surprisingly empty.

It turned out I had two voicemails. The first was from Jenna, bubbly and joyful, the result of picking five out of six winners at the Sports Book. She and Ben were having a wonderful time but would I please quit leaving so many messages and being such a worrywart. I didn't know whether to be relieved the kids were having a great time with Hank or annoyed that I'd been reclassified as a smothering mother.

The second message was from Stan. It was unintelligible and incomprehensible. According to Stan, he had gone door knocking but there weren't any doors to knock on. I dialed his number.

"Ah-choo."

"Hey, it's Laurel. Are you okay?"

"Go away and leave me alone in sneezy peace."

"I'm sorry, but your message didn't make any sense. What do you mean there weren't any doors to knock on?"

His next sneeze exploded into my eardrum. "I drove around and around those streets but there were no houses at any of the addresses you gave me. There's only one huge home with a for-sale sign on it and a sales trailer located on a knoll at the top of the subdivision."

"Are you sure you drove through the right subdivision?"

He honked again. "Hey, I may be on my deathbed but I'm not delirious. Yet. Bella Lago. Off of Salmon Falls Road. I'm going back to bed."

The dial tone buzzed in my ear while a gazillion questions buzzed inside my brain. None of which would be answered in the ladies' room. Something fishy was going on and I was beginning to have an inkling where the stench was coming from.

I returned to the table and apologized for my absence. Peter was empathetic about my maternal concerns. "I can understand why you'd be concerned about your children's safety. When are they supposed to return home?"

"Not until Monday night. But I think I may have been worrying over nothing. My daughter left a message and it sounds like both kids are having a great time."

Peter looked thoughtful as he sipped his wine. "So no more doubts about the ex."

I shrugged as I took a bite of my pesto mashed potatoes, which tasted far better than they looked. I had a lot of doubts about my ex but I seriously couldn't imagine him as a murderer.

In the meantime, a million questions milled around my brain. "My mother mentioned you're a developer. How are sales going in this market?"

"It's been kind of slow. But we think things will pick up again soon." Peter ran a finger around the rim of his wineglass. "The lots have the most incredible views of Folsom Lake. Nothing else like it in the area."

"What's the name of your subdivision again?" I snagged a piece of salmon as I waited for his answer.

"Bella Lago."

The salmon I was gnawing on landed with a sick thud in my stomach.

Peter latched onto my free hand. "I'd love to show you the property sometime. The view of the lake from the top is spectacular." He ran his finger lightly down my palm. "And romantic."

His touch made me tremble. But not in a good way.

"So do you have any partners?"

"I do." He drained his wineglass and smacked it down on the table.

Peter's reticence was most unusual. Was it due to the typically competitive nature of real-estate agents or something else entirely? I felt like a dog with a bone and I would keep gnawing until I got all of my answers. It was time to find out whose names the "L" and "C" stood for in the TLC partnership.

"How many houses have been built so far?"

He dropped his fork and knife on his plate. "Would you excuse me for a minute?" He stood up and walked away from the table heading, I assumed, to the men's room.

I stared at the mound of pale green potatoes on my plate. They resembled miniature hills. I thought about the subdivision Peter had developed. And the three delinquent loans I'd uncovered. And the empty lots Stan had driven by. What would it mean if Mike Clark prepared appraisals on multimillion-dollar homes that didn't exist? Who would benefit from the fraudulent sales?

Our eyes locked as Peter returned to the table.

I had the answer to my question.

THIRTY-ONE

PETER RESTED HIS HAND ON TOP of mine. "Laurel, sorry if I seemed a little testy. Bella Lago has become a real sore point. We've had one problem after another. First there were huge excavation costs because of more bedrock than the engineers anticipated, then the county made us realign some of the water lines, which was another unexpected expense. Then..." He reached for the bottle of Syrah and poured the remainder in his glass. "But I've taken care of all my issues. Finally."

The waiter arrived to clear our plates producing dessert menus for each of us. Peter snatched the menus and gave them back. "Sorry to end our evening so quickly, but I received a page when I was away from the table and unfortunately we need to get going." He turned to the waiter. "We'll take the check."

Fine with me. I needed time to evaluate the information Peter had divulged. And the information he'd been reluctant to disclose. We both remained silent as we entered his luxury sedan and headed back to my house.

I had no idea what Peter was thinking but I hoped he didn't have the ability to read minds. Because my cerebral cortex was processing the information that it was very likely I was sitting next to a murderer. And the murderer was about to deliver me to an empty house.

My heart was pounding so hard it was a wonder Peter couldn't hear it. There had to be someplace safe he could drop me off. Somewhere I could call the cops.

My mind was mulling over a variety of safe havens when Peter interrupted my thought process. "Laurel, do you mind if we stop at the Centurion office before I take you home? It's right on the way."

I nodded. It was perfect. Peter wouldn't be expecting me to run away and there was a gas station just around the corner from the building.

We arrived at the office in less than ten minutes. We parked in front of the Centurion building and Peter turned off the ignition. I was almost afraid to make eye contact with him, but he grinned at me, his left hand resting on the polished wood steering wheel.

I wondered if my imagination was getting out of control. Maybe I had read too many mysteries. An hour ago my ex-husband had been my number-one suspect. Now my date had moved into the first-place ranking.

I rummaged through my tote, making sure my cell phone was close at hand. One of Ben's leftover cherry gummy bears dropped on the immaculate floor of the car. I picked it up and dumped it in the side pocket of my purse.

Peter pushed open one of the frosted-glass double doors and I followed him inside. By now I desperately needed to use the bathroom. A full bladder would not be conducive to a speedy getaway. Plus the bathroom would provide a convenient excuse to disappear for a few minutes.

"Peter, I'm going to use the ladies' room."

He nodded and headed down the hallway to his own office. The overhead lights above the large brass-plated Centurion Realty sign barely lit the space. The empty desks shape-shifted into distorted monsters ready to jump out at me from the shadows.

My nerves were completely shot by the time I reached the rear of the building. My hand was pressed against the ladies' room door when a creaking sound startled me. I turned around to a terrifying sight, one I'd read about in many a murder mystery but never expected to experience myself.

THIRTY-TWO

I was staring at the wrong end of a revolver. Boy, those mystery novels had it all wrong. When faced with a gun, I didn't want to flee.

I wanted to pee.

Peter grabbed my shoulder and spun me around, the hard end of the gun digging into the small of my back. He prodded me down the corridor into his office then shoved me into one of the visitor chairs. My purse dropped, some of the contents rolling on the navy tweed carpet.

"You killed Garrett," I blurted out. "And Jeremy."

Peter laughed. Not a pleasant sound. He walked around the uncluttered desk and sat down. The gun never wavered. "Laurel, I swear you are as nosy as your mother. I thought if I took you out to dinner I could find out what you'd discovered. But you just wouldn't stop asking questions."

"I am not as nosy as my mother." Nobody is as nosy as my mother. I looked at the weapon pointed at me. Maybe my nosiness wasn't the real issue right now.

"Whatever. You've been poking around. I could tell at dinner you were close to figuring it all out. My plans have been screwed up ever since you joined that stupid Love Club. What are the odds you would be out on a date with each of the men I killed on the night they died? If it weren't for you, no one would have tied Garrett's and Jeremy's deaths together."

He cocked the gun right at my heart, making me feel like an invisible bull's-eye was emblazoned over my left breast.

"But then it turned out the detectives considered you the primary suspect so it ended up working out in my favor. The only hitch was Mike Clark. Mike was under the impression you accidentally killed Garrett with the cell phone. One day we were talking and I slipped up and mentioned Garrett and I had fought. Mike figured out I killed him. Eventually he realized I must have murdered Jeremy, as well. He tried to blackmail me. His partner. Can you believe it?"

Peter looked hurt that one of his merry band of fraud fugitives had tried to extort money from him.

"So you killed Mike," I stated in a voice far calmer than I felt.

He smirked. "Right again. I'd agreed to pay him in cash and we arranged to meet at the Bella Lago sales office at midnight. Once he took off, I jumped in my truck and followed his motorcycle out of the subdivision and down Salmon Falls Road. You know how windy that road is?"

He looked at me for confirmation.

"It's a dangerous strip of road. What did you do? Ram him in the back of his motorcycle?" I asked.

He nodded. "Yep. Just as he rounded a curve I smashed into his bike and it crashed down into the canyon. I was sure he was a goner but I climbed down the hillside to make sure and he was still breathing. I grabbed the money then hit him on the back of his head with the pipe wrench. You can see I had no other choice, can't you?"

I bobbed my head in agreement. I wasn't sure Mike's blackmail was a perfect rationale for murdering him, but nodding seemed the most expedient response since the gun was still pointed at me.

"I was worried about using the same weapon I'd used on both Garrett and Jeremy but I figured the buzzards would have him for dinner long before his body was discovered.

I sure didn't expect those two teenagers to find him so quickly. Don't kids have curfews anymore?"

The subject of curfews was a continuing debate in my house but not a top priority right this second. I balanced on the edge of the chair, my hands clasped together, unable to resist asking the obvious. "The murders are all tied to Bella Lago, aren't they?"

He hesitated. I didn't know if it was the bottle of wine he downed at dinner or the fact he had nothing to lose by sharing his confession with me.

"You were right on target about the sales at Bella Lago. We had expectations for huge profits. But we incurred all those additional expenses from the water lines the county made us move, which delayed the grand opening by six months."

"By then the market had changed and the economy was heading downhill fast," I said.

"You got it. When we finally started selling lots, home prices were decreasing. Foreclosures were mounting. Not a lot of folks were looking to buy expensive lots to build multimillion-dollar homes.

"That subdivision drained me with all the cost overruns. We couldn't even sell our spec home we built. Everything I'd worked so hard for. We still had bills to pay to the bank, the subcontractors. There was only one thing we could do."

"Speaking of 'we,' does TLC stand for Tyler, Lindstrom and Clark?" I asked.

"Your mother was right. You are smart." He leered at me. "As well as hot."

My mother said I was smart? Peter thought I was hot?

I looked at the muzzle of the revolver and shivered. Regardless of how smart and hot I was, the gun was still pointed in my direction.

"So who came up with the idea? Garrett?" I said.

He nodded. Of course. Garrett had tons of wealthy clients. As their CPA, his files contained not only their tax returns, but copies of their W-2 forms, 1099 statements, and complete bank and investment company year-end statements.

"He could create an entire loan package with authentic documents." He smiled wickedly at me. "No one could tell they were fakes."

He was right. Neither Mary Lou, a senior underwriter, nor Earl had noticed anything amiss.

Peter continued to gloat over the deviousness of their scheme. "Garrett forged their signatures on the loan application and the closing documents. I'm a notary so that wasn't a problem. Mike produced fake appraisals with photos of other million-dollar homes in the area. All these Tuscan-style houses look alike anyway. And no one ever inspects the houses."

That was true. Banks used to rely on their approved appraisers to protect them from fraud. It was only recently the government decided they probably should intervene and regulate that aspect of the lending business more carefully.

"But how could you make sure the borrowers didn't catch on?"

He smacked the desk with the palm of his free hand. I curled back in my chair.

"Garrett was supposed to pick wealthy retirees, people who were set financially and who wouldn't be buying another house or applying for a new loan. We planned on making the mortgage payments for a couple of months then pay off the fake loans when lots sold and we had the extra cash. We figured if they ran their credit report someday, it would just look like a bank error, a loan that was on the books for a brief period of time then paid off."

"But what about the collection letters the servicing department sends out?" My analytical mind couldn't stop looking for the flaws in his scheme.

"Not a problem. We used different fake post office boxes for each of the borrowers."

Peter looked at me with reproachful eyes. "It was an excellent concept. And those big view parcels would have brought in profits of at least half a million each. It wasn't our fault the lots didn't sell and we couldn't pay off the fake loans. It was all due to the crappy economy."

Of course it wasn't his fault the fraudulent loans became delinquent. Totally due to the economy, which meant the list of people he could blame was endless.

"Okay, I understand your financial problems. And even though I don't agree with what you did…" Peter glared at me. "I realize you needed cash." Fear was placed aside by curiosity. "But why did you have to kill three men?"

Okay, maybe I am a little nosy.

My captor started rummaging through his desk with his free hand, managing to keep the gun pointed at me with the other one. "One of Garrett's clients, Jeremy Slater, fit our profile—successful doctor with a nice home in Serrano. He had tons of money in the bank and no need to apply for an equity line. We didn't think he would need to run a credit report."

"But Jeremy decided to buy the vacation home in Tahoe," I said. "When his application was declined by the bank he discovered there was a jumbo loan in his name on a property he didn't own."

Peter nodded as he slammed the first drawer shut and opened another one. "Right again. We put that loan through Worldwide Bank. Jeremy contacted them and discovered they had a full file on him, tax returns, verified assets. I guess at first he thought his partner committed the fraud because that guy was siphoning cash from the practice to cover gambling losses. When his partner assured him he had nothing to do with the fake loan, Jeremy realized no one else could have produced that information other than his personal CPA. Jeremy accused Garrett of creating a fraudulent loan and the dummy confessed."

That dummy Garrett.

"Jeremy and Garrett argued about it just hours before you and Garrett went out to dinner. He called me right after he got home. He was not in a good mood."

Good.

"Garrett was drinking heavily to ease the pain from your hitting him…" Peter paused a minute in his search and looked at me with admiration. "You really are quite a woman, Laurel."

Much as I appreciated the compliment I was still terrified.

And I still had to pee.

"Anyway, when Garrett admitted he'd confessed the entire scheme to Jeremy that afternoon, I drove to his house to see if we could come up with some type of damage control. Garrett was freaking out. He picked up the phone to call the police so he could come clean. I had to stop him. That pipe wrench was lying on the kitchen counter by the sink—and when Garrett turned away, I grabbed it, swung and it was over."

His lip curled in satisfaction. "Just like that. I'd fixed my problem in an instant. Your little encounter made you the perfect suspect so I stuffed him back in his car, threw the wrench in my trunk and took off."

"So you killed Garrett with the pipe wrench. A red-handled wrench?" I guessed.

He nodded. "Craftsman. The finest tools money can buy." Yup. Craftsman produced excellent tools. For contractors like my ex-husband. And killers like the man sitting across from me.

"Did Jeremy figure out you were involved in the scam with Garrett? Is that why you killed him?"

He smirked, the fluorescent lights in the office making his emerald eyes glitter. "I had no choice. I told Jeremy I would take care of everything but he kept nagging me. He casually mentioned he was having dinner at the River Inn that evening although I had no idea you were his date. I realized that would be the perfect place to remove him from the picture. All I had to do was lure him out of the restaurant."

"So Jeremy responded to your page and met you outside the restaurant," I said.

"Yep. We walked over to the bluff to talk. The wrench had been so effective on Garrett that I stuffed it in the pocket of my cargo pants just in case. All I had to do was distract Jeremy then hit him on the back of his head. It momentarily stunned him then I shoved him into the river. I figured the rocks and the water would take care of him once and for all. Everyone would think it was an accident. There was just one little complication.

"Always the complication, aren't you, Laurel?"

I was about to defend myself when lights flickered on throughout the outer office.

My heart dropped all the way down to my flat feet as the sound of a familiar voice echoed from the hallway.

THIRTY-THREE

CENTURION REALTY'S TOP producer strolled into Peter's office. "And here I thought I was the only one who stopped in on Saturday nights. Peter, you shouldn't be working when you're out with my daughter. Are you trying to snatch that number-one spot from me?"

Peter and I looked at each other. I didn't know what to say.

He did. "Barbara, you and your daughter will be the end of me yet."

Or vice versa.

Her eyes widened as she zeroed in on the gun. "I don't understand. I thought you two were on a date. I realize Laurel can be a little difficult at times, but you don't have to point a gun at her."

"Mother, Peter killed Jeremy. And Garrett. And Mike, the appraiser."

"Mike who?" she asked, as usual focusing on the most irrelevant part of the conversation.

"Never mind. It doesn't matter. What does matter is that Peter is a murderer and he's holding a gun. On both of us."

Her face paled and she dropped into the chair next to me. For once, she looked all of her sixty-two years. Peter drummed the fingers of his left hand on the desk although his gun hand remained steady. Was he trying to figure out what to do with us? Maybe I could give him some ideas.

"Peter, please let us go. You've got the money. Why don't you leave the country?"

Mother chimed in, "Wonderful idea. I'd be happy to service your listings for you while you're gone."

One would think that when one's mother is facing a gun, she would not be tabulating real-estate commissions in her head.

"Right. I'm sure neither of you would inform the sheriff's department about any of this. But I can't leave until Monday. Two more fake loans are recording at 8:00 a.m. Once the sales proceeds are wired into the partnership account I'll transfer the money into my personal account."

He shifted the gun to his left hand and opened another drawer. "I already booked a flight. By Monday afternoon I'm off to Rio. Now all I need to figure out is the best way to dispatch you two."

I didn't care for the way he used the word *dispatch*. Who would know if we were missing? Hank and the kids wouldn't be home from Tahoe until Monday night. Tom knew I was on a dinner date so the earliest he might check on me would be tomorrow. And my mother, who wouldn't hesitate to intervene, had already done so.

"Wait a minute. The guy I saw with Jeremy on the riverbank had a bald spot."

"Just in case anyone saw me from a distance I chose to go au naturel that evening." Peter lifted the top of his thick blond hair. Damn. That was a great-looking hairpiece. If we'd ever reached the kissing stage I guess I would have realized it. The thought of kissing a murderer made my pesto potato–filled stomach lurch.

Peter pulled something out of the drawer. He smiled in satisfaction as he waved a plane ticket at us. He motioned for both of us to stand.

I rose slowly, racking my brain for a way to extricate us from this mess. How could I get the gun away from Peter without either of us getting shot?

What would a kick-ass female detective do in this situation? And wouldn't it be great if one of those kick-ass women were here right now?

Peter herded us out of the office, turning off the lights as we walked ahead of him. No evidence of any midnight oil–burning real-estate agents was left behind. He hesitated as we stood in front of the cars then reached into the pocket of his slacks for his keys.

Peter beeped open the trunk of the Jag, indicating we should throw our purses inside. Darn, that eliminated any chance of us using our cell phones. He motioned to my mother to get behind the wheel. He ordered me to climb in the front passenger seat then he slid into the backseat of the car.

"Barbara, if you try anything funny I won't think twice about putting a bullet in the back of your daughter's head."

Multiple shivers slithered down my spine as he stroked my cheek with the gun. I didn't doubt him for a minute. The man had already killed three people.

I thought about my children. At least I no longer had to worry about their father being found guilty of murder and removed from their life. Now all I had to do was figure out how to keep them from losing both their mother and grandmother.

THIRTY-FOUR

WE DROVE OUT OF THE PARKING lot then took the entrance ramp heading west on Highway 50, exiting five minutes later on El Dorado Hills Boulevard. At first I wasn't sure of our ultimate destination. Once we crossed Green Valley Road and headed north on Salmon Falls Road, I realized where Peter was taking us.

Bella Lago.

After a silent and tortuously short drive we arrived at the massive stone entrance.

"Barbara, hit the red button to the right of the visitor phone. That will open the gate. Then drive to the top of the hill."

The driver's window rolled down and my mother stretched her left arm toward the intercom. Her knuckles gleamed white in the moonlight as she punched a round red button on the control panel.

The gate creaked out an eerie greeting as we drove through. The large car glided up into sheer dark nothingness. The roads were steep and during the day I imagined there would be beautiful vista points.

I shifted and felt the cold metal caressing my neck. Moments later we arrived at the summit. The hilltop had been leveled to make room for a small modular trailer that served as the sales office. As in most of the subdivisions in El Dorado Hills, there were no streetlights. A smattering of stars sprinkled the dark velvet sky.

I felt as if I was in a dream. No, make that a nightmare.

What good was all that mystery-novel reading to me now? Nothing less than a miracle could get us out of this alive.

Mother braked, shifted into Park and turned off the ignition. Peter seemed lost in thought and I wasn't sure if I should interrupt him. That didn't stop Barbara Bingham. She twisted her head and looked directly at Peter. "If you harm us they'll hunt you down."

"No one will connect me with the two of you."

"But Peter," I objected, "I told several of my friends I was going out with you. My mother probably told everyone about our date."

"Of course I did. I thought you two made a great couple. You have so much in common."

Yeah. I dated the men Peter murdered—some common denominator.

Peter nudged the back of my neck with the gun. "Get out of the car, both of you. No sudden moves."

We eased the car doors open carefully. I wasn't going to do anything to upset Peter. At least not while he was holding that gun.

Even though I had on my black leather coat, the gusts of wind chilled me on the inside as well as the outside. My mother shuffled forward, rounding the front of the car. I reached out and clasped her slender frame to mine.

"Hey, stop that!" Peter hollered. "Stay at least three feet away from each other."

We pulled apart and followed Peter up a makeshift wooden staircase to the sales office. Our captor turned away from us to fumble with his key ring. I looked around for a possible weapon. Off to the side of the trailer was a small pile of lumber.

As Peter attempted to open the door, I winked at my parent, placed my finger against my lips, and tiptoed back down the steps.

Creak.

Never try to make a stealthy getaway treading on cheap plywood.

Peter wheeled around and pinned his left arm around my mother's neck. Her eyes bulged with fear as he shoved the gun into her side.

"Try that again and your mother is history. Now open the door." The keys clanged together as he threw them at my feet. Her eyes implored me to do as he instructed. I picked up the key ring from the foot of the stairs and trudged back up.

Lucky me. My first choice opened the door. I hesitated at the entrance but Peter pushed me into the trailer. He hit a light switch illuminating the office then shoved my mother against a battered beige metal desk.

The sales office wasn't much to look at but that wasn't unusual for the early stages of a building project. Peter motioned for us to sit. I dropped into one of the dark green plastic chairs and scanned the scratched surface of the desk. The desk was sadly lacking in potential weapons. I found a staple remover—which would be useful if Peter shot us with staples—and a glue stick.

Maybe I could glue his hands together.

Peter banged desk drawers open and shut. He finally held up a large black metal flashlight. "All right, ladies, this will make your hike a little easier."

I pleaded with him one more time. "My ex and the kids will be trying to get hold of me. If I don't answer, I'm sure they'll call the police."

He smirked. "Didn't you say they weren't coming home until Monday evening?"

Lucky me. I finally met a man who listened to my babbling.

"I'm supposed to have dinner with Detective Bradford

tomorrow," Mother said. "Certainly he'll wonder what happened to me."

I sensed my eyes bulging out of their sockets. "You have a date with Bradford? How could you? The guy thinks I'm a murderer."

She stiffened in her chair. "Robert is a very capable detective. I'm sure eventually he would have determined you were innocent."

"Well, I wish he'd discovered it a little quicker," I responded, nodding in Peter's direction.

"Laurel, dear, I—"

"Focus ladies!" Peter waved a flashlight in one hand and the gun in the other. He grabbed my mother's arm and shoved her out the door. "It's time to take care of a few loose ends."

I didn't need to be clobbered over the head to know the two of us were the loose ends. We were quickly running out of options. All that wine Peter had drunk should be fuddling his thinking but so far he hadn't missed a thing.

Mother was right. Peter would be the chief suspect if I vanished. But how long would it take before anyone realized we were gone? Would Bradford be concerned if she didn't show up for their dinner date? Would Tom wonder where I was? Would he even care? By the time the sheriff's department put everything together, the killer would be thousands of miles away.

On a beach in Rio clasping a delicious mojito in his murderous hands.

Peter handed the flashlight to me. The three of us hiked down the road away from the trailer, Peter behind us, the gun still aimed at my back. The moon was a toothpick-size sliver of light and the few stars didn't provide much illumination. The subdivision was supposed to have fabulous view lots but the lake was invisible to my naked eye.

Massive shapes loomed alongside the road. The huge machines they used for site development.

I increased the length of my stride; my mother followed my lead. I gradually veered to the right, hoping Peter wouldn't notice. As we reached the enormous vehicles, I directed the flashlight to the opposite side of the road and screamed. "Rattlesnake!"

Peter turned and pointed the gun in that direction. I took advantage of his momentary lapse of attention and bonked him on the back of his head with the jumbo-size flashlight.

A gunshot rang out.

I clicked off the flashlight and grabbed my mother's hand. We raced to the earthmover closest to the road and hid behind one of its gigantic rubber tires.

I peeked out. Peter was still upright although rubbing the back of his head. I calculated how many bullets he had remaining. In the old Westerns there were only six bullets in each gun. What was the norm these days? Next time I read a mystery I would pay better attention to weaponry.

Assuming I would ever have the opportunity to read a mystery again.

We crouched behind the earthmover. It was so cold we could see our breath. My body felt like there was ice in my veins and I didn't know if it was from the cold or my fear.

"C'mon, ladies. You know I wasn't going to hurt you. I just wanted a place to detain you until I left town."

Yeah, right. Shove our bodies in a shallow grave in the beautiful Bella Lago subdivision. That would detain us for a lifetime.

I edged away from the earthmover. Could we make a run for it and escape back to the sales office? I remembered seeing a phone on the desk. How long would it take 911 to get someone out here? And how would we keep Peter from shooting out the lock? And us.

Distracted, I slipped on a piece of gravel. The noise sounded as deafening as a boulder rolling down a mountainside.

Crack!

A bullet whizzed past my cheek. I picked up a fist-size rock and threw it across the road.

Peter turned and fired toward the direction I'd thrown the rock.

With his attention temporarily diverted, I grabbed my mother's arm and we darted over to one of the mammoth backhoes. She clambered up the metal ladder and entered the small glass enclosed cab. I went around to the other side, scrambled up and squeezed into the enclosure. The tiny space was a tight fit and I made a contract with God that if I survived this ordeal I would drop another ten pounds.

Mother looked perplexed as she gazed at the controls. Did we need a key to operate this thing? "There's no ignition. I wonder how we start it."

I pointed to a square numbered keypad on the console. What combination should I try? I pressed 123 and the engine roared. Would we be able to escape and reach the safe haven of the sales office?

A shot rang out. The window exploded.

THIRTY-FIVE

THE GLASS WINDOW OF THE backhoe disintegrated into a spiderweb of cracks.

"That SOB isn't going to hurt my baby." Mother yanked on some type of lever and we started moving forward. I couldn't decide if I was more stunned by the bullet hitting the window or my mother swearing. We rumbled onto the road. If I hadn't been so terrified I might have enjoyed the ride.

Peter stood in the middle of the pavement, his mouth gaping. Good thing he drank all that wine. Otherwise his brain might have relayed a message to his legs to react more quickly. We were on the verge of mowing him down when he came to his senses. He ran to the side of the road and scaled the ladder of another big machine. No wonder his development costs were so high. Half the heavy equipment in the county resided in his subdivision. Our own backhoe was careening downhill, away from the sales office—not the direction we needed to go.

"How do we turn this thing around?" I asked over the roar of our machine.

Mother looked down for some type of braking mechanism. She must have found something because we jerked to a sudden stop. She paused, trying to find a lever that would allow us to switch directions.

Bam. The grinding sound of metal hitting metal resounded through the night. My head hit the roof of the cab. The evening sky glimmered with the brilliance of a zillion stars before I blacked out.

When I came to, my head felt like it had been run through a trash compactor. The ringing in my ears sounded like a chorus of sirens.

"What happened?" I gingerly prodded a rapidly expanding lump on the top of my head.

"Peter rammed us." She looked at me tearfully. "I was so worried about you."

Wham. Another enormous jolt threw us into each other.

"I can't believe we're being rear-ended by a backhoe." I shook my head in disbelief. Bad idea. I almost blacked out again. The siren sounds grew louder. They were accompanied by the sound of a hundred chain saws buzzing in unison. Suddenly an enormous beam of light pierced the dark sky. Was I losing consciousness again? Was that cosmic shaft of light radiating from heaven?

I peeked out the side window. Neither.

A helicopter from the California Highway Patrol hovered overhead, its searchlight focused on both our vehicles. The clang of a bullet bouncing off metal resounded through the night.

The searchlight had turned us into sitting ducks—target practice for Peter. I swiveled in my seat. There must be a way to outfox him. Peter stood in the door of his cab, his left arm clasped around the metal frame, his right hand holding the gun leveled in our direction.

"Mom, do something."

She looked flummoxed by the array of levers. Technology has never been my forte but one of the joysticks had a drawing of a claw on it. It reminded me of the helpful drawings on my computer keyboard. When in doubt, go for it.

I shoved the lever back.

Bingo.

The immense clawlike attachment on the rear of our backhoe telescoped out and crashed through the front windshield of Peter's machine. Perfect timing. The impact knocked him from his precarious perch. He fell off, landing in a flurry of gravel on the side of the road.

"Those sirens are getting closer. I see headlights coming up the main road," Mother said.

"Thank God. I thought I had permanent ringing in my ears." The spotlight illuminated the killer, his face eggplant-purple with anger and pain, as he rocked back and forth, clutching his ankle.

I was petrified he still had possession of the gun. Then Peter crawled across the asphalt surface, his leg dragging behind him, in a desperate attempt to retrieve his weapon, which must have landed across the road.

My mother maneuvered the throttle and before you could say "Bella Lago," the huge front bucket lowered. She expertly scooped Peter up and within seconds he was trapped nine feet above the ground.

Four vehicles with flashing beacons of lights crested the hill. The noise of the sirens diminished as the cars abruptly stopped. The helicopter briefly touched down in an open area and an officer jumped out, racing in our direction. Sheriff's deputies, their guns drawn, surrounded the backhoe. One of them bellowed through a megaphone, "Put your weapons down. Leave the vehicle. Now."

Okay with me. My entire body trembled from PTD-MSS—post-traumatic dating a murderer stress syndrome. Mother opened the door and gracefully descended the ladder. Of course, she's taller and slimmer, and was dressed in a pair of slacks and flat-heeled shoes. I slipped on the second step, losing one high heel in the process. I almost landed on my well-padded posterior when someone caught me, keeping me from exposing my legs all the way up to my bikini wax.

Engulfed against a broad chest, my heart rate went into overdrive as Tom's arms wrapped around me.

"Uh, what should we do with this guy?" one of the deputies asked, pointing up to the bucket of the backhoe where Peter peered over the edge. Tom reluctantly released me.

"I'll take care of him." With the agility of a teenager, Mother climbed up into the backhoe. We applauded as she lowered the bucket. Two of the deputies grabbed Peter and handcuffed his hands behind his back.

As the officers marched the prisoner past Tom and me, Peter's face contorted in anger. He spat at me, his spittle landing on my bare foot. "You stupid cow."

Stupid cow?

That was the last straw. I limped over and kicked Peter in the balls. The deputies couldn't stifle their grins as he bent over from the impact of my one remaining pointy-toed stiletto.

Tom drew me close and whispered in my ear, "Laurel McKay, you are one hell of a woman."

I was still in a state of shock, but it didn't keep me from asking, "How did you find us?"

"Brian called Liz to tell her he would be working late. He suggested you girls go to dinner. When she told him you were having dinner with Peter Tyler he came unglued. He knew we were trying to put together a case against Tyler."

I shot an accusing look at him. "You never told me that."

He matched my look with one of his own. "You never gave me a chance."

Oh.

"We were suspicious that Tyler had something to do with Mike Clark's death. He claimed he didn't know him, but Clark's fingerprints were in the sales trailer. It took a while to follow the paper trail but we finally ascertained that TLC was a partnership between Tyler, Lindstrom and Clark. With Tyler the last man standing we knew he had to be our guy. We just didn't know why."

Good thing Tom knew an amateur bank detective. I'd fill him in on the details of the loan fraud case later.

"The minute Brian heard you were out with Peter, he called me and we raced to Placerville. I couldn't remember who you were dining with, but I remembered last week you said you were going to the Sequoia House."

After a lifetime of being ignored, I'd met two men who actually listened to me. Of course, one of them also wanted to kill me.

"When we arrived at the restaurant you'd already departed. We sent deputies to Peter's house and the real-estate office. The deputy who checked out the Centurion office noticed a red gummy bear on the recently vacuumed carpet in Tyler's office. That locked it up for me."

Good thing I hadn't gotten around to cleaning out my messy tote. Next time I'd leave a trail of colorful gummy bears. Although hopefully there wouldn't be a next time.

"How did you think of looking in Bella Lago?" I asked.

"What better place to stash a body than a beautiful but deserted lakeside setting? I hopped in the copter and we kept in touch with the other units. I didn't care how long it took. I was going to search every ravine in this county if I had to." His hand trembled as he lightly traced his fingers down my face. I sensed he wanted to kiss me but not with an audience comprised of El Dorado County's finest watching us.

We stood next to each other. The heat radiating from the burly detective warmed me up as we watched Mother climb down from the backhoe. She pulled her coat close and ambled over to where we waited.

"Well, that was quite an adventure." Her eyes gleamed as she brushed her hands in satisfaction. I merely stared at her, this woman who never failed to amaze me.

"When did you learn to operate a backhoe, and why didn't you tell me you could drive one?"

"I don't recall you ever asking me, dear. For your information, your father used to work construction during the summer while he attended college." A wistful look passed across her face. "Sometimes I'd come out at night and we'd..." She hesitated and blushed. "We would fool around with the machines."

Fool around with the machines? Hey, I was her thirty-nine-year-old daughter. I'll bet they were fooling around on the machines.

"Ladies, I hate to make you do this but we need you to come down to headquarters." Tom briefly put his arm around me and gave me a quick squeeze. "I know you both must be exhausted but this can't wait. We want this guy locked up for good."

"That's fine. There's just one urgent thing I have to do first," I said.

"Retrieving some evidence?"

I shook my head and raced into the sales office.

After we took care of that tactical maneuver, we walked over to Peter's Jag. Tom located the trunk release button on the Jaguar's console and we collected our purses. My hero had to coordinate the enormous force that had come to our rescue so we climbed into the back of one of the squad cars. Deputy Sam would take us to headquarters where the sheriff was waiting to interview us.

The back of the patrol car wasn't the most aromatic place but I couldn't have cared less. I leaned my head against the leather seat and shut my eyes. My mother slid in and grabbed my hand in hers. We held on tight, exchanging weary smiles.

This was a Mother and Daughter outing we would never forget.

THIRTY-SIX

THE NEXT FEW HOURS WERE A BLUR. Once Peter sobered up, he lawyered up, refusing to say anything until his attorney was present. Because Peter had divulged his motive to me, I had to repeat my story numerous times before the sheriff was finally satisfied. My voice broke occasionally when I realized how close my children came to losing both their mother and their grandmother.

Detective Bradford sat next to my mother during my entire recital. He remained silent, gnawing away at a toothpick, with an occasional glance at her profile. When I got to the part where she lowered the backhoe bucket to scoop up Peter, he threw his head back and guffawed.

I wasn't too tired to miss the wink she gave him. Was she planning a romantic backhoe assignation with him? There was only one question yet to be resolved, at least, one question relating to this case. I had a ton of questions about this budding relationship between my mother and Detective Tall and Bald.

"So what's the deal with Dr. Radovich? What about his gambling losses?" I asked.

"I'm happy to say we caught up with the doctor at a facility designed to help those with gambling addictions. For whatever reason, I think Jeremy's murder made him realize he needed help."

Or maybe Dr. Radovich had a little encouragement from the Sopranos duo. Either way, I was glad he was on the road to recovery.

At two-thirty, my mother and I were finally released. Tom arranged for one of the deputies to drop us off at our respective houses. He promised to call me first thing in the morning.

We were both exhausted and spent the drive in silence.

The deputy pulled into my driveway. I opened the door to exit the car, then leaned over and hugged my mother. "I don't know what to say. You were completely amazing tonight."

"Honey, I wasn't half as incredible as you. You were the one who figured out Peter was the murderer." Her eyes started to tear as she clutched me close. "I am so very proud of you."

I frowned at her. "I still can't believe you set me up with a killer."

She chuckled. "Hey, every good real-estate agent has to have a killer instinct." I decided to ignore her and eased my tired body out of the squad car.

"Don't forget your purse." At last count my mother had reminded me not to forget my purse approximately 4,580 times. But after tonight's adventure, she could remind me as often as she wanted.

I grabbed my tote. "Thanks, Mom."

I let myself in the house and walked to the kitchen. Miniature tremors coursed through my body as I realized that only a few hours earlier I'd stood in this room with a murderer.

Food, I needed food. No, make that carbs. I needed lots and lots of carbs. I opened the freezer and smiled. A gallon of brownie chunk ice cream beamed back at me.

I slid into a chair, dug my spoon into the chocolate delight and raised it to my lips. A blur of fur landed next to me, her reproachful green eyes meeting mine. I couldn't tell if Pumpkin wanted a snack or if she was my reminder that I had vowed to lose weight if I came out of this alive. I sighed and put the tub back in the freezer.

Pumpkin was right on my heels as I climbed up the stairs. Fine with me. I could use a cuddle tonight although I'd prefer to cuddle with a handsome detective who thought I was a helluva woman.

I walked into the bedroom and undressed, hanging my leather jacket next to my red blazer. Suddenly I remembered the slip of paper I'd retrieved from Earl's office. The one I'd stuck in my blazer pocket then forgotten about.

I reached in and grabbed the minuscule piece of paper with its microscopic print and held it up to the light. Would the tiny fortune end up being a clue?

I read the words out loud.

The love of your life is right outside your door.

The front doorbell pealed. I chuckled and tucked the tiny slip of paper into my pocket.

* * * * *

REQUEST YOUR FREE BOOKS!

2 FREE NOVELS
PLUS 2 FREE GIFTS!

Your Partner in Crime

YES! Please send me 2 FREE novels from the Worldwide Library® series and my 2 FREE gifts (gifts are worth about $10). After receiving them, if I don't wish to receive any more books, I can return the shipping statement marked "cancel." If I don't cancel, I will receive 4 brand-new novels every month and be billed just $5.24 per book in the U.S. or $6.24 per book in Canada. That's a saving of at least 34% off the cover price. It's quite a bargain! Shipping and handling is just 50¢ per book in the U.S. and 75¢ per book in Canada.* I understand that accepting the 2 free books and gifts places me under no obligation to buy anything. I can always return a shipment and cancel at any time. Even if I never buy another book, the two free books and gifts are mine to keep forever.

414/424 WDN FEJ3

Name	(PLEASE PRINT)	
Address		Apt. #
City	State/Prov.	Zip/Postal Code

Signature (if under 18, a parent or guardian must sign)

Mail to the **Reader Service**:
IN U.S.A.: P.O. Box 1867, Buffalo, NY 14240-1867
IN CANADA: P.O. Box 609, Fort Erie, Ontario L2A 5X3

Not valid for current subscribers to the Worldwide Library series.

Want to try two free books from another line?
Call 1-800-873-8635 or visit www.ReaderService.com

* Terms and prices subject to change without notice. Prices do not include applicable taxes. Sales tax applicable in N.Y. Canadian residents will be charged applicable taxes. Offer not valid in Quebec. This offer is limited to one order per household. All orders subject to credit approval. Credit or debit balances in a customer's account(s) may be offset by any other outstanding balance owed by or to the customer. Please allow 4 to 6 weeks for delivery. Offer available while quantities last.

Your Privacy—The Reader Service is committed to protecting your privacy. Our Privacy Policy is available online at www.ReaderService.com or upon request from the Reader Service.

We make a portion of our mailing list available to reputable third parties that offer products we believe may interest you. If you prefer that we not exchange your name with third parties, or if you wish to clarify or modify your communication preferences, please visit us at www.ReaderService.com/consumerschoice or write to us at Reader Service Preference Service, P.O. Box 9062, Buffalo, NY 14269. Include your complete name and address.

WWLI1B